TAILS

OF THE SMOKIES

JIM PARKS

ISBN 978-1-64468-686-7 (Paperback)
ISBN 978-1-64468-687-4 (Digital)

First Edition

Covenant Books, Inc.
11661 Hwy 707
Murrells Inlet, SC 29576
www.covenantbooks.com

ACKNOWLEDGEMENT

The writing of this book has been a journey, not unlike the journey taken in my personal life of fly-fishing. For this dedication, I begin with my mentors who, without their time, patience, and instruction in the intricate aspects of fly fishing in the Great Smoky Mountains, I would never have continued the journey. First, there is Ernie Maxwell who taught me the finer arts of working a stream. Second, is the late Charlie Murrell who passed along an appreciation for the history of the Smokies and third, is the late, legendary Kirk Jenkins who taught me to tie flies from his basement just down the street. It is in their honor that I've made a point of paying it forward by teaching the next generation and then the next, with the goal of shortening their learning curve, which can be difficult for a young beginner, and to respect the resource.

To my wife, Trena, who though she has never fished, has supported my passion which at times has become an obsession. She's been asked, "How do you put up with him?" more times than I wish to consider. Without her love, patience, and wisdom I would not be the person I am today.

Finally, to Jesus Christ who watched over me and guided my path even before I knew Him and to Him, I owe it all.

Proverbs 3:5-6 Trust in the Lord with all thine heart; and lean not unto thine own understanding. In all thy ways acknowledge him, and he shall direct thy paths.

CONTENTS

THE REUNION

It was common knowledge around these parts that Jason McMahan and Dillon Webb shared the same birthday. As they were growing up, it was often said they were joined at the hip as you rarely saw one without the other. The fact that they were born on April 15, which to the outside world is income tax day but around Laurel Cove was the opening day of trout fishing in the Great Smoky Mountain National Park, seemed a precursor for what lay ahead in their lives. As many small-town boys do, they spent their early years running in the woods, swimming the streams, building tree houses, swinging from grapevines, and fishing for whatever was biting. These early years were void of trout and instead consisted mostly of smallmouth bass, bluegill, carp, and catfish. To this day, both are immune to the scent of stink bait, fermented doughballs, and rotten chicken livers as a result of the production and constant exposure to said baits. As with all young boys, there are turning points or events that forever change who we are or what we are to become. It was not until Jay's and Dillon's thirteenth birthday that Dillon's grandfather, Harvey "Pop" Powell, figured it was time to share his passion with that of his maternal grandson and the next closest thing, his sidekick. Though not a drop of Jewish blood coursed through the veins of either of the parties involved, Pop felt it was time to make men out of the boys he had watched grow up, and to him, taking them fly-fishing was his idea of a southern-style bar mitzvah. Gifts were even presented as each received his own fly-fishing outfit special ordered from Webb's Hardware, at a modest cost of $20 each.

And so it was that Dillon and Jay arose before the chickens on their thirteenth birthday, were picked up by Pop, presented with the birthday fishing outfits, and treated to a man's breakfast at Smoky's Café complete with sausage, gravy n' biscuits, and strong black coffee. Both unwilling to forgo any aspect of the initiation to manhood, they drank the strong black coffee only to learn the concept of free refills, much to their dismay. The trip up to Big Creek was a quiet drive as Pop always listened to the local news on the radio. "Need to know who done what and who got caught," he'd remark.

It was a cold morning, on that first April 15th, the first of their teenage years, fly-fishing careers, if you want to call fly-fishing a career, and by some standards, their manhood. With temperatures hovering around the freezing mark in Laurel Cove, it was at least five if not ten degrees cooler walking up the trail that parallels Big Creek. They walked the mile or so up to Midnight Hole. Fortunately, this time of year, the pool is void of swimmers and, being daytime, also void of high school-aged skinny dippers. Pop proceeded to show the boys "how it's done" using the Smoky Mountain flip to cast the weighted nymph into the deep emerald green water. Being a good caster was advantageous even on the small creek considering none of the members of the fishing party had waders. Pop believed waders were much too dangerous. "They'll fill up and kill ye, sure as shoot! And besides, if'n ye cain't stand the cold water, ye ought not be out here."

That first day ended with Pop's creel filled with his limit. Jay and Dillon got skunked. Of course, this day wasn't without its lessons nonetheless. Jay, for example, learned that it's not wise to crawl on your belly on a rock sloping downward into a deep hole just to see if there were any trout resting beneath. Without immediate assistance, the likely conclusion is falling in over your head and having to swim out. Dillon didn't fare much better. In trying to get the first of many tangled flies out of the trees, he learned that in early spring, some tree limbs are not as strong as they ought to be. Naturally, the tree limb just so happens to be hanging out over a deep pool, and like Jay, he found himself swimming in some mighty cold water. So Jay's and Dillon's first lesson in cleaning trout was conducted by Pop with the two boys shivering as ice crystals formed on the outer edges of their clothing. Pop was a realistic man. He neither expected nor wished the boys to learn fly-fishing on that first trip. Pop believed in the journey, not the destination. "The best thangs er worth waitin' fer." He believed the most important aspect of the journey was the experience and, more importantly, the first-time experience. Each first-time experience in life could only be lived once, and while some were best not to be remembered, most were to be seen as a joyful aspect of life and hopefully a lesson. To Pop, there was knowledge and wisdom. A good "schoolin'" would hopefully bring about some "smarts," and the right take on experiences, if properly applied, would handle the wisdom, a.k.a. common sense. Though he taught Jay and Dillon many of the important aspects in trout fishing, he knew too much information was both a hindrance and a waste. Like trying to teach a first grader quantum physics, it was not possible for the first-time fly fisherman to master the perfect cast. For now, they only needed to know a few basics. The most important of which was stealth.

For anyone joining Pop in the mountains, drab clothing, keeping a low profile, and slow movements were not hoped for; they were expected. While the boys handled the basics fairly well considering their youthful exuberance and lack of experience, the thing that most impressed Pop was not their ability to cast, or catch trout, since neither did, nor was it in their rock-hopping ability. Instead, it was in their perseverance. After each took a swim on this cold, overcast April day, Pop gave each of them one of his shirts to go under their wet clothing, leaving him with one dry shirt for himself. Fortunately on this day, Pop dressed in three layers. Though they were cold and a bit disappointed in getting skunked the first time out, neither wanted to call it a day on Big Creek. Before heading back down the trail, Pop made a brief side excursion to dig up some ramps, which he loved to eat scrambled with eggs, to go with his mess of trout. Ramps, a member of the garlic family, are known for the pungent odor they leave not only on the breath but also through the sweat glands of the consumers for at least a few days. As they dig up the short, two-leafed plants, Pop tells of days when he was in school as a boy. It was not uncommon for his classmates to be sent home for reeking of ramps. In fact, as Pop puts it, "I wuz known to eat ramps fer dinner from time to time, so's I would git sent home. It worked purt near every time!" Filling a bread bag each for their trip out, the threesome made their way back down the trail. The main topic of discussion on their walk out was about the next fishing trip.

Sociologists and anthropologists would conclude in their assessment that Jay's and Dillon's desire to fish is a result of thousands of years of human evolution in which the males of the species become the hunter-gatherers. Others would say it is the desire of best friends to do things together. Pop figured it was the boy's love of the Smoky Mountains and the fact they can't stand to be bested by a wild fish with pea-sized brain, even if it was a trout.

From an early age, Jay and Dillon exhibited a drive to excel in whatever occupied their time. Either that, or they were stubborn beyond their years and hated being bested by anything or anyone. They loved a good challenge, particularly one involving fishing in the mountains. Now, on the thirteenth anniversary of their birth, this unrelenting drive had become focused on the pursuit of wild, stream-bred mountain trout.

When summer finally came and school was out, Jay and Dillon found themselves occupied in the typically mundane world of summer jobs. To their chagrin, both spent more than their share of time bailing hay, usually as a team, for ole man Frazier. However, this year things were different. They had stuff to buy and not just the usual stuff desired by teenage boys not yet old enough to seriously consider what kind of car they wanted. They found themselves looking to buy equipment to help them catch more trout. From the outside looking in, that equipment wasn't geared toward trout fishing as would deem appropriate to the untrained eye.

True to their nature, they had a plan, a long-term plan. It began with the realization that they were in this for the long haul. Their goal was to someday be as good as Pop, and they had the potential, ambition, and most importantly, the drive to see it through. Seeing as how trout had to be caught, they knew the first basic need was bait, or in this case flies. According to Pop, the "yallerhammer" was the ticket, and he proved this to them on Big Creek. Every trout fisherman in Laurel Cove and most within a twenty-five-mile radius knew about the "yallerhammer." While there were several variations of this local favorite, the main ingredient was the feathers from the wing of a "yellowhammer" or, as they're known by ornithologists, the yellow-shafted flicker. And as Jay and Dillon learned early in life, few things were without a catch. The catch in this case was that the yellow-shafted flicker was a protected species of woodpecker.

Since the source was somewhat limited, they were expensive if not difficult to get. Pop had his own source, and tied his favorite pattern, which consisted of the hackle from the split feather wrapped around the front of the hook with an insect-green body. So the first few months, Jay and Dillon had to develop a strategy to procure their own supply. Being thirteen made it somewhat difficult to find a source, so they spent their first few hard-earned dollars buying some much-needed equipment to increase their chance of acquiring the birds.

Lady luck called out their name one hot May afternoon when they spotted several hanging out in a small stand of dead trees along a fence row separating two fields full of hay bales waiting to be hauled to the barn. At the end of one long and hot afternoon, they "found" two yellowhammers and a crow that had succumbed to gunshot wounds, a fortuitous afternoon indeed. The next afternoon, Lady Luck revisited the boys as they found the ingredients for the body of the fly strutting around behind one of ole man Frazier's barns in which they were loading the afternoon's trailer full of hay. Fortunately, it didn't take long for them to "borrow" several long quills, making everyone happy, except for the angry peacock with the gap in his tail. While Pop preferred the green yellowhammer, another popular choice was the peacock body yellowhammer, also known as the yellowhammer wooly worm.

With the main ingredients in hand, the next challenge presented itself in acquiring the necessary tools and equipment to produce said trout fly. Borrowing some of his mom's black sewing thread and his dad's needle-nose pliers, Jay held the hook while Dillon gave it his best shot. However before they began tying the real deal, Jay had the idea of some practice flies. For this, they chose the feathers of field wrens and meadowlarks, of which there was an ample supply in the hayfields, and they borrowed some of their mom's black cross-stitching thread for the bodies. As they took turns holding the number 8 hooks while the other tied, the first several dozen flies were less than perfect. In fact, they were terrible. After several consultative lessons with Pop, improvement came about fast. The next major acquisition was a Thompson Pro Vise, for which they scraped up enough money to get one to share. The game was on.

Before long, they had improved their fly-tying skills enough to risk the process with the precious yellowhammer feathers. Hooks, being a scarce commodity with the lack of funds and all, were reused by disassembling their previous attempts. With their recycled hooks, they made their first attempts with the yellowhammer feathers.

For their next on stream foray, Pop took them for a Memorial Day weekend camping trip to Elkmont. It was here they would learn the effectiveness of their efforts. It didn't take long. Elkmont campground was crowded as always on Memorial Day weekend. While the campfires were plentiful and well-tended at night, each day began with a mass exodus of the campground to nearby Gatlinburg where plenty of stuffed bears, tacky T-shirts, and hillbilly souvenirs could be found for overly inflated prices. Meanwhile Dillon, Jay, and Pop made their way up the old train bed along the Little River among the cool, clear waters dropping into the dark plunge pools and waterfalls accentuated by white rhododendron blooms.

Pop, dressed in his dark-blue Dickies with his wicker creel strapped around his neck and resting against his left hip, slowly made his way across the stream, leaving the boys on the near side to leapfrog as they progressed upstream. As Pop flipped his line into one run after another high sticking his way from pool to pool, Dillon and Jay learned the hard way just how impossible it can be to avoid the overhanging rhododendron and mountain laurel. Pop's movements were slow and deliberate, and like those of a Great Blue Heron stalking dinner, each movement possessing purpose and precision. Each motion commenced only after the previous was concluded. When still, Pop could be hard, if not downright impossible, to spot. Blending into the surroundings often crouching behind a boulder or hugging the back side of a tree, even his fly rod resembled that of a tree limb, albeit a straight tree limb. He even went so far as to dull the sheen from his rod to prevent any glare or flash from giving away his location and intentions.

Meanwhile, Dillon and Jay bounced from rock to rock with movements similar to the random motions of downy woodpeckers. Looking over his shoulder, Pop couldn't help but smile at their youth and innocence in both life and fly-fishing. *Youth is wasted on the young*, he thought as he paused to light his cigar. Every so often, he would make his way to Jay or Dillon to offer some advice. Typical comments were "try this" or "cast over thur" or "Move ye rod this way to get 'che line to go thur." And the ever popular, "Don't do that er that'll happen ever time." At that time, neither realized the significance of what Pop was trying to teach them. Both were too busy pursuing the next trout.

Pop knew 99 percent of his advice was falling on immature, teenage boy ears, but he believed it would be helpful when that special moment arrived where all the pieces came together for each boy. When that would come, he didn't have a clue, but he was certain of one thing, it would come. Like an action adventure movie where scene after scene of thrills and suspense would be intermittently broken by the comedy break, Jay and Dillon provided additional priceless entertainment that kept Pop anticipating their next fishing trip just as much as they did.

That camping trip, Memorial Day weekend of their fourteenth year, was a milestone that neither Jay or Dillon realized 'til years later at a time when they sat around the fireplace on a cold winter day reminiscing about Pop and their early days of fly-fishing. It was that weekend that both Jay and Dillon caught their first trout, both nine-inch rainbows, their first "keepers," which was a nine-inch or longer trout, their first limit of four nine-inch fish, and their first trout on flies they personally tied, all under the ever watchful eye of Pop. He always seemed intensely focused on the pool or run he was fishing, but he also always knew exactly what Jay or Dillon were doing or not doing. Pop was mindful that experience was the best teacher and thus allowed the boys to make their own mistakes, to learn themselves, and to make their own discoveries. He always seemed to know just how much wisdom to impart and when. Years later as Jay and Dillon sat around their campfires, they could recite word for word some of the stories shared by Pop—the time he caught the three big browns at Metcalf Bottoms on the same day, and his one hundred plus fish days on Eagle Creek, all on his green yellowhammer. Those were fishing trips Pop took when he was a boy before the Park was created.

The day Pop died was another milestone for Jay and Dillon. It was the summer after Jay and Dillon finally got their driver's license and now had the ability to drive, which potentially meant more fishing, if only they had wheels. Although Pop was Dillon's maternal grandfather, Pop kept Jay just as close. Both of Jay's grandfathers passed away before he was born; thus, Pop became his surrogate. A couple of days after his funeral, Mamaw Powell asked the boys to come over. She wanted to follow Pop's wishes by giving the boys what remained of Pop's fishing equipment, a couple of short, stiff graphite rods, his wicker creel, his fly-tying kit, and his old, rusty pickup truck. Pop never had much equipment, never needed much, but he sure caught the trout. It was on this day, Jay and Dillon began to realize what a blessing they had in Pop and how much they missed him. From this day forward, they knew their lives would be ever entwined in both their friendship and in their fly-fishing. They had a legacy to carry on and now the equipment to do it. No, it wasn't worth much on the market, but they wouldn't trade any of it for the world. What they now shared had been once Pop's. Now, it's was theirs, and it was their responsibility to use it. In a way, they felt responsible to Pop for all he taught them. It was knowledge of which he had plenty and shared frequently, and they were blessed to have been on the receiving end.

For the next few years, Jay and Dillon spent most all of their time in the mountains chasing trout, honing their fly-tying skills, and making a lifetime of mistakes along the way. Fortunately, they learned from a few and remembered most. Pop's old pickup got a lot of use and became well known among the park rangers as it was a frequent site along Smoky Branch and Big Bear Fork. By their senior year of high school, Dillon had bought his own wheels, a '69 Nova. While the particular vehicle wasn't known as a muscle car, Dillon had allowed the engine to be tweaked in automotive shop class to vastly improve the horsepower. Still, it was a work in progress. What wasn't rusted was bondo, but it would fly!

One beautiful, sunny early May morning found Jay and Dillon hanging out at their usual post in the hallway just outside the school cafeteria waiting for classes to begin. As usual, Jay was thinking about fishing, Dillon was thinking about fishing and Luanne Davis's tight jeans and V-neck blouse. Both had a bad case of "senioritis" and were just biding their time 'til graduation day, which was still a long three weeks away. Since the semester began in January, which they repeatedly pointed out as their last semester, their motto had been "D for diploma." As long as they passed their classes, they were out of here. Dillon and Luanne had been the "on again, off again" relationship of the high school year, culminating in their being voted the prom king and queen. Jay casually mentioned, "I sure bet the trout are bitin' today. The weather man says it's gonna be sunny and a high 'round seventy-five. Man! I'd sure like to be on the west prong of Little River bringin' 'em in."

Those words were not lost on Dillon whose arm was around Luanne's shoulder. At once, his eyes shifted from her dark hazel eyes and over her shiny indigo hair to someplace distant. She knew that look. It was a look that only Jay seemed able to instigate, a look that once embedded, no amount of cuddling, pouting, or whining could cure. She was resigned to what was next. Dillon turned toward Jay, "Let's hit it!" Without another word, both took off down the hallway toward the back door leading to the parking lot and Dillon's Nova. On the way, they spotted Melvin Cody heading their way. Melvin was the class salutatorian and self-proclaimed fishing guru of the school. Most everyone knew he was full of "BS" but did not bother arguing the point as he was too annoying to carry on the amount of conversation required. Stopping in their tracks, Jay and Dillon began talking about nothing, trying to give the appearance of an involved conversation, hoping he would pass them by, but no such luck. Melvin was in a talking mood this morning, which wasn't unusual as long as the conversation centered on him or fishing or preferably him fishing and the knowledge he possessed about the subject.

"Hey, guys. You wanna see my newest invention? It'll catch trout like nobody's business." Slightly overweight but believing himself to be husky in the manly sense that an overweight, overconfident teenager would be, Melvin nervously adjusted his thick, black-rimmed, "Coke bottle" glasses every other sentence as they tended to slide down his nose, which was usually sweaty. He was a real momma's boy but tried to exude confidence to cover his insecurities. The problem was that he tried too hard, resulting in overcompensation to some sub-infinite degree.

"Not really, Melvin. Dillon and I are talkin' about the history test on Monday," Jay replied, trying to politely excuse himself and Dillon from Melvin's dissertation they knew was imminent on the virtues of the trout's inability to resist his newest creation.

As they began walking toward the back door, Melvin trotted toward them. "Hey! Where you guys goin'? School's about to start, and you don't want another tardy, do you, Dillon? I'd hate to see you suspended with a month to go before graduation," Melvin stated more in a nagging parental tone than one of concern.

"Shut up, Melvin! I can tell time! We'll be back. Just don't say nothin' to nobody," Dillon replied as he and Jay closed the door behind them.

Suddenly, the door swung open, and it was Melvin. "You guys ain't going fishin', are ye? If so, I wanna go. I'll even let you have one of my new secret weapons!"

Sharing that "well now what" look, Jay and Dillon considered the consequences of their next decision. They could walk back into school now and forget the whole idea, they could go fishing and leave him behind knowing full well he can't keep a secret, or they could take him along and tolerate him as best they can. "You know, Dillon, we don't have to fish with him. We can always walk upstream a ways and keep a buffer zone. Once we get him up there, we can threaten to tell his mom on him if he tags along too close."

Dillon grins. "You know, fer a second I thought you were going to say once we got him up there, we could kill him!" Both let out a loud laugh as they looked back toward Melvin. "The problem is the drive over to West Prong will take a while, and I can't stand listenin' to him that long."

Jay patted Dillon on the shoulder giving him a reassuring look. "I got an idea." Looking back toward Melvin, he yelled, "Come on, Melvin, let's go!"

The three climbed into Dillon's Nova, with Melvin in the backseat. Immediately, Jay pops in the new eight-track tape from The Knack. Spinning gravel out of the parking lot as they made their getaway, "My Sharona" was blaring over the speakers. From the back seat, Melvin shouted, "Hey, guys, the music's too loud. I can't talk!" Jay and Dillon shared a grin.

The hooky-playing threesome made their way home to get their fishing equipment. Knowing Melvin would have the most trouble getting his stuff together, gathering his many secret weapons and self-proclaimed brilliant ideas, Dillon dropped Melvin off at his house while they drove on to their respective houses. Within minutes, both were out the door and ready to hit West Prong. As they neared Melvin's house, they spotted a commotion from a block away. Ms. Cody came stomping out of the front door, her hair in rollers with little sideburns "dippity do'd" and taped to her cheeks. She was wearing an old pink housecoat with pink fuzzy house shoes and was walking briskly toward her brown AMC Pacer with car keys in her left hand and Melvin's left ear in tow in her right hand. They couldn't hear what she was yelling, but they knew it wasn't pretty. With every syllable of every word, the cigarette hanging out the left side of her mouth bounced up and down like the end of a jackhammer. Poor Melvin was taking short choppy steps trying to stay up with Momma, knowing the slightest stumble meant a 50 percent reduction in hearing. They almost felt sorry for Melvin… almost. For a moment, a wave of fear swept over Jay and Dillon. Should they sneak back into school and risk another tardy or continue their current path? While stopped at the corner of Melvin's street weighing their options, the passenger side door of the car opened momentarily startling both Jay and Dillon who were focused on the decision at hand. Both quickly realized it was only Mr. Hopkins.

"Over," says Hoppy as he slid into the front seat, moving Jay into the middle. Tall and slim, with unkempt gray hair, Mr. Hopkins, aka Hoppy, wore his usual navy slacks and vest with a white long-sleeved shirt and navy tie. An eccentric, retired landowner, Hoppy got his money the old-fashioned way. He inherited it. Though never quite possessing all of his marbles, he lost most of what he had some time back when he had a "nervous breakdown." As Pop always put it, "What in tarnation did he have the nerves over, he never did a honest day's work. And which nerve wuz it that broke down anyway?" Since his "breakdown," Hoppy walked with a cane, but it never stopped him from his only known occupation, hitchhiking between the local communities.

As was his usual modus operandi, Hoppy would simply wait on a street corner for a car, any car, to stop at which time he would promptly open the car door and bum a ride. During such "lifts," Hoppy rarely spoke. When he did, it was limited to one word. Beyond that, either Hoppy did not desire to expound in more depth or figured anything worth saying could and should be covered in one word, no more no less. Other than being sort of an odd ball, he was harmless and generally liked and trusted by all.

With Dillon at the wheel, Jay in the middle, and Hoppy riding shotgun, their thoughts returned to the topic at hand.

"What d' ye think we oughta do, Jay?"

"We're done in it up to our waist. I'd say let's wade the rest of the way in and go on to West Prong. Just because Melvin's been busted don't mean we gotta call it quits. Them trouts still callin' my name. Hell, there might be one or two calling your name as well. As Momma always says, anything worth havin' is worth fightin' for. Besides, now we don't have to put up with his yakkin' the whole way over."

"Well, what if'n he tells Principal Baxter. Ye know he's been dyin' to do me in before I graduate."

"Well, Dillon, you know when I thought you were talkin' 'bout killin' Melvin a while ago? I guess we'll have our excuse. Besides, Melvin knows better'n to rat us out. If'n we don't kill him, he knows we'd never go fishin' with him again, not that that would be bad."

Dillon nodded in agreement and shifted it into third gear, and the threesome made their way toward West Prong as the sun began to break through the early morning fog over the Great Smoky Mountains. As they made their way up the winding curves of Wears Valley Road, Dillon and Jay were jamming to the thirty-seventh rendition of "My Sharona" when they came upon a tractor pulling a wagon full of poles to be used in building a fence. Dillon downshifted and slammed on the brakes. Never one for patience when driving, especially when going fishing, Dillon knew they might be stuck since the curves do not lend themselves to an easy pass even though the tractor is barely doing twenty miles per hour.

"Come on, man! Get out of the way!" Dillon yelled as he punched the steering wheel with the palm of his hand.

"Calm down, Dillon, we'll get there," Jay replied in a calm voice. "We've got all day."

"Not at this rate! I'm gonna blow his straw hat plum off when I punch it past him!" The curves continue.

Finally, a short straight comes up, still a double yellow line, but Dillon couldn't hold back any longer. He punched the gas, shifted gears and spun his wheels as he took off around the tractor and trailer going from twenty to fifty before the end of the straightaway. Unfortunately, Dillon and Jay were not familiar with the nuances of Wears Valley Road and did not realize the sharp right hand curve coming up at the end of the straight away. Dillon hit it wide open now going nearly sixty-five. He hit the brakes hard, but his momentum carried him across the oncoming lane and over the embankment getting airborne briefly. For a fraction of a second, all was quiet. Only the rumble of the engine, the wind whistling by outside, and their screams broke the silence. As they passed over a fence, they came to a hard nose first landing into a soggy pasture. Their speed failed to decrease sufficiently as water and mud sprayed from beneath the Nova. The windshield became covered in brown water, like that of a dirty, high-speed carwash, grass, and mud streaming up the glass. *Bam, bam, bam, bam!* It seemed the banging and rattling never stopped. Then, as suddenly as it began, it ended. Dillon looked at Jay. Jay looked out through the opaque windows trying to get his bearings. Suddenly, Hoppy opened the door and stepped out into the muddy pasture.

"Idiots!" comments Hoppy as he storms away from the mud-covered car back to the pavement of Wears Valley Road. Once there, he assumed his usual position, right thumb out while standing on the side of the road headed back toward home.

After sitting in the car for a moment, "Ooh you make my motor run, my motor run. Gun it comin' off the line Sharona," was still blaring on the eight-track, but all else was quiet. Dillon turned the key and attempted to fire up the Nova; miraculously, it started. He gently pressed the accelerator, but the rear wheels only spun. "Man, we are royally screwed!"

Jay stepped out of the passenger side door. A few curious cows standing around the car now trotted away. Apparently, all the excitement scared the heifer as she left him something warm and moist to step into. His first step was a bull's-eye. "Oh man!"

Dillon looked over from the driver's seat. "What's wrong? Is it bad!"

"No, I just stepped into a fresh cow pile with my new tennis shoes!"

"Screw the shoes, man! What about my car!" Dillon got out and took a look for himself.

As both walked around the Nova surveying the car, they were surprised and happy to see little damage. The only problem was a dent in the front bumper and some scratches on the hood; otherwise, very little could be seen under the mud covering the car except for the obvious—they're deeply mired in mud and on the verge of sliding into an opaque brown pond.

"Ye know, if you'd succeeded in drivin' off, we'd be in the middle of that pond 'bout now." Jay observed as he looked up from the car.

"Well, how 'bout pushin' on the front of the car while I try to back away and out of the mud."

By now, Jay realized his hope of keeping his new shoes clean was over as he sloshed around to the front of the car in ankle-deep water and mud from the overnight rain that apparently hit Wears Valley but missed Laurel Cove altogether, something not unusual in the Smoky Mountains.

Dillon sat back in the driver's seat with the engine still idling and put the Nova in reverse.

"Ease on it slowly," Jay yelled from the front bumper, "and don't furget to put 'er in reverse."

"Yeah, yeah, I ain't stupid!" Dillon eased on the gas but to no avail. The car would not budge. His only accomplishment was digging the rear wheels deeper into the mud now up to the axel.

Dillon slammed his hand against the steering wheel. "Man, we're screwed! Our parents are gonna find out, Principal Baxter's gonna find out. When he finds out, we'll both be suspended and spend the entire friggin' summer in school! Do you know how dead I'll be when I don't go through the graduation line with the rest of the class! Man, it's over!"

Now sitting on the hood, Jay, ever the calm optimistic balance to Dillon was already thinking about what it would take to get the car out of the field.

Unnoticed by both, the farmer had pulled down a dirt road off the highway and had opened a gate driving his tractor over to the fence row now missing. He unhitched the wagon, slowly climbed back onto the tractor, and headed toward Jay and Dillon.

Jay pointed toward the oncoming tractor and optimistically commented, "Maybe farmer Brown will lend us a hand."

As Dillon shut off the engine and stepped out of the car, the tractor pulled up and stopped. The old farmer eased the tractor to a halt, shut off the engine, and stepped off the tractor. He walked toward the Nova and looked over the sunken rear wheels of the mud-covered car, wearing grungy overalls with the legs stuffed down old muddy rubber boots and a dirty brown jacket; he adjusted his hat, spat tobacco juice on the ground, and wiped the excess off his gray, bearded face with his right sleeve. "Looks like you boys could use some help!" he said as he grinned and nodded toward the back wheels mired deeply into the pasture.

Dillon casts a sarcastic look at the farmer, "Naw, we're jus passin'..."

"Shut up, man," Jay said quietly to Dillon as he stepped in front of him.

"Yeah, we're in it purty good," he said smiling at the farmer.

Jay turned around and quietly whispered to Dillon, "Right now, this guy's our only way out." Jay stepped a little closer to the mud-covered farmer. "We'd sure appreciate a little help. My buddy here got in a little bit of a hurry and didn't make that last curve."

"What're you boys doin' out here?"

Jay glanced over at Dillon. "We were hopin to head up to the Park to do a little fishin'. My buddy here gets in a little bit of a hurry sometimes when on the way to a fishin' trip."

"Well, mix that with a wet road, and it spells nothin' but trouble. I don't know much 'bout fishin', but I do know thar ain't none in that thur pond," he replied as he chewed on the wad of "backer" and nodded toward the pond in front of Dillon's car.

Jay glanced toward Dillon and then back at the farmer. "Well, we'd sure appreciate any help you could give us in gettin' out of the mud and back on the highway."

Dillon, having been quiet up till now, stepped forward and asked, "Mister, ye wouldn't know who owns this farm, would ye?"

"Yer, lookin' at him," he replied, spitting tobacco juice on the muddy ground.

"Well, I figure we owe ye a new fence."

The farmer looked both boys over, looked at the Nova again, and glanced at the missing fence behind him. "Tell ye what. Ye boys seem like purty good fellers. I'll make a deal with ye. That ole fence was purty rotten, and I figured I'd be replacin' it sometime soon after I got done addin' the fence I've been workin' on. I'll help ye get out of the mud if'n ye help me fix the fence."

Jay and Dillon look at each other, then the missing fence, and back to the Nova. Both come to the same conclusion that they don't have much of a choice.

Jay nods at Dillon and Dillon replies, "Well, mister. Don't see how's we got much of a choice, and it's only fair that we help repair the damage."

Dillon walked over to the farmer, shook on the deal, and said, "My name's Dillon. This here's my buddy Jay."

Jay reached out to shake the farmer's hand. The farmer gave it a strong shake with his calloused hand, "Name's Walker. Elijah Walker. Look, before we get goin', you boys need some decent work clothes. Hop on the back of the tractor, and I'll take ye over to the barn. I have some ole overalls and a couple o' pairs of work boots that might jest fit the both of ye."

Jay and Dillon did as they were asked by hopping onto the back of the tractor and holding on for the bumpy ride to the barn. There they found extra pairs of overalls and rubber boots that loosely fit, good enough though to get dirty in. After changing into the oversized, dirty farming clothes, they walked back outside the barn where they found Mr. Walker sitting on his back porch in a rocking chair with a cup of coffee.

Looking at the newly clad farm boys, Mr. Walker finished his coffee, stood up, and commented, "You boys look a mite out of place, but I reckon you'll get by. We'll, daylight's burnin', and we ain't getting much done."

Jay and Dillon climbed back on the tractor for the ride out to where the car was still mired to its axel in mud. Using a chain brought out by Mr. Walker, Jay hooked one end to the back of the tractor and the other to the rear bumper of the Nova. Dillon sat in the driver's seat of the car, feathering the accelerator as Mr. Walker pulled him out of the soggy field and onto the dirt road coming off Wears Valley Road. The three then headed over to the trailer with the fence poles, hitched it up to the tractor, and rode it over to where portions of the fence poles still stuck out from the ground. The demolished poles were strung out along the pasture, some still attached to the barbed wire.

As the day wore on, Jay and Dillon were amazed at Mr. Walker whom they agree had to be pushing eighty years old, if a day. The weatherman had predicted a high of seventy-five today. As usual, he missed it, by about ten degrees. It was now sunny, clear, and nearly eighty-five! Through nearly four hours of steady work, Mr. Walker had held his own with the boys. Initially, Dillon was sandbagging hoping the old farmer would do most of the work. It wasn't long before he was being put to shame by this ole timer.

With Mr. Walker working at the far end of the fence row, Dillon paused for a moment, stretching his back, working the fatigue out of his athletic arms, and wiping the sweat off his forehead. "Dang, ole Mr. Walker's killin' me! How the crap does he keep goin' at his pace. I mean, he ain't stopped since we got started!"

Pausing for a minute from fighting a pair of posthole diggers, Jay stopped and stretched. "I don't know, but I got too much pride to let him put more poles in the ground than me. I mean, I didn't really want to help but knew we had no choice but Mr. Walker's wearin' me down and puttin' you to shame!" With that, Jay laughed at Dillon condescendingly and went back to digging his hole.

"Shut up, Jay! I'm only two poles behind, and I'm gonna outdo him if'n I gotta cheat somehow."

"Well, don't take no shortcuts. Somehow he'll know and dog us 'bout it." Around lunchtime, Mr. Walker gave the boys a ride on the tractor to his back porch where Mrs. Walker, the epitome of the perfect grandmotherly type, had boloney sandwiches, tater salad, and sweet tea ready. It was the only time Mr. Walker stopped working. While they ate, Mrs. Walker continued to coddle the boys, meeting their every need, the perfect southern Appalachian hostess. The real treat was the stories Mr. Walker shared with the boys. Though they got a kick out of the tales of his early days in the Smokies before it became a park, it was not until years later that they truly relished their chance meeting with the Walkers. Elijah and Mary Walker talked of their early days going to school at the Little Greenbrier Schoolhouse just across the ridge near Metcalf Bottoms. "I 'member walking up that ridge in the snow when I was ten," Mr. Walker reminisces.

"I bet it was uphill both ways," joked Dillon, ever the sarcastic comedian.

"Matter of fact 'twas, 'eh, Momma?"

"Eya," Mrs. Walker answered and smiled at Ms. Walker as she refilled their tea glasses.

"From whur we lived up thar in the valley, we walked the trail up over the ridge, down the holler to get thar, then up the ridge and down the holler back home. So I'ma guessin in a way, it wuz uphill both ways."

Trying to show his limited knowledge of Smoky Mountain history, Jay asked, "Did ye know the Walker sisters?"

"Know 'em. They's cousins of mine. They went to school thar too. Been dead a while though, all five of 'em that lived over next to the school. When weather wuz bad, I stayed thar in that cabin a time or two. Independent women, they wuz, and proud of it."

Standing up, Mr. Walker finished off his sweet tea. "Well, boys, let's hit it. Time's 'uh wastin' and daylight's 'uh burnin'."

As the afternoon wore on and Jay and Dillon wore down, Mr. Walker kept his horrid working pace, which Dillon made every attempt to match but in the end found it futile. The work wasn't too bad as Mr. Walker kept them humored with his stories of the "olden days," as Jay called it. Dillon called it "the corn cob days," describing them as when a corn cob was used in place of a roll of Charmin in the nearby outhouse.

Thinking back to his youth, Mr. Walker told stories of "catchin' specks by the hunnert and keepin 'em by the sackload. Back then, we used a fly called the Clay Hart and a gray fly with guinea feathers."

A sudden jolt hit Jay and Dillon when Mr. Walker mentioned that he used to fly-fish for trout, realizing the old farmer had been holding out on them all day.

With a serious look on his face, Jay asked, "Did you say you used flies to catch specks back then?"

"Eya, it wuz that 'er worms, and I saw a flatlander ketch the tar out of 'em on flies once when I wuz a kid. Couldn't believe my eyes at how many he caught. I ordered me some hooks from a catalog, got me one of them fly-fishin' poles, and got started. It took a while, but I got the hang of it. I found it to be better'n throwin' worms in the long run. Didn't have to bait yer hook so often."

After a long day, they finally got the job finished, and while Jay and Dillon were tired and relieved, they found themselves not wanting the day to end. All of the stories Mr. Walker shared about camping, hiking, horseback riding in the mountains, and most of all fishing had left them wanting more.

Reaching out to shake their hands, Mr. Walker said, "Well, I shore thank ye boys for a hard day's work in fixin' my fence."

"We're shore sorry for bustin' it up, Mr. Walker," replied Dillon as he shook the gnarled, ole hand. "I wanna thank ye for pullin' us out of the mud."

"I 'spect ye maw and paw's waitin' on ye boys."

The three gathered up all of the tools and damaged poles. As Jay and Dillon rode on the back of the trailer on their way to the barn, they looked up toward Cove Mountain overlooking Wears Valley. While it was a wasted day in terms of trout fishing, all was not a loss. In fact, it wasn't bad at all. While they were sure to be sore tomorrow, it was Friday, and if nothing else, they could work the soreness out fishing up Big Bear Creek at home tomorrow. At the barn, Jay and Dillon took turns pumping the hand pump on the well while the other washed up. They walked into the barn and took off the muddy boots and overalls. As they walked out of the barn and toward the muddy Nova, Mr. Walker was on the back porch hugging two young, beautiful blonde girls.

Their mouths dropped open looking first at the girls, then at each other. Dillon asked, "Jay. Am I see'n double, or are there two hot babes huggin' Mr. Walker?"

"Maybe we're both see'n double, 'cause I see 'em too. Farmer's daughters?" Jay asked with a sneaky smile.

"Nah. Gotta be granddaughters at the least. Maybe great-granddaughters," replied Dillon, not removing his eyes from the two girls apparently in their late teens and obviously identical twins. "Mr. and Mrs. Walker both got to be in their seventies, at least. More likely their eighties"

"You boys gonna stay fer supper?" Mrs. Walker asked from the front porch while wiping her hands on her apron. For the first time, the twins see Jay and Dillon standing in the doorway of the barn. They smiled.

Jay and Dillon smiled back. Jay, still focused on one of the twins, didin't matter which one as they were identical, said to Dillon, "I don't care if they're havin' pig's feet and possum gravy. I'm stayin' fer supper."

Dillon, likewise stared at one of the twins, replied, "I heard dat!"

Over a delicious home-cooked country dinner of fried chicken, mashed potatoes and gravy, green beans, and homemade rolls, the Walkers were the perfect dinner hosts. Though a freshly baked hot apple pie sat on the windowsill cooling, Jay, and especially Dillon, had a different post-dinner dessert in mind, the blonde kind. They learned the twins, Mandy and Candy, had just completed their first year of college and were spending the next week with their grandparents. They further learned, the twins attended a girls-only college, and though they weren't certain, all signs pointed toward the fact that they had sorely missed male companionship. Of course, that observation was duly noted by the two possessing the highest testosterone level at the dinner table, and quite possibly within a ten-mile radius, though Winston, the horny, Black Angus bull on loan to Mr. Walker might give them a run for their money.

Settling for the apple pie dessert for now, Jay and Dillon worked what little magic they possessed between them in setting up a date with Mandy and Candy for tomorrow night. Sore muscles be damned, there were two blondes in their immediate future.

A full day's work repairing the fence, dinner, working up a date with the twins, the drive home, and washing the mud, a.k.a. evidence, off the Nova before driving back into Laurel Cove meant a late arrival at home for Dillon and Jay. For Jay, little explanation was required. For the most part, he was a trustworthy teenage boy, at least in the eyes of his parents. Any occurrence outside the "norm" was filed into the "boys will be boys" category. Dillon on the other hand had a different problem.

No sooner had he walked through his door that he was told by his mom, "Luanne's been callin' all afternoon. She's wonderin' where ye been and so am I." Dillon had little trouble talking his way out of his absentee afternoon with his dad, who understood the deadly recipe of youth, senioritis, sunshine, and trout fishing, as well as he did corn, sugar, yeast, and copper tubing. However, he did not understand how his boy could come back with an empty creel. "Boy! I figured if'n ye spent all day in the mountains, ye'd have somethin' to show fer it." Unlike Jay, Dillon was in deep trouble. Luanne was jealous, and she was pissed. It would take some sweet-talking and no small measure of groveling to get back in Luanne's arms and good graces. After spending a good hour and a half on the phone, Dillon had made some progress but still had a long uphill climb. There was no way he could keep his date with Mandy or Candy, whichever it was. Jay would have to go at it alone.

Jay did go solo the next night driving back over to Wears Valley for a date with Mandy, or was it Candy. It didn't really matter as he could never tell them apart. Fortunately, they didn't pull the Doublemint twins routine by wearing identical clothing. Still, they could've left the room switched clothing, returned, and he wouldn't ever know the difference. In fact, the date was a real letdown of sorts.

After leaving Luanne's house Sunday afternoon, Dillon stopped by Jay's house to get the scoop. "So how'd it go?" Dillon asked, starved for details.

"Aw right, I guess," Jay replied.

"What d'ye mean, aw right? Man, they're hot! Which 'un wuz it, Mandy or Candy?"

"I believe it wuz Candy," Jay replied somewhat dejected. "Don't matter though. I ain't goin back."

Trying not to choke on his words, a stunned Dillon asks, "Not goin back! Man, you crazy! I'd be all over it. I mean if it wasn't fer Luanne."

Jay, acting real casual about the events of the previous evening, began to tell the story. "Well, I went to pick her up and told them about you gettin' in trouble."

"You didn't tell 'em bout Luanne, did ye?"

"No, I ain't stupid. I told 'em your parents got all out of sorts and wouldn't let you get out fer a month. I told 'em how bad you wanted to come over but how you bein' a bad boy and all, this was yer last straw. Anyway, I found out it was Candy who decided to go, leaving Mandy all dressed up an' nowhere to go. Man, she had it bad for you."

"Thanks fer rubbin' it in," Dillon replied sarcastically.

"I took her up to Gatlinburg, and we drove around a bit. I even took her to a fancy dinner at Howard's. Afterward, we walked to one of the candy factories, and I got her a candy apple. Ironic, ain't it. I got Candy a candy apple!"

The irony was all but lost on Dillon who was only interested in the more amorous details of the previous evening. "Man, did ye get any dessert fer yer money?"

"Ye know the term, smoked salmon? It was more like smoked Candy. Right after we ate, she lit up a cigarette."

"Uh, what?"

"A cigarette, you know like a Virginia Slim er somethin'. One of those little girly cigarettes. Man she smokes!"

"She smokes!" Dillon can't believe his ears. "You know what they say, if she smokes...she pokes! She's H-O-T, hot!"

"I don't care. I cain't take smokin'. I feel like I'm kissin' an exhaust pipe. I swear! I believe I could blow smoke circles after every kiss. 'Bout made me sick. If she'd dipped Skoal, it wouldn't have been much worse. Might've tasted better, wintergreen over menthol!"

Trying to weigh all the possibilities, Dillon asks, "Well, what about Mandy? Does she smoke? Maybe she don't smoke, and we can figger a way for you to work your way to her er somethin'."

"Naw. She smokes too," Jay replied already resigned to give up on the twins.

After that weekend, Jay and Dillon rarely spoke of the smoking twins and never around Luanne. They spent the remainder of the summer doing what most graduating high schoolers do, enjoying their last summer of carefree fun. Both Jay and Dillon graduated with honors, Jay the class valedictorian and Melvin was the salutatorian. Even as they spent that last summer balancing summer jobs and fishing trips, with a few camping trips in the Smokies thrown in for good measure, both knew things were about to change. Though still kids, they were mature enough to know that the only thing sure in life, besides death and taxes, was change.

Jay had applied to and been accepted, with the aid of an academic scholarship, to Duke University in Durham, North Carolina. Dillon, though excelling as a linebacker, turned down a scholarship to East Tennessee State University. To him, twelve years of schooling was all he could stand. While Jay worked toward a liberal arts degree and into medical school, Dillon began doing what he did best—building things. In the eight years since that summer, Jay finished his medical training to become a family practice physician with plans on returning to Laurel Cove to assume the practice of ole Doc Hembree as the only physician in town.

Doc Hembree had gradually spent more and more time out of the office and in the mountains enjoying trout fishing. As the gradual change from sewing sutures and closing up wounds evolved to tying flies to catch trout, so did his desire to get out of the office and among the hemlocks and rhododendrons of Big Bear Fork. The timing of everything seemed to work out for all parties involved. Doc Hembree wanted to wind down his practice, easing his way into retirement while he still had the legs and wits to fish, and Jay wanted nothing more than to come home. Home, where he grew up, where his family lived, where the trout were intelligent but plentiful, and where Dillon lived.

While working on his undergraduate degree, Jay crossed paths with a cute little brunette for which there was no cure. From the first time they met at a fraternity-sorority party, Debbie, an education major, seemed to have Jay's number while Jay seemed to get her goat like nobody's business. Growing up in Portsmouth, Virginia, Debbie grew up as the daughter of a naval officer and was conditioned to having her dad gone for periods of time and her brothers spending days on end away on fishing trips. Fortunately for Jay, Debbie never fully grasped the reasons but did understand the need for a man to spend time outdoors. As her mom always said, "I'd rather he join the men fishing, than the ladies dancing." After Debbie finished her degree, she and Jay married, with Dillon stepping in as the best man.

Dillon had been busy as well, having made quite a name as a residential construction contractor, specializing in log homes. Many attributed his special skills as an outdoorsman to his ability to construct beautiful houses so that they blended so well into the mountains they were nearly invisible to all but the closest observations. The summer after Jay left, Dillon and Luanne had finally called it quits. Dillon could no longer handle the volatile relationship they shared brought about by Luanne's jealous streak and Dillon's smooth ways with the opposite sex. Like Jay, Dillon had met someone special; unfortunately, it seemed his marriage was always in some state of turmoil. Regardless of its status, Dillon continued to make every effort to maintain peace at home with one exception. Unlike Debbie, Mrs. Webb did not care much for Dillon's outdoor escapades and made every attempt to deliver the proverbial guilt trips dished out by a self-centered young bride.

The eight or so years had not gone by without more than a few visits by Jay to Laurel Cove. They were typically centered around the holidays, except for a few years when he was forced to stay near the hospital for on-call duties during his medical residency. And though Jay had spent very little time fishing in the Smokies, he did get in some time casting the fly rod. Though unable to spend the hours he so desperately wanted at times chasing trout, he did have a few opportunities to improve his casting. Occasionally, he had the good fortune to join a couple of the physicians, with whom he worked, on bone fishing trips to the Bahamas. It was in preparing for these trips that Jay developed his casting stroke, with the aid of some Lefty Kreh books, a gift from his father-in-law, allowing him to make long casts that were seemingly never needed in the Smokies but a must on the bonefish flats of the Andros Islands. Jay also spent numerous hours unwinding from the torturous hours of residency expanding his skills as a fly tier. No longer was he limited to yellowhammers, guinea flies, and crow flies in size eights, now he was known among the medical staff as one heck of a dry fly and midge tier in all sizes. Jay was also blessed with a father-in-law who, like Jay, loved to fly-fish, albeit on larger rivers and among the estuaries of Chesapeake Bay.

While Jay was learning new skills in healthcare and honing his abilities as a fly caster and dry fly fisherman, Dillon was perfecting his small stream tight line abilities using heavy nymphs to trick the monster browns known to live in the bottom of the deepest pools in the Smokies.

One night, Dillon received the call from Jay learning that Jay was moving back home. As tickled as he was, Dillon found himself just as nervous. Perhaps anxious is a better term, but Dillon was both excited and somewhat apprehensive as to what the future held. A few days later, Dillon read the blurb in the *Laurel Creek Banner*, "Dr. Jason McMahan will be returning home to assume the practice of the retiring Doc Hembree." Dillon found his gaze locked on the phrase "Dr. Jason McMahan." Something just didn't seem right about that. Deep down, Dillon knew this was the same Jay that he'd grown up with, the same kid with whom he'd learned to fish with Pop, played on the football team, chased bikinis below Hemlock Falls, and camped up on Big Bear Creek and Hazel Creek. This was the same Jay who caught his first trout on Elkmont and with whom he learned to tie trout flies with. Still, had Jay changed? For that matter, Dillon wondered if, well not if, but how had he changed.

Suddenly, he realized he was looking at himself differently. What would Jay think of him? Should he call him Jay, Dr. McMahan, or Dr. Jay? *Growin' up is hell!* Dillon thought as he laid down the paper. *Don't get yerself bent out of shape. This is Jay, the same Jay, at least he seemed the same on the phone. I don't have to call him doc er nothin',* Dillon thought. Still, Jay sounded different. He talked different. Gone, it seemed, was his East Tennessee accent characteristic of the southern Appalachians as noted by Horace Kephart in *Our Southern*

Highlanders. Had he been away that long? He sounded more like a city slicker, not the country boy he grew up with.

Like Dillon, Jay was also somewhat apprehensive. While it was great that he was able to return home, he knew he was returning as a different person. No longer is he "little Jay McMahan." Now he will be expected to treat patients, many of whom he'd known his whole life. Will they have the same confidence in him that they do Doc Hembree? If not initially, when?

During his years away from home, Jay had sorely missed the peacefulness of Laurel Cove and the easygoing, slow-paced lifestyle of the townsfolk. How he had longed to drive down Main Street where everyone waved and where he could walk into Webb's Grocery or Smoky's Drugstore and Café and know everyone and everyone know him. Surprisingly, he missed Hoppy and how he'd jump in the car without notice just to ride down the road a few miles. How he yearned for the beauty of the tumbling streams of the Smoky Mountains, with their moss-covered rocks dotted with white and burgundy trillium blooms and the early morning mist that hung low among the rhododendron blooms in early June. How his soul ached for the cleansing feel of the cool mountain water against his legs as he wet-waded up Big Bear Fork on a warm July afternoon. He missed sharing a can of Vienna sausages and crackers on a rock in the middle of Deep Creek as a kingfisher chattered by making its way upstream. Man, he missed fishing! He missed fishing with Dillon.

Jay wondered what Dillon would think of his fishing skills. He was certain that over the years, Dillon's skills had advanced far beyond those of his own. He had learned some new techniques over the years but had not been able to spend the time he wanted, and he was certain not the time Dillon had, in pursuing the advancement of his skills. He wondered what Dillon would think of his propensity to use dry flies. How would his ability to cast seventy-five feet help or was it something he could even manage in the often tight fishing confines of the Smoky Mountain streams? Only time would tell, and if he had his wish, that time would not be too far into the future, once he got settled into his practice.

Driving the moving van down Highway 15, Jay first notices the sign beside the road, "Welcome to Laurel Cove Pop: 278," followed by the "Pop" Powell Bridge, named after the same Pop that taught him and Dillon how to fish and tie flies in what seems now like a lifetime ago. Jay steals a quick glance at the clear waters of Big Bear Fork, summing up the conditions in his mind, *Conditions look just perfect for a number 16 parachute Adams*. Suddenly, he hears the horn from Debbie who is following behind in their red Jeep Cherokee. Jay's focus centers back on the road where he has drifted across the center line into the oncoming lane. He immediately swerves back to the right and is now headed directly toward a newcomer to town who he would soon learn is Homer.

Homer is always at his "post" every Tuesday and Friday selling copies of the *Laurel Cove Banner* to anyone arriving in town. Homer sort of appeared out of nowhere one day looking for odd jobs, the first of which became that of a newspaper boy. Though somewhere in his fifties, Homer did not physically qualify as a boy, but his mental capacity did. Working other menial jobs and being looked out for by the townsfolk, Homer always seemed to have just enough to get by. Instinctively, Jay slams on the brakes of the big truck, stopping just shy of his unintended target. He is suddenly greeted by Homer who steps up to the side of the truck and extends a newspaper. One part surprised by the newspaper sticking through the window and three parts embarrassed, Jay promptly pays a dollar for a twenty-five-cent newspaper.

As Highway 15 enters town, it becomes Main Street before turning left at the lone traffic light onto Church Street. Church Street crosses Big Bear Fork, which is the town boundary, and resumes its way as Highway 15. Resuming his drive down Main Street, Jay first comes to Webb's Grocery on the left, owned by Dillon's uncle, Leroy. Leroy steps out into the doorway wearing his usual stockman's smock smiling and waving as the big yellow truck rolls by. Jay waves back. All the ole timers sitting on the whittlin' bench in front of the grocery pause momentarily on their latest creations to stare and raise their knives-in-hand to salute. Jay recognizes Selma Mitchell, Reverend Mitchell's wife. Selma pulls double duty in town as the church pianist and town gossip. As usual, she is yakking away at some poor bag boy as he unloads groceries into the trunk of her car. *I wonder who she's gossipin' 'bout now*, he thinks as he shakes his head in pity at the helpless recipient. *Dang, that woman never shuts up. Reverend Mitchell preaches to us on Sunday, and she preaches to us the rest of the week.*

On the right is Jeb's Hardware, the largest building in town. Jeb's motto is, "If 'n it's hardware ye thank ye need, I got it. If 'n I don't got it, ye don't need it." Next on the left is Boots' Barber Shop. The front of the barber shop has a large brown boot on the left followed by the words "Barber Shop." With a name like Boots, Jay always wondered why he never got into shoe repair; though, he does dabble a bit in moonshine. Driving by, Jay notices Boots waving through the large front window with a pair of scissors in his hand. Smiling, Jay chuckles, *I bet he just cut a chunk out of somebody's hair. Sure wouldn't be the first time and sure won't be the last.*

Beside Boots' Barber Shop is Smoky's Drug Store and Café. *I wonder if Luanne still works there*, Jay thinks referring to Luanne Davis, Dillon's ex-girlfriend. Jay brings the moving van to a halt at the traffic light. Though no more than a three-way flashing light, yellow on both directions down Main Street, which continues straight, following Big Bear Fork toward the National Park, the light flashes red for traffic coming from the left across the Big Bear Fork and entering town from the north on Highway 15. While pausing at the traffic light, Jay looks to his right at the Laurel Cove post office and gas station.

After checking for traffic, there is none as usual, Jay makes a left turn onto Church Street where the first building on the right is the First Fidelity Bank. Jay remembers that he must go there first thing tomorrow morning to open an account. Crossing the Big Bear Fork again, Jay takes a shorter peek than before to notice the shoals, not wanting to repeat his earlier mistake. Driving up Highway 15, he passes by River View Baptist Church. Reverend Mitchell is out front changing the letters on the sign giving everyone a preview of Sunday's message. "The Prodigal Son," Jay reads, a possible coincidental if not divinely timed message. A bit overweight, Reverend Mitchell sweats a lot, especially during a well-delivered "hellfire and brimstone" sermon during which he habitually rakes back his jet-black hair with his left hand. Using a great deal of hair gel, his church followers are relieved that he performs the "right hand of fellowship" after each service. Preacher, as most of his flock refers to him, is a pretty good trout fisherman in his own right. When short on inspiration for a Sunday sermon, he heads to the mountains. "Moses talked to God on a mountain, I figger it'll work fer me."

Reverend Mitchell stops to look at the large yellow moving van passing by. "Hey, Reverend!" Jay yells out the opened window as he drives by.

Reverend Mitchell waves and yells back, "See ye Sunday!"

After another mile or so down Highway 15, Jay turns the big yellow moving truck right onto Jenkins Cove Road where a short distance later he turns left into his drive. At the end of the gravel road is the white two-story frame farmhouse with its large back porch facing Balsam Ridge and the Smoky Mountains. A strong selling point for both Debbie and Jay, the porch is complete with swing and rocking chairs.

The next morning, with unopened boxes aplenty, Jay leaves the arranging of housewares to Debbie as he runs his first errand to First Fidelity Bank. Walking in the front door, Jay stops for a moment to look at a plaque so familiar to him. The plaque "commemorates" First Fidelity Bank's claim to fame.

> Frank Sullivan, aka John Dillinger "Public Enemy #1," robbed this bank on December 27, 1933 while on his way from Chicago to Florida, brandishing his favorite Tommie Gun.

What the plaque fails to mention is that having built his status as "Public Enemy #1," the take from the bank was so little as a result of the Depression, that Dillinger returned the money in order to save his reputation as a big-time bank robber. He was rumored as saying, "Hell, I can take more than this from an ice cream parlor! Anybody here ever blabs, and I'll come back!" This episode was kept from the public for fear of Dillinger's return until after his death on July 22, 1934.

Notifying the teller of his desire to open a new account, Jay is pointed in the direction of a small cubicle. A small sign on the side of the cubicle signifies it handles accounts. Hearing no one in the cubicle, Jay peeks around the wall where a heavyset, balding man in Coke-bottled glasses looks up. "Hey, Melvin!"

"Well hello, Jay. What can I do for you?" Melvin Cody motions for Jay to take a seat across the desk. Jay notices from the nameplate on the desk that Melvin is now the assistant accounts manager. Having graduated class salutatorian, Jay was valedictorian, Melvin went to the nearby community college where he received his associate's degree in business. This collegiate path allowed Melvin to maintain his apparent lifelong goal of living at home with his mom. A goal thus far he has met. His time in college and years of brown-nosing has advanced Melvin to where he is today. On the wall behind Melvin is a framed photograph from the *Laurel Cove Banner*. In the image, Melvin is holding what the caption says is a "16-inch brown." According to the story given to him by Dillon, Melvin caught the large trout using the "Blind Hog Theory" that states "even a blind hog finds an acorn eventually."

Jay knows that even though Melvin is putting on his best professional appearance, Melvin has always been envious of him and trying to get the better of him, always losing, and thus has always possessed a strong jealous streak, which he's sure has done nothing but simmer over the past eight or so years. As he reflects back on their high school years, Jay notices the same thick black-rimmed Coke bottle glasses and how Melvin signed his and everyone else's yearbook, "Future World Champion Fly Fisherman." Only time will tell how much Melvin has matured, but realizing that Melvin still lives at home with his mom, Jay doesn't have high expectations.

After completing their business, Melvin asks, "Been doin' much fishing?"

"Nah. I've not had much time. It doesn't look like I'll have any for a while," Jay replies partly telling the truth, mostly hoping to avoid being asked to go.

"Well, the first chance ye get, give me a shout. We'll go out and rip some lips!"

The only thing you can rip is a pair of waders, Jay humorously thinks as he stands up to shake Melvin's hand. "Well, thanks for your help, Melvin. I better get back to helping Debbie move into the house and setting up the office."

Arriving back at his house, Jay notices a late model Ford pickup truck with mud splashed along the sides. Knowing immediately that Dillon has stopped by, Jay feels a slight wave of sudden nervousness. *What do I say?* Jay asks himself. Walking into the house, Jay notices a couple of pizza boxes and a six-pack of beer. *The perfect moving-in gift,* Jay thinks as he opens a bottle and grabs a slice of pepperoni. Washing a mouthful down with a Budweiser, Jay hears Debbie giving instructions to Dillon whom she has already put to work carrying items upstairs.

As Debbie returns downstairs, she notices Jay with a mouthful of pizza. "Well, I'm glad you stopped by, Dillon. As you can tell, Jay isn't much help in getting things moved in," she says with a laugh.

Dillon walks over, faces Jay for a moment with a serious expression, then grins ear to ear as he gives Jay a bear hug and pats him on the back. "Welcome home, doc!"

Returning the gesture, Jay replies, "Give it a rest, Dillon. I'm Jay, the same Jay you've always known." Stepping back, Jay sizes up Dillon who in high school was a second team all-state linebacker and fullback. Though several years have passed, Dillon has maintained his conditioning as a construction worker. At an even six feet and 210 pounds, Dillon has broad shoulders and well-defined, muscular arms. Dillon has dark, slightly wavy hair, a mustache, and with brilliant light-blue piercing eyes that always melted any girl's heart and a tan from working outside on sunny days. As usual, Dillon is dressed in his trademark blue jeans, cowboy boots, and long-sleeve button-up shirt with the sleeves rolled up his forearms. And as in high school, Dillon maintains a can of Skoal in his left rear pocket.

Compared to Dillon, Jay was always a bit lanky. Unlike Dillon's linebacker build, Jay was slightly taller at six feet two inches and about twenty pounds lighter. Built more like a basketball player, Jay was a wide receiver and defensive safety for the Laurel Cove Bears, and like Dillon, Jay has maintained his physical condition not so much in strength but in riding a bicycle, mostly on a trainer and indoors due to his long and odd hours while in his medical training. Jay notices that compared to Dillon, he has fair skin and soft hands, both of which he finds himself a little embarrassed but realizes it is a product of his profession. And unlike Dillon who is more like a modern-day Marlboro man, Jay has a more clean cut intellectual look with short brown hair and glasses.

As the evening wears on, Jay and Dillon laugh, eat pizza, reminisce through old memories, and catch up on the local news and happenings of Laurel Cove. Every so often, the teacher would come out in Debbie as she would threaten to place the "boys" in timeout as she would any of her rowdy, misbehaving students.

Jay spent the next few weeks getting him and Debbie settled into their house and him into the medical clinic. Though Debbie is fairly compulsive about having every box emptied and every item in its rightful place at record speed, Jay isn't so efficient. Compounding Jay's laidback style in getting things organized is the fact that the small clinic built for one is being shared by two physicians and would continue to be so until Doc Hembree worked his way out of a job and into retirement. Fortunately, at the moment, the office is not experiencing a community-wide pandemic, allowing his first days to run relatively smoothly. Jay's first patient happens to be someone with whom he is not familiar as a Laurel Cove resident.

Chester Barnes had moved into the area from Nashville a few years back. Chester had hoped to make it in "The Music City" at first as a studio musician, eventually making it *big* in the country music business. Unfortunately for Chester, his money ran out before opportunity came a knocking. Though forced to give up his plans, he has never given up his dream and continues to pick anything with strings. Having excellent manual dexterity and digital flexibility, Chester took up fly-tying and saw a great opportunity to pay his bills, save a little, and practice his stringed skills by opening and running a fly shop on the fringes of the Great Smoky Mountains National Park. Chester named his new venture "The Hatch." To the uneducated, "the hatch" refers to the entomological life cycle exploited by fly fishermen, but in reality, it was Chester's idea to spawn his attempt at a musical comeback. Only time would tell if the plan hatched into his dream. Though not a devout fisherman like his customers, Chester is a craftsman with fur and feathers and can tie quality, durable masterpieces with the best of them. Spending even brief time browsing through his shop will reveal several "works in progress" created by Chester's skills and insight into tying and creativity coupled with the input and field experience of his customers.

One of the skills so important to a family practice physician, but seldom taught in medical school, is tying the psychological and emotional aspect of the patient's well-being to the physical realm. Few "ailments" are found to be totally created and maintained strictly within the scope of human physiology. All too often, illnesses in the modern, industrialized world in which we live are created or adversely affected by the plague of modern man—stress. Such is the case with Chester. Chester came to Jay complaining of headaches and difficulty sleeping. After completing an eye exam to check his vision, which by the way is worsening as a result of age and hours at the fly-tying bench, Jay begins peeling away the layers of Chester Barnes. He found that after leaving Nashville, Chester was in deep debt and on the verge of bankruptcy. As Chester puts it, "I believe in paying my debts, Doc. Besides, what better way to write music and play it from the heart than to go broke and lose it all! Fortunately for me, I didn't have to lose my wife, little girl, and dog." Chester finishes with a laugh. What Jay did determine was a bad case of stress, brought about by Chester's financial woes. Jay gives Chester some samples of a sleeping medication to help him get some much-needed rest and a contact name and phone number for some free financial counseling. He also prescribes some therapeutic time in the mountains, if not fishing, then picking, but preferably fishing as it would provide a greater distance from his stress-inducing past. Only time will tell how well his first patient will accept the prescribed treatment. On his way out, Jay makes a promise to drive out to The Hatch soon.

Eventually, enough time had passed for Jay to say he was moved in at both his office and his house. Not so for Debbie, as it would be some time before she considered herself to have moved in, but for Jay, it was close enough. For both, they were moved in enough to allow Jay some "downtime" in the Smokies chasing trout. It has been a long time since Jay has been fishing, way too long. It was now early June, and it seemed a lifetime ago, but in reality, it had been since last fall. Between finishing his training, moving, and getting settled in to his office and house, most would not have had time to think about fishing, but not so for Jay.

On the short drive to and from work each day, he thinks about fishing. Each day since moving home, as he crosses the Big Bear driving into town, he sizes up the river and ponders on what he believes the fishing conditions would be. This morning, he has his gear ready and is sitting on the back porch finishing his second cup of coffee, enjoying the view up Jenkins Cove toward Balsam Ridge. There is a light haze moving along the valley with early morning fog shrouding the tops of the mountains. Today's sunshine will burn the fog off soon enough. His attention is broken by the sound of Dillon's truck coming up the gravel road. Throwing his gear into the back of the truck alongside Dillon's, Jay hops into the truck and says, "Mornin', Dillon."

"Mornin', Jay." Dillon backs the truck out onto the dirt road as the two make their way to town. Turning left onto Church Street, the white Ford pickup makes its way down toward the bridge crossing the Big Bear Fork. As they reach the bridge, they come to a complete stop as both survey the river. "Looks purty good," Dillon surmises.

"Yeah, the fishing ought to be pretty good," Jay comments as he looks over Dillon's shoulder and upstream along the shoals of the river.

They continue on a short distance, stopping at the red light briefly before turning right onto Main Street and coming to a stop in a parking space in front of Smoky's Café. The two walk into Smoky's, settling into a booth against the wall across from the soda bar, both turning their coffee mugs right side up to let Luanne know they wanted coffee.

Looking around, Jay begins to notice how little things had changed. The same décor, same stools and soda bar, as well as booths.

Looking over Dillon's shoulder onto the wooden surface above the padded back of the booth, he recognized a carving from years back, "DW + LD." Jay tries to hide the grin on his face as Luanne walks up filling their cups with hot, black coffee.

"Do you boys need a menu?" Luanne asks.

"Naw, we'll just have the usual," Dillon answers with a grin knowing what will happen next.

Luanne knows when a customer is trying to give her a hard time, and with Dillon, that's pretty much any time. "So for Dr. Jay, that is country ham and a side order of biscuits and gravy, and for Dillon, that is French toast with low-calorie syrup and a poached egg white."

Burning his lips as he tries to choke down his mouthful of coffee, Dillon looks embarrassingly at Jay and then angrily at Luanne. "What're you talkin' 'bout! I don't want no French toast, and I ain't never had low-calorie syrup. Bet it don't taste right. Besides, I don't even know what it is!"

Jay recognizes his time to pile on even this early in the morning. "Dang, Dillon. You done went soft on me while I wuz gone! Luanne, bring him a bib while you're at it. And do you mind cutting the French toast up in little pieces for him before you bring it over? He has such a difficult time with a knife!"

"Sure will, hun," Luanne replies as she walks away to place the order.

"You know I want what Jay's havin', don't ye?" Dillon shouts out to Luanne. Then looking back at Jay, Dillon asks, "What're you grinnin' bout?"

"Oh, I don't know, Dillon. It seems some things have not changed, like you and Luanne arguing and me sitting here looking at carvings in the woodwork," Jay replies as he nods toward the carving Dillon made years ago when he and Jay used to come down to the café mostly so Dillon could flirt with Luanne.

Dillon turns to take a peek at what Jay is referring to. "I done fergot that wuz there. That's from back in high school."

Luanne returns shortly with two orders of country ham and biscuits and gravy placing them in front of her two customers. Dillon lays three one-dollar bills on the side of the table just in front of Luanne.

Luanne looks at Jay, then Dillon. "So, Dillon, are you gonna eat big boy food since Jay's here this morning?"

Dillon answers back, "Smell that? That's the smell of your tip slippin' away," as he slides one of the three bills away and places it in his shirt pocket.

Luanne grabs the other two bills as she walks away. "I see you're giving a big boy's tip today too. Much better than the usual quarter."

Laughing, Jay looks at Dillon. "She still gets the best of you, doesn't she, Dillon?"

The two finish their breakfast with a few more jabs between Dillon and Luanne during the coffee refills. They hop back into the pickup and drive back down Main Street and head up Big Bear Fork.

Pointing at the fly shop, Jay says, "Hey, Dillon. Let's stop by The Hatch. I promised Chester that I would stop by sometime and check it out."

As they walk into the fly shop, a small bell chimes overhead as it makes contact with the opening door. Chester peeps at the new arrivals while in the middle of tying hackle on a parachute Adams.

Ready to give Chester a hard time for tying anything small, Dillon asks, "What's that fer, Chester? Ye know big fish eat big flies!"

"Well, some of those big browns need to go on a diet and eat smaller bites. This is my Slim Fast special!"

Three older gentlemen are sitting around the fireplace, no fire going as it is late spring. Jay recognizes them as the as the "ole farts" from the whittlin' bench in front of Webb's Grocery. Apparently, they migrate to The Hatch on weekends where there's a higher probability of more lies being told. After perusing the racks of flies and looking over the long, limber rods, Jay grabs a spool of 5X tippet and pays at the counter, as Dillon fills up his mug of coffee.

"Good luck, boys! Save a few fer the rest of us," Chester yells as Jay and Dillon walk out to the tune of the chiming bell over the door.

Dillon and Jay continue their way up Main Street, which turns into River Road and follows the Big Bear Fork upstream into the Park. As the road turns to gravel, Dillon rolls down his window to listen to the flowing rapids of the stream. Likewise, Jay rolls down his window more to feel and smell the fresh air gently blowing into his window as they drive into the ever dense forest of hemlock and yellow poplar trees.

Arriving at the parking lot, both gear up and begin walking up the trail, which parallels the water. The trail, a remnant of the 1920s, is an old train bed that was used to carry the logs from the high ridges through the deep valleys and down to the sawmill. The forest has recovered somewhat, though nowhere near its pre-logging majesty. Gone are the towering poplars and huge chestnut trees, the diameter of their trunks measured in feet. What chestnuts were not logged out were subsequently lost to the chestnut blight which made its way down to the southern Appalachians. Remaining are tall hemlocks reaching heights of over one hundred feet, along with white oaks, and yellow poplar trees that were too small at the time loggers passed through but have survived to reach great heights. With the removal of tall trees came increased sunlight to the forest floor spawning the growth of numerous brush and flowers. Fortunately on this early morning, holdover blooms of the yellow trillium decorated the edges of the trail and into the woods, their mottled green leaves appearing camouflage against the thick, brushy backdrop. The bright yellow flowers in the center of three large leaves often give off a lemon scent, which even now makes Jay's mouth water just a bit.

As they walk upstream, Jay begins to sense a feeling of dread. Though tickled to be fishing again, the first time in what seems like an eternity since he's been on his beloved waters, a part of him realizes he has lost something. He no longer feels the absolute comfort of being on his home waters. Instead, it all seems like an uncomfortable family reunion where he recognizes someone but cannot quite remember from where. He knows they are related and they have a shared past, but the details are just beyond his mental reach. No amount of reflection will reveal the answers. All that is left is the awkward conversation, where no doubt the "stranger" will know every aspect to the finest detail, leaving him to piecing the puzzle together without embarrassing himself. *That's it! Embarrassment!* Jay thinks as they walk toward the Splash Pool at the base of the twenty-five-foot Hemlock Falls. *I don't want to embarrass myself in front of Dillon!*

Knowing Dillon has spent many hours mastering his fly-fishing skills on this very stretch of water and knows if not all then most of the trout on a first-name basis, Jay has only been here a few times in the past eight years and none in the past three. But oh, how he's thought about it. Stopping at the benches overlooking the emerald-colored Splash Pool, Jay looks at Dillon. "You know, I think I'll give it a try right here."

"Okay, I'll go ahead and cross over to the other side," Dillon replies. When growing up, they always fished together but on opposite sides of the stream. Initially, Pop made them stay together more for safety than anything. However over time, they realized the enjoyment gained by simultaneously plying the waters for their hidden secrets and sharing in each other's triumphs and dogging each other for the fish lost and sudden dunks into the cold water.

With a bit of a sheepish grin, Jay replies, "If it's okay, I'd like to work the pool alone for now. Get my fishing feet under me."

"Sure. I'll go above the falls and work some of the pocket water." Dillon walks up the trail while Jay looks into the deep pool, spotting a few small trout apparently feeding in the current.

Making his way down to the streambed, Jay follows a trail winding his way through patches of dog hobble. Found only in the southern Appalachians, dog hobble is an evergreen shrub with shiny tooth-edged leaves. Its name comes from local lore in which hunting dogs became ensnared in the dense shrubs, but the larger black bears were able to pass through, leaving the bear hunters behind to retrieve their entangled canines. Arriving at the tail out of the Splash Pool, Jay is careful to stay back into the woods and among the rhododendron to conceal his presence. Jay decides to sit for a moment on a rock covered with velvet-smooth crown moss. Somewhere in the distance, a pileated woodpecker is hammering a tree. Jay ponders the amazing acoustics of the sound created by this bird and a tree, while looking at the beautiful pool with Hemlock Falls tumbling down from the other side at the upper end of the pool. More of a cascade than a waterfall, the water splashes its way down crashing into boulders spraying a mist nearly halfway across the main stream of the pool. At the base of the falls, the water is turbulent, leaving prime feeding lanes on both sides. Peppering the large pool are dozens of fallen rhododendron blooms floating along the surface following the current to eventually drift past where Jay is sitting. Observing the procession of floating flowers reminds him of the Japanese Obon services in which lighted candles are floated down rivers in memory of deceased ancestral spirits. He begins to feel perhaps the spirit of Pop welcoming him home. Jay's focus is broken by Dillon, who has already caught his first trout just upstream. Catching Jay's glance, Dillon gives him a thumbs-up.

As that sense of dread returns, Jay begins to analyze the situation. The memory of Pop oscillating through his mind. "Focus on the basics," Pop would say. "Let the fish tell ye what they want."

The basics. What do the fish want? Jay asks himself. Sitting on the rock, gazing upstream into the pool, Jay begins to break the water down into small segments. Instead of a large overview of the whole pool, he changes his focus to the tail out just before the water rolls into the small set of rapids. Suddenly, his eye catches a small yellow pair of upright wings attached to something struggling on the surface. *Slurp!* A small rainbow noses up to take the hatching insect. Knowing Dillon is already now into his third fish of the morning, undoubtedly on a large nymph, Jay has more experience in recent years using dry flies. Searching through his fly box, he finds a number 16 yellow stimulator. *This appears about right*, he thinks. Tying it on, he prepares for his first cast as his eye catches a glimpse of another rising trout. To get into a better casting position, he steps into the pocket water just downstream from the Splash Pool.

By staying out of the pool, no waves will spook any trout in the pool, but he is still conscious to maintain a low profile. Feeding out what he figured to be enough line to reach his intended target, he performs a short false cast to the side, not directly over the target. As his line sails downstream on his back cast, he waits to allow the line to extend behind him before starting the forward presentation. As the rod tip moves forward, it suddenly becames taut. "Damn! Stupid rhododendron!" The first sign of his absence from fishing in the Park, he has forgotten to always, always consider the flora, especially rhododendron. Walking over to retrieve his tangled stimulator, he glances back toward Dillon who is into yet another trout.

He refocuses on his prior objective, another rise by what appears to be the same trout. Crouching back into position, remembering the rhododendron behind him, Jay makes a good cast just upstream from where he's seen the rising fish. Through the surface, he sees the trout rush up toward the yellow stimulator, studies it for what seems an eternity, then noses up to sip it into its mouth. With a sharp but soft lift of the rod tip, Jay makes contact with the rainbow, which immediately leaps out of the water. After a couple of runs and even more leaps, Jay slips the rainbow into his net.

Observing the beautiful red band along its side, the bright red gill plate, and black spots along the back and tail, he pauses as he realizes that finally, he is home, where he belongs. All that he has worked for has brought him full circle to where he now stands in the cool water of the Big Bear Fork. Looking upstream above the waterfall, he sees Dillon who has stopped fishing and is watching from a distance, not moving, not fishing, simply sharing the moment. Giving Jay a nod of acknowledgment, Dillon also senses that something has happened, something that he too has waited for—Jay is home.

Slipping the young trout back into the water, Jay takes in a deep breath of fresh air, feeling its coolness within his lungs along with that of the water on his legs. He feels goosebumps on his arms, the result of tactile and emotional celebration. Since those carefree summer days of his youth, he acknowledges the fact that he has changed, as has Dillon. Both are adults now and have responsibilities. For now, however, in this world of rhododendrons, hemlocks, purple dwarf iris blooms, and trout, all is as it should be. Here, along the Big Bear Fork of the Great Smoky Mountains, indeed, nothing has changed. It is as it was.

EVERY DOG HAS HIS DAY

Great Smoky Mountains National Park Headquarters

Having not seen her friend in a few years, Doris Wentworth becomes ever so anxious as she and her husband drive along the winding Highway 15. It has been a long drive up from Atlanta, not so much the miles driven but the Memorial Day weekend interstate traffic fought along the way. Even though the traffic dissipates as they exit Knoxville and make their way to Laurel Cove, the curvy road is not well liked by William. William is used to big cities, having lived in either New York or Chicago his entire life and recently moving to Atlanta. Now he is fighting carsickness as he drives the last few miles into this backward village to visit her friend. The only consolation is the hope of an Arnold Palmer or Jack Nicklaus grade golf course somewhere in the vicinity; though he has agreed to go fishing with a couple of country hicks entirely to satisfy Doris.

Rounding that final curve, they notice the sign on the side of the road that reads "Welcome to Laurel Cove, Pop: 278." The directions given to them by Doris' friend, Debbie McMahan, are not very clear once they enter Laurel Cove. However, their first glance as they roll into town quickly tell them they do not need any directions. There is not much to the town, especially when considering their hometown of Atlanta. Having spent very little time outdoors with the exception of his weekly golf outings, William Wentworth III barely notices Big Bear Fork as they cross the Harvey "Pop" Powell Bridge. What did catch his eye is the strange homeless-looking man selling newspapers just across the bridge. As usual, Homer is there every Tuesday and Friday selling the day's edition of the *Laurel Cove Banner*.

William Wentworth III does notice a few people sitting outside in front of Webb's Grocery. He has never seen older men sitting on a wooden bench carving objects with their knives. Even if he did concern himself with what they are actually doing out on the bench, he will never understand why they spend time carving on a stick. Whittlin', as the locals call it, is a favorite pastime of the retired farmers, if there is such a thing. When there are no crops to plant or harvest and no tobacco to work, the group, affectionately known as the ole farts club, comes to Webb's Grocery. Those who do have work often make trips into Jeb's Hardware.

As they watch the shiny black Mercedes SUV slowly roll by from their right to left, in unison they all take a look back to their right down Main Street for the trailing of the funeral procession. Around town, there's only one large, shiny, black vehicle, and it belongs to the funeral home. Taking a left at the town's one traffic light, which is actually a flashing yellow light for Main Street and a red light for Church Street, they pass between the Smoky's Café and the First Fidelity Bank, once again crossing the Big Bear Fork. Just up the road on the right, past the church, is Jenkins Cove Road. From there, they drive to Jay and Debbie McMahan's house. William is none too happy to have to drive his clean SUV onto the final fifty yards of gravel road to the McMahan residence, ruining the fresh wash job that he paid $30 for yesterday. But at least he is here, wherever here is.

Jay has been dreading this moment as much as his wife Debbie has been anticipating it. Unfortunately, Jay cannot allow his lack of enthusiasm to show, thus ruining Debbie's moment. After all, it is her friend and a long weekend only lasts three days—three long days.

Debbie and Doris meet halfway between the Mercedes and the front porch, embracing as two lifelong friends do when they've not been together for a while. William is surveying the car for any gravel dings and aching over the collection of dust along the sides and rear of the car as well as the splattered insects on the shiny chrome grill. Finally, after some coaxing, William strolls over to the girls for proper introductions. Debbie had met William at the Wentworth wedding a few years back when she served as matron of honor, thus returning the favor to Doris who was her maid of honor. Jay has to this point been able to avoid meeting Mr. Wentworth, as he was unable to attend the wedding. Jay figures William to be about his age but is unsure due to the capped shiny white teeth and a few cosmetic procedures.

"Good to see you again, Doris," Jay says as he gives her a hug.

"Jason, I'd like you to meet my husband, William Wentworth III."

Jay, reaching out his hand, says, "Happy to meet you, Bill. Everyone calls me Jay. How was the drive up?"

"The name is William," he answers as he shakes Jay's hand. "William Wentworth III. The drive was fine, thank you," he adds with a stoic expression.

Jay, sizing up William for his potential outdoor prowess, especially since he has to spend time with him in the mountains, is wondering how much babysitting would be required. William, a stockbroker for a major brokerage firm, is dressed in pleated cream-colored golf slacks, wearing no socks under his wicker loafers. Covering his white short-sleeved polo shirt from last year's Masters Golf Tournament is a light beige cardigan sweater tied around his neck with a perfect loop hanging over his chest. William's slim physique gives the appearance of a once anemic, if not pampered, child. With skin so fair, Jay wonders if it has ever seen direct sunlight except for trips from beneath the roof of a golf cart to the green. His perfectly styled hair swept over to his left side refuses to move against the mountain breeze. Jay knows this is going to be a trying few days of holding William's hand as they work along the river.

After dinner of fried chicken, mashed potatoes, green beans, and dinner rolls topped off with blackberry cobbler and homemade vanilla ice cream for dessert, Jay and William sit out on the back porch in rocking chairs watching the day's last rays of sun fade along the Smoky Mountains. As Jay sips sweet tea and William finishes what's left of the bottle of Broadbent 10 year Malmsey Madeira, which he brought for dinner, Jay admires the rhododendrons slowly reaching their peak bloom around the perimeter of his property. William gently, though frustratingly, swats at a few gnats with his monogrammed, silk handkerchief. Jay notices the monogram "WW III." Though he wants to make some sarcastic remark about the coming third world war, his sense of hospitality and William's arrogance persuades him otherwise. Out in the back of the house is Jay's workshop. One side has an assortment of tools used around the house. The other, a separate room ten feet by ten feet, faces east toward the mountains. This is Jay's fishing room where he ties his flies as well as piddles with his equipment.

"So, William, Debbie tells me you'd like to do a little fishin'. Do you need any equipment? I've got an extra of pretty much everything. It's yours to use if you need it."

"I do not believe I will need to borrow anything, Jason, as I brought my own equipment. On second thought, I may need to borrow some lures."

Jay, cringing at how William uses the word *lures*, replies, "Well, you'll probably need some flies as the trout here can be tricky to figure out most of the time, especially if you're not familiar with the water. I believe Debbie is interested in some trout for dinner tomorrow evening. She has a special buttermilk and beer batter recipe given to her by her grandmother that is great with fresh trout. She'll probably add some fried potatoes and onions along with buttermilk cornbread. Oh man, that's eatin'!"

"Sounds wonderful," William replies flatly as he sips his wine and he gazes off to somewhere he'd rather be.

"We typically don't keep any except on occasion when one of us has a craving for them. The trout we'll be catching tomorrow are gonna be rainbows and browns. There may be an odd brook trout, but they typically live in higher elevations where the water is cooler. Since we'll be fishin' in the Park tomorrow, I want to make sure you know the regulations. We'll get you a license tomorrow down at The Hatch. We need to remember to take our creels tomorrow to keep the fish in. I usually put a Ziplock bag in the creel with a little bit of water to help keep the fish fresh. For the most part, the trout will be in the seven- to ten-inch range. However, there are fish well into the twenty plus inch range, especially the browns. Those big browns though are hard to catch. My friend Dillon, whom you'll meet tomorrow, always says, 'Big trout don't git that way by bein' caught!'" Jay continues, "While you can keep up to five fish seven inches or longer, I prefer to not keep any under nine or ten inches. Whatever you do, don't keep any brookies. They're protected and cannot be kept."

As William's eyes begin to get that glazed over look that comes with drinking more wine than he can handle, he asks, "What is so special about brook trout? Why can we not keep them?"

Jay gazes up into the mountains and points toward Jenkins Cove, which leads to Balsam Ridge. The sun is casting its last moments of brilliance and irradiating the slopes resulting in a green glow overlooking the shadowy coves. "Around the turn of the century, there was nothing but tall trees measured by the feet in diameter all along that ridge. The logging companies moved in and cut down the huge chestnuts and poplar trees. They took out millions of feet of lumber. In a matter of twenty years, give or take a few, the big trees were gone, leaving old train beds, logging roads, and exposed hillsides prone to erosion. Naturally, the silt from runoff built up choking the streams. My granddad told me the canopy on those big trees was so thick you'd think it was nighttime in the middle of the day. When they took out the big trees, the once thick canopy that provided shade to the creeks was gone. The water conditions became warm so that the brook trout could no longer survive except in the highest elevations. Up there, the water was cool enough for 'em. Eventually, rainbow from out west and brown trout were brought in and stocked in the streams. The rainbows and browns are more tolerant of the warmer water temperatures. Unfortunately for the brook trout, the rainbows were more aggressive and further reduced their range forcing them even farther up into the higher elevations. When the park service discovered the problem back in the early seventies, they stopped stocking trout. Now, all of the trout caught in the Park are wild. You'll hear the locals refer to them as native. What they really mean is not native but wild as compared to stocked."

Jay, glancing over to William, asks, "William, can you tell the difference between the different species of trout?"

"Nothing to worry about, Jason. I've caught enough to know one from the other."

"Well, I just want you to be prepared and have a fun time tomorrow. I believe it's gonna be a good day to be on the water."

The next morning, as William uses his cell phone to check his messages, Jay loads their equipment into the back of his Jeep Cherokee. In doing so, he notices that William's waders and boots are still in their original boxes, having never been opened, much less tried on for proper fit. When finished, Jay looks at William with a smirk as though telling William to leave his security blanket behind. "You can leave the cell phone here, William. Where we're going, it won't work anyway."

Much to his chagrin, William tosses it into his Mercedes and hops into Jay's Cherokee.

As they make the short drive back to town, they cross the Big Bear Fork. As always, Jay looks at the river for a quick assessment as only a seasoned fisherman can. The river is slightly up and a bit off color, telling him of an overnight shower somewhere up in the mountains. They pull up alongside Church Street and park in front of Smoky's Café.

Stepping into the café, the bell over the door rings, telling Luanne more customers have arrived. Luanne is the town flirt and was the high school beauty queen back when she, Jay, and Jay's friend Dillon were teenagers. She went to the prom and dated Dillon briefly during and after school. Since then, she's worked for her parents at Smoky's. She is single, five feet and nine inches tall, with dark eyes, and long black hair. She's never been brave enough to leave town.

She's still waiting for Mr. Right to come in for breakfast. Her Mr. Right is handsome, rich, and has no kids.

Luanne's dad, the town pharmacist, wants his baby girl to marry well but realizes Dillon is probably the best she can do and has tried to get the two together over the years with little luck. Her mother cooks in the café. "Good mornin', Jay," says Luanne with her usual bright 6:00 a.m. smile.

"Good morning, Luanne. This is William. He's in town for the weekend visiting."

"Welcome to Laurel Cove, William."

"Good morning," replies William, not quite comfortable with the small-town surroundings.

Jay looks around the café, giving "good mornings" to the customers as he walks over to the table where Dillon is nursing a cup of black coffee. "Good morning, Dillon. This is William."

"Good mornin', Jay, good mornin', Bill," replies Dillon.

"The name is William, William Wentworth III. I am very glad to meet you, Dillon."

As Jay sits across the table from Dillon, they share a quick glance and a raise of eyebrows acknowledging their mutual understanding of the superficial and arrogant personality of William Wentworth III.

After settling in, Luanne pours a cup of black coffee for Dillon and asks William. "Would you like a cup of coffee, hun?"

"Yes, could I have a double latte, light on the cream?"

"I'm sorry, hun, we only have regular and decaf."

"Well, I guess I will settle for a cup of decaf with cream and Equal."

A few minutes later, Luanne returns with a pot of decaf coffee and a small container of cream. "Here you go, shug."

"Do you have any nondairy creamer? I am terribly lactose intolerant."

"Sure, hun, I'll be right back."

After another trip, Luanne returns with a small cup containing nondairy creamer and Equal. "What can I get y'all for breakfast this morning?"

Jay, pouring his second cup, says, "I'll have the usual, Luanne."

"Same here," Dillon replies as he sips his coffee.

"William, do you need more time?"

"No, I will take a bran muffin and a bowl of cereal."

Luanne returns with breakfast consisting of fresh, hot biscuits smothered in steaming sawmill gravy with a side order of grits and country ham for Dillon and Jay as well as William's muffin and cereal.

Dillon, thinking of William's frail frame, suggests, "William, why don't ye try some of the biscuits and gravy, son? They'll stick to ye ribs. Besides, they serve the best biscuits around, made from scratch."

"I had better not, Dillon, I have a delicate stomach."

Dillon, sipping his coffee while observing William, thinks, *Everything about you son is delicate...except your snootiness!*

After Jay and William pay at the cash register, Dillon lingers for a moment. At the opportune time, he picks up an additional item, a small gift for William, which he adds to his check.

As they walk out of Smoky's, Jay and Dillon stop by to chat with Rangers Kowalski and Patterson. Ranger Kowalski has been a ranger in the Smokies for over ten years. He transferred down from Glacier National Park. After a brief time, he fell in love with the area and a lady in Gatlinburg. He enjoys working with the area's people and has blended in nicely. He is well liked by the locals for his fairness and concern for the Park. His new partner, Ranger Patterson, is a recent addition to the park staff. This is his first assignment since using his family's political clout to gain his position. Seen as a brownnoser to anyone within the system that can fast track his career to superintendent, he is not a favorite of the locals. He is often flexing his power to anyone he deems to not be following the law to the letter. He is known as "Possum Patterson," a name he despises, for reputedly climbing trees with binoculars to spy on park visitors in the hopes of making an arrest. He seems to generally look down on the locals as a bunch of illiterate rednecks. To them, he's a smart aleck Yankee.

Jay looks at Kowalski. "Morning, Kowalski." Then out of manners of obligation, he speaks to Ranger Patterson who has his nose buried in the *Knoxville News-Sentinel* morning edition. "Morning, Patterson."

Ranger Patterson grunts his reply without looking away from the newspaper.

With a smile, Ranger Kowalski replies, "Morning, Jay. Morning, Dillon." He notices their camouflage clothing and asks, "You guys heading up today?"

Dillon, with no lost love, glances spitefully toward Patterson behind the newspaper, then back at Kowalski, and with a smile answers, "Yeah, we're gonna walk up Big Bear Fork a ways and try and catch a few."

"Well, I've not seen anybody up there the past few days, so fishing should be pretty good. There's been a good hatch coming off every day about midmorning."

Jay, realizing he forgot to introduce William, adds, "This is William Wentworth III from Atlanta. He's gonna be joining us today."

Shaking William's hand, Ranger Kowalski asks, "So, Bill, do you fish much."

"The name is William. No, I do not get many chances to get out much."

"Well, hope you guys enjoy it. Be careful."

As they walk out, Ranger Patterson, peeking around his newspaper, casts a suspicious look over the stranger, in addition to his distasteful glare at Dillon with whom he's had more than a few arguments.

After breakfast, Dillon loads his gear into Jay's Cherokee. The three ride over to The Hatch where Chester Barnes is just turning the sign hanging on the door to "Open" as he unlocks the door. Chester owns The Hatch fly shop and is known as the best and most prolific fly tier this side of the Smokes but never gets to use them. Unfortunately, he never gets to go fishing as his life is bogged down in a mortgage on his house and a second mortgage on the shop in addition to paying for his wife's shopping habit. Instead, he lives vicariously through the exploits and adventures of others, particularly Dillon and Jay. Chester is liked by all, except for Melvin Cody. Melvin is jealous of Chester's fly-tying skills. But Chester, being the nice guy, allows Melvin to sell his flies in his shop, though rarely does any sell except to outsiders who are unaware of their tendency to tear apart as though they are water-soluble.

The three walk into The Hatch where Chester is gathering the materials to tie a number 16 bead-head pheasant tail, his fly du-jour. "Morning, guys."

Jay leads William over to the sales counter. "Morning, Chester. This is William Wentworth III. He's in town for the weekend and needs his fishing license."

"Glad to meet ya, William." Jay breathes a sigh of relief as someone finally gets William's name right the first time and is spared the formal correction. "Let's see, a three-day nonresident license is twenty dollars. I need to see your driver's license to get some info."

Reaching for his wallet, William states, "I would prefer to buy a resident license, if you do not mind. No need to pay the full nonresident fee for a few days."

"Sorry, William, I can't do that. Not only would I be breaking the law and possibly lose my ability to sell fishing licenses, but it would cost you more. Besides, there is no three-day resident fishing license. You'd have to buy a one-year resident license, which would cost thirty-three dollars."

William, obviously miffed at not getting some sort of discount, tosses his platinum card onto the counter next to the register. Chester raises an eyebrow as he picks up the card for a closer look in the light. This is the first platinum card he's personally seen.

While Chester is working up the license for William, Reverend Mitchell walks in. Reverend Mitchell is an old-fashioned Baptist preacher. He's been preaching up at River View Baptist Church since before Jay and Dillon were teenagers. Now in his early sixties, every time they meet, Jay and Dillon can't help but wonder if he dyes his hair black to keep the gray out, a sign of religious vanity perhaps. As usual, Reverend Mitchell has a few beads of sweat on his forehead, which turns into steady streams as he works up his sermon every Sunday morning, Sunday night, and Wednesday night. Dillon always feels a bit uncomfortable around Reverend Mitchell as he typically goes to church on Christmas, Easter, and of course the annual church homecoming. Homecoming is held every August and is attended by nearly everyone in Laurel Cove, if not for the sermon, then for the large assortment of home-cooked delicacies brought by the ladies of the congregation. The only exception to Dillon's comfort level around Reverend Mitchell is when they're on the stream, as it is there he feels at home and believes he has a slight advantage over the reverend.

"Good morning, gentlemen. What a blessed day the Lord hath made!"

Jay glances toward Reverend Mitchell. "Good morning, Reverend. You headin' out this mornin'?"

"Yeah. I need a little bit of inspiration for tomorrow's sermon, and what better place than on the river." Reverend Mitchell dabbles in fishing when not involved in church business and is a skilled angler who often joins Jay and Dillon when time permits.

"What's happening on the river, Chester?"

Chester, handing William his license, replies, "There was a good rain up in the mountains, Reverend. The water's got a bit of color in it. They should be bitin' purty good. I'd try some weighted Tellico Nymphs. If the water clears, an Adams should be productive."

Reverend Mitchell, recognizing a new soul in town, walks toward William. "Sounds like a plan. Good morning, young man. I'm Reverend Mitchell."

William, caught off guard by the plump pastor now standing directly behind him, responds, "Good morning, sir. My name is William Wentworth III."

"Glad to meet you, William. Are you visiting the area?

William, beginning to squirm at the fast invitation and strong handshake, says, "I have come up for the weekend. My wife and I are staying with Jason and Debbie."

The reverend, recognizing the opportunity to increase his flock, says, "Well, we're glad to have you. I preach over at River View Baptist Church. We'd love to have you visit us tomorrow morning at 9:45. Perhaps you can accompany Jay, Debbie, and Dillon." He answers casting a glance toward Dillon.

Dillon, quietly sifting through the selection of flies tied by Melvin is wagering to himself how long the flies would last until full disintegration, grins slightly while running the theme to *Mission Impossible* through his mind, *This fly will self-destruct in ten seconds.* He recognizes an opportunity to get moving before Reverend Mitchell gets him cornered and utters a quick, "Well, boys, let's get er goin'," and heads out the door. Jay and William are close on Dillon's heels heading out the door and into Jay's Cherokee.

At the city limits, Main Street turns into River Road. Driving down River Road, they pass through rolling green farmland with the folding Smoky Mountains in the background. Off in the distance, the mountains appear blue with a faint smoky haze hovering over the valleys, giving them their namesake.

Jay suddenly gets on the brakes to avoid a cow wandering on the side of the road. "Well, it looks like old man Frazier's got a hole in his fence again. Hey, Dillon, remember when he used to give us a quarter for each cow we rounded up and herded back onto his farm?"

"Yeah." Then a sly grin crosses Dillon's face beneath his thick mustache. "Remember that young bull you tried to round up and it wound up comin' after ye? You had to jump the fence to get away from him, and you landed in that steamin' cow pile?"

Jay tries to keep a serious face. "You know, ole man Frazier said someday I'd laugh about it. That day ain't got here yet!"

"Man, I'd work a week for free just to see that again! Your mama wouldn't let you come into the house 'til she washed you off with a hose and then made you take your clothes off outside."

William looks up on the hillside at a herd of Holstein cattle grazing. Just beyond the cattle sits a bright red barn with an adjoining silo. The barn's roof is black with the words "See Rock City" painted in huge white letters. "Jay. What is the significance of Rock City and where is it located?"

"Well, William, that barn roof has been painted that way since before Dillon and I were born. Rock City is a tourist attraction in Chattanooga."

"Now that you mention it, I do recall some billboards describing Rock City while driving up from Atlanta."

"Yeah, you can about find them all over. Years ago, Rock City paid some guy to drive around the Southeast and paint the words 'See

Rock City' on the side of as many barns as he could for advertisement. Now, it's become somewhat of a novelty. It seems most of the barns are painted red on the sides and have black roofs. I assume he painted the barns red to attract attention. It seems to have done the job."

As they work through the curves a few miles outside of town, William notices dozens of barrels on a hillside. "What is the purpose of those barrels on that hill?"

"Well, those barrels are to house the roosters used in chicken fights?"

"Do you mean those are for cockfighting?"

"Cockfighting or chicken fighting, it's all the same thing. Anyway, those belong to Lester Blalock. He raises the roosters and fights them at various rings around the area."

"Have you ever been to a cockfight, Dillon?"

"Yeah, a few times, when I was a teenager. It was sort of a family outing. It was interesting at that time, but looking back, I don't care much for it now. Pretty gruesome." Dillon laughs and says, "A waste of a good fried chicken dinner."

"Or hot wings," adds Jay.

"Why do the police not arrest him?"

"Well, William, there's no law against raisin' chickens. Not even if they're all roosters. The law cain't do nuthin unless they catch 'em actually fightin' 'em. The organizers move the rings around to different locations, typically staying one step ahead of the good guys."

"So I guess Mr. Blalock has remained out of jail?"

Jay swallows a sip of coffee. "For the most part. Lester's our local poacher. He's been busted a time or two, but only by the local game warden. Trouble is, small-town politics work in his favor. At worst, he's lost his hunting privileges for a year. Usually, he gets probation and stays out of trouble 'til his probation is up."

Dillon, leaning forward from the back seat, asks, "Hey, Jay, isn't he on probation right now?"

"Yeah, I think so. He got caught turkey hunting out of season. Now, if he ever gets caught poaching in the Park, then he's in big trouble. That'd be a federal crime!"

As they near the Park boundary, the rolling farmland suddenly gives way to noticeably taller trees and a more densely covered landscape.

The sudden change is not lost on William who begins to experience a sensation in the pit of his stomach last felt when his stock portfolio went south a few years ago. With a deepening sense of dread, William's arrogance is slowly unraveling to an unbridled fear. He realizes that for the first time in a long time, he is no longer in control. Here, his wealth and his privileged upbringing cannot adequately protect him from the unknown. It is an unknown that is coming all too soon. William begins to grasp a totally foreign concept. He must rely totally on two strangers, two country hicks from the mountains, for his safety, if not his absolute survival. To top it all off, he is without his cell phone, his last trustworthy lifeline. In an effort to quell his fears, William verbalizes the root observation of his uneasiness, "My, this is a thick forest." After a short pause, he adds, "By chance are there any bears out there?"

Jay glances in the rearview mirror and catches the eyes of Dillon who is sitting in the backseat. For the first time, both simultaneously confirm their suspicions of William's outdoor inexperience. The same naiveté William has been trying to conceal but, as with all things outdoors, has failed to accomplish.

Dillon leans forward to relay the news that will surely break down the arrogance of the rich city slicker and says, "Well, William, they don't call it Big Bear Fork fer nuthin'."

Jay, realizing his duties as unofficial town host and babysitter for the husband of his wife's childhood friend, answers in a more protective voice of reason, "Yes, William, there are black bears in the Park. Fortunately, they are not as dangerous as grizzlies, and they're much smaller. For the most part, they will go out of their way to avoid you. If you do come into contact with a bear, just make some loud noise to let 'em know you're there. You'll be all right."

Dillon, wanting to inject his dose, says, "Just make sure ye don't git between a sow and her cubs. If ye do, son, you're in deep trouble."

Having no doubts in William's climbing inabilities, Dillon offers, "Don't think climbin' a tree will help. Black bears can climb trees fastern you." Pausing for effect, he continues, "Oh yeah, and playin' dead don't help none either."

"Why not?" a solemn William asks.

"Black bears like their meat freshly killed…at least typically killed." Wanting now to give William the full dose, he continues, "And don't forget that we also have wild hogs."

Feeling as though he's falling into a bottomless pit of fear, William asks Dillon, "Wild hogs. Do you mean boar?"

"Yeah. Years ago, some fella had a game preserve on the top of one of these mountains. He stocked it with some Russian wild boar. Some of the pigs, they call 'em feral hogs, rooted their way out of the fence and mated with domestic pigs owned by the mountain farmers. They've been on the loose ever since. The park service tries to get rid of 'em, but there's way too many, and they're too spread out. You can see rows of dug up leaves about anywhere they've been rootin' along the roads and trails."

Catching his breath while letting the last bit of trivia sink into William, Dillon adds, "But what I really hate are the rattlers and copperheads. The rattlers are more poisonous, but the copperheads make up for it with their tempers. I swear, sometimes I believe they look fer somebody to bite."

Just as Dillon finishes, Jay slows the Cherokee as the paved road turns into gravel. Simultaneously, Jay and Dillon lower their windows to listen to the sounds of the river. Immediately, they notice the higher than usual volume from the risen water. As they pull into a small parking area, the not so distant rapids rumble their tune for the fly-fishing connoisseurs, the sound of mountain music to the two outdoorsmen. In contrast, William only hears the dreadful sound of sure and impending death.

As they put together their gear, they notice William pulling his waders out of the plastic bag from inside the box. He pulls the feet on and adjusts the shoulder straps with some confusion and difficulty. Next, he pulls out his wading shoes from their box and begins working on lacing them up. Dillon patiently nurses his cup of coffee and gazes at the river for any activity that may give away a trout's position as he waits for William to assemble his gear. Jay tries to lend

William a hand when possible. Finally, William is all together, relatively speaking, and ready to go fishing.

Dillon turns from his gaze of the river to the visual shock that is William, nearly coughing his last sip of coffee through his nostrils. Fortunately, it has cooled considerably by now. "Well, it's William the Conqueror!" After a short pause, he adds, "The third!"

As they turn to begin walking up the trail that parallels Big Bear Fork, Dillon ceremoniously adjusts his camouflage Dale Earnhardt ball cap, a.k.a. his lucky fishing hat, thus turning serious to the business at hand—fly-fishing.

Walking up the trail, heading upstream, after about twenty yards, William says, "Oh, I forgot my bait. I believe I left it in your vehicle, Jason." He walks back to the Jeep and fumbles around in the backseat where he pulls out a small can of cream-style corn. "Do either of you have a can opener?"

With a laugh in his voice, Dillon asks, "What do you need a can opener fer?"

"Well, I forgot to get the can with the pull tab on top."

Dillon answers, "Dude. You cain't use corn up here. In the Park, it's artificial only. No live bait."

"I beg to differ, Dillon. Corn is not live bait. It is indeed dead," replies William.

Jay, playing the mediator in a calm voice, says, "You're right, William, it is no longer live, but it is not artificial and thus is illegal. Leave it in the Cherokee. We've got plenty of flies for you to use."

William returns the corn back to the Cherokee. With that, the three begin to walk upstream. As they make their way up the old train bed that follows the river, Jay and Dillon discuss their plan for the day's trip.

Jay looks at Dillon and asks, "Well, master strategist, what do ya think?"

Dillon, staring at the river says, "It looks a bit high and off colored a dab. Perhaps if we walked up above Hemlock Falls, it might clear up a bit. The water's a little flatter up there and makes for easier wadin'."

"Sounds like a plan, Dillon." Jay looks over at William who is looking all around as though expecting something to leap out of the dense rhododendron and dog hobble undergrowth and drag him into some hidden lair. "Does that sound good to you, William?"

"I am with you two gentlemen. Whatever you decide is fine with me."

As the three continue up the trail, Jay shares more of the logging history of the Smoky Mountains. He tells William of the trail on which they are walking, of the hundreds of men who once rode the small piston-driven steam engines that once carried the massive chestnut and poplar logs down from the steep ridges. He shows William the remains of an old settling pond, now drained, on the side of the path opposite the river. Unfortunately, all is lost on William who feels more powerless by the minute. If not physically, he feels ever more attached to his chaperones in a mental need-to-survive sensation.

After a short walk, they hear the roar of a waterfall up ahead. They arrive at a widened area on the trail where a few benches are positioned on the left side of the trail overlooking the river. On the opposite side of the river is the twenty-five-foot-high Hemlock Falls, named after the tall Hemlock trees that still stand in the area. As with most falls in the Smokies, Hemlock Falls is really a cascade. From the benches, the falls seemingly appears from between two large hemlock trees. The clear water pours over a rock face where it glides at an ever-increasing speed bouncing off a few ledges on its way down resulting in a stream pouring into the creek surrounded by a thick mist. On clear winter days, after the leaves have fallen off the trees permitting sufficient sunlight to enter, a distinct rainbow can be seen hovering over the pool. For reasons unknown, the loggers, leaving an awesome reminder of how the forest of the Southern Appalachians once appeared, bypassed the trees in this area. At the base of Hemlock Falls is a large, deep emerald pool called the Splash Pool. During the logging days, it was the site of a large splash dam. Splash dams were constructed to pool up water. Once logs were cut and brought to the pool formed by the splash dam, the dam would be blasted away resulting in a surge of water that would carry the logs downstream.

As the three study the pool, Jay and Dillon for rising trout and William for its depth in which he imagines himself drowning, Jay says, "William, how 'bout you and me startin' here. You can practice your casting a little before we head on upstream. There's a few rising on the lower end that will be a good chance for you to hook up on one early."

Dillon adds, "I'll just head upstream a bit." He takes a few steps up the trail, then stops, turns around, and walks up to William. "I got somethin' fer ye, William. I picked it up fer ye at Smoky's this morning. Who knows, it may come in handy." He reaches and pulls a small can out of a pocket in his shirt and hands it to William, then turns and begins walking up the trail.

"Why thank you, Dillon," William says with a puzzled look on his face. Reading the can out loud, "Potted possum. Ingredients, choice snouts and tails in distilled swamp water."

"Save it fer later. Ye know they say what don't kill ye makes ye stronger!" Dillon yells back over his shoulder from up the trail.

Jay and William walk down a footpath taking them to the tail out of Splash Pool. At streamside, Jay looks over the surface of the pool from ground level at that perfect angle where the slightest disturbance is most easily detected. He pauses for a moment to admire the vibrant purple of the wild dwarf irises growing along the stream bank. As happens every year at this time, he marvels at the white blossoms in high contrast to the shiny green leaves of the rhododendron. He watches as a few fallen blossoms float by on the surface of the water as he thinks of the fishing gods sprinkling their blessings on this day. William only sees tall trees, deep water, slippery-looking rocks, and dark places where a snake, boar, or bear could hide waiting to kill him.

Jay shows William how to sneak up on the pool to within casting range. As he exhibits a roll cast, William shows little interest until Jay has his first hookup of the day on a number 16 Thunderhead. After a short fight, Jay lands a feisty eight-inch rainbow. He then backs away to let William give it a try. William reluctantly steps up and begins flailing his line around, nearly hooking Jay on a back cast.

Fortunately he misses, but his line becomes heavily tangled in some overhanging rhododendron.

"It's best if you get used to it now, William. Otherwise, it might be a long day," Jays says, referring to casting among the overhanging limbs.

He begins walking over to help untangle William's line when William waves him off. "Do not worry, Jason. I can handle this."

"Have you ever tried a roll cast, William? It really helps when you don't have room for a decent backcast." William sits down on a rock beneath the rhododendron and the snagged line as he watches Jay's masterful cast and another hooked fish. "Looks like they're really on today, William," Jay yells as he fights the trout. This one's a twelve-inch brown. "You sure you don't need any help?"

"No, thanks, Jason. I will be fine. I think I will watch you fish for a little while. You know, get the hang of the techniques you are using." Jay catches another rainbow at the head of the pool and walks back to William.

"Do you want to move on upstream? There's some good water there."

"You go ahead, Jason. I'm going to sit here and enjoy the scenery a little while. I will catch up to you shortly."

"Well, if you want, walk back up to the trail and walk upstream until you see me or Dillon. We shouldn't get too far." As Jay works his way upstream around the bend, he looks back at William who is still sitting on the same rock, busily swatting at gnats with his handkerchief.

After a couple of hours of fishing, Jay catches up with Dillon and asks him if he's seen William. When he learns he hasn't, they head back down looking for William with their catch of five trout each. Dillon has the biggest of the day, a nice fifteen-inch brown. Jay catches most of his on Thunderheads as he prefers dry flies since he used them mostly during his minimal fishing days at medical school; whereas, Dillon remained true to Pop's teaching, catching most of his on weighted Tellico Nymphs. He never gave up on the use of nymphs, mastering the technique he saw as having the greatest potential for regularly catching large trout. Dillon is considered by most in Laurel Cove as the best trout fisherman around.

Meanwhile, William breaks off his fly instead of going through the effort to untangle it. He ties on another and dabbles a little bit, making a few half-hearted casts. On his third cast, if you want to call it that, he gets tangled on the same rhododendron branch. In his frustration, he tries to break his line again by pulling back on his rod. Unfortunately, in his anger, he does not pull straight back but instead yanks his rod tip backward in a sharp motion. Just below his first ferrule, his rod snaps. Two pieces of the rod land on the moss-covered bank on the edge of the stream with the last few inches of the tip landing in some shallow water.

As he reaches down to grab the pieces on the bank, a large bullfrog makes a short hop out of the way. The sudden movement scares William who jumps back, tripping over a rock at the edge of the stream and landing on his back in a shallow pool. His anger, now intensified, causes him to throw a spoiled-brat-all-grown-up-style tantrum. He grabs the two pieces of the broken rod and crashes into the woods in the direction he believes will lead him to the trail. In his rage, he forgets about the pathway taken on his way down. He tumbles through the woods and into a rhododendron thicket. Instead of turning around, he stubbornly continues toward the thickest part of the patch.

After jerking his way through, over, under, and around rhododendron branches, he pulls sharply against his snagged leg and rips a gaping hole just above the right knee in his new waders. Lying on the ground surrounded by the nearly impenetrable rhododendron, he now realizes that he is alone. He's not sure where Jay and Dillon are. He's clueless to the location of the trail, now resting some fifty feet above him on the hillside. He sits down and reaches into a pocket. From his vest, he pulls out a small flask of Hidalgo Cream Sherry, which he sips to calm his nerves.

After a brief time to calm his anger, William begins to assess his situation. He realizes he is in a large, dark forest by himself and unsure where to go. Because of the thickness of the rhododendron all around him, he is unsure what dangerous creatures are sizing him up at this very moment. He feels claustrophobic but open and somewhat vulnerable at the same time. Another sip of Sherry, and William regains some composure but zero courage. Somewhere beyond the thickness of the undergrowth, he hears a faint, thumping noise.

At first, he thinks it might be Indians. Alas, too many movies. But if not wild Indians, what could it be? He goes through a mental rundown of Dillion's wildlife options, bears, boars, and snakes. No, not snakes but rattlesnakes and copperheads with attitudes. Suddenly, he feels like a choice buffet item, but for what creature? *Thump, thump, thump*. The repetitions get faster until it is a solid hum, then silence. William cannot think what a bear sounds like and is clueless to anything regarding the habits of wild boar. Rattlesnakes do rattle, but that noise is not a rattle. Another sip of Sherry provides him with a smidgen of nerve to explore the mysterious thumping sound.

Now on his hands and knees, he crawls quietly through the thicket toward the thumping noise. Without warning, it stops again. Unsure of the distance to the source of the sound, William pauses. As the thumping starts up again, he quietly crawls further through the brush into a small clearing. The thumping speeds up, hums, then stops again. William again pauses, looking in the direction from where he believes the sound is originating. Just on the other side of the clearing, William's eye catches movement. He focuses his eyes onto something moving along a fallen log.

At first, it looks like a wild chicken, its mottled black and brown colors blending into the surroundings. The "chicken" walks back and forth along the log, then suddenly stops and begins to flap its wings, pausing ever so briefly between beats. The strong beats and sudden stops of its wings create the thumping noise. As it repeats the process ever faster, the multiple thumps combine into one harmonious hum. *Thump, thump, thump, hum.* That wild chicken is making that strange sound. Another sip of Sherry allows William to stand upright. The bird, known as a ruffed grouse, disappears in a thunderous flight.

Laughing at his fear, William continues uphill. Just as he is about to stop for another rest, William looks up to see a short, agile-looking man who is the stereotypical hillbilly type. This strange-looking character has a short, unkempt beard with a tobacco stain at the corner of his mouth, old baggy clothes, and a well-worn grease-colored ball cap pulled down over his graying hair. Perhaps the most striking feature is his boots. While obviously this man has been fishing, his pants still wet from wading in the creek, he is wearing a fairly new pair of wading boots. This little guy is standing on the edge of the trail looking down at him. He reaches down giving William his hand. William reaches up and is pulled with ease by the small but stout man onto the trail.

Letting go of William's hand, the strange man asks, "How do?"

"Not too well. I got tangled up and tore my stupid waders trying to get out."

"Looks like ye got tangled up in 'rhodo-hell' and got a broken rod fer ye troubles."

"Oh yes," William replies having forgotten he was holding the pieces in his left hand. "That happened when I was down in the creek."

"Ye ain't from around here, are ye?" the man asks noticing William's northern accent.

"No, I am visiting from Atlanta." Reaching out to shake hands, he says, "My name is William Wentworth III."

"Glad to meet ye. My name is Lester."

Squirting a mouthful of tobacco juice on the ground, Lester wipes his mouth then gives William a strong handshake.

Wincing from the hard shake, William removes a handkerchief from his pocket and wipes his hand.

Chewing the tobacco stuck in his right jaw, Lester looks at William who has tears in his waders and is covered in leaves and mud. "Well, I hope ye caught some."

William, ashamed of his failure and subsequent panic, responds, "Yeah, I caught a few little ones."

"What happened to yer pole?"

"I was fighting a big brown when it snapped. Those gentlemen at the shop are going to get an earful from me. How about you? Did you catch many?"

Lester, looking up and down the trail, answers in a lower voice, "Yeah, hit was a purty good day. I got a lot of 'em. Mostly smallens though." Lester, glancing at William, asks, "Are ye headin' out fer the day?"

William, now realizing he is no longer lost and alone and wanting to get out of the forest, says, "Yes. I am finished. Besides, I do not believe I can catch many with a broken rod."

They begin to walk back down the trail toward the parking lot. William is glad that his ordeal is nearing its end. At least that's what he wants to believe. He just hates to go back to the Cherokee and wait for Jason and Dillon both empty handed and with a broken fly rod.

With a bit of gratitude for saving him from his plight, William looks over at the short, stout, country-looking man. "Did you say you caught a lot of trout."

With a prideful grin across his face, Lester looks over at William. "Yeah I got my limit. 'Course, I usually do."

His curiosity getting the best of him, William asks, "What did you catch them on?"

With a sheepish grin showing his poor dental hygiene, Lester spits some tobacco juice to the ground and says, "Well, keep this 'tween you and me. I use what's called a crow fly. I tie a crow feather around a hook with some black yarn on hit. If'n that don't work, I add a pinch of night crawler. Gets 'em every time."

With a puzzled look on his face, William asks, "Is that not against the regulations?"

"Only if'n ye gotta follow 'em. Ye see, my folks is originally from Scotland. They came over here and owned a lot of land up'n this here holler. Then the government came in an stole it from 'em. The way I sees it, they owe me somethin'. Besides, they's not smart enough to catch me."

Lester stops walking, looks up and down the trail, and with a serious look on his face, says, "Ye wanna see 'em?"

"Well, sure."

Lester makes a quick glance up and down the trail, then pulls a plastic bag out from behind his back. "These here's a good mess of fish."

William, looking at the trout with envy, replies, "They sure are."

"I like these because they's the best kind to fry up. Roll 'em in some corn meal with some fried taters and onions. Feller, that's eatin!"

William, admiring the small trout, replies, "They sure are pretty fish."

"Yeah, them's what we call specks. They's the best kind for eatin'. They's the only real trout in these mountains."

"Well, Lester, I am sure impressed. I wish I would have caught some today, but unfortunately, a faulty rod has put an early end to my fishing." William thinks for a moment. "Lester, would you be willing to sell me your trout. I'll gladly give you a hundred dollars?"

Lester casts a glance up and down the trail, hands the bag of trout to William, and with a smile says, "A hunnert dollars? Sure! I still have plenty of time to catch me some more fer dinner. The sun won't be down for a while yet!"

With a smile, William reaches into his pocket retrieves a crisp one-hundred-dollar bill and hands it to Lester who accepts the gift with a smile showing a few dark teeth and his chaw of backer. With that, Lester quickly makes a 180 and heads up the trail. William watches Lester walk away and yells, "Thanks for the specks, Lester," as Lester waves his hand back at William.

With his newfound fortune, William walks toward the parking area. He smiles as he thinks of how he's going to brag on his catch and the success. Now he's only got to think of an explanation for his broken rod. Perhaps he can say that he hooked into a big brown trout and in the epic struggle, his rod gave way under the immense weight of the trophy. William can hardly wait to show Jason and Dillon, the experts, his catch. Their envy will be worth every minute of his struggle in the forest and every cent of the hundred dollars. He thinks, *Yeah, I may not be in my element, but I'm a survivor. Even here, I can come out on top with some fish for dinner. And Doris did not think I could bring anything home. Well, this will show her.*

Meanwhile, Jay and Dillon are walking quickly down the trail looking down into the creek for any signs of William.

With a frustrated look on his face, William says, "Man, am I gonna catch it from Debbie!"

"Oh, don't worry, Jay. He's gotta be here somewhere. I mean, he is a grown man, ain't he?"

"Well, if you hadn't scared him with all your tales of the wild animals. I mean, man Dillon, you went a little too far."

"Oh, don't get your waders in a wad, Jay. Besides, everything I said was true, wasn't it?"

Making his way back up the trail, Lester hears a loud whistle and veers off the trail and into the woods to see what is going on up ahead. He sits in the woods, listening to Jay and Dillon's conversation. As they walk away, Lester looks around, and realizing that the coast is clear, heads on upstream.

As they approach the Splash Pool, Jay heads down the trail to the base of the pool while Dillon stays up on the main trail. Jay looks around for any signs of William. Something in the rhododendron catches his eye. He reaches up and pulls on a broken leader. He looks around and sees a broken rod tip in the water at the edge of the stream when he hears Dillon whistling from the trail.

Jay heads back to the main trail with the rod tip in his hand.

"Hey, Jay, it looks like William the Conqueror made his way up the bank right here. Man, he does things the hard way, don't he?"

"Look what I found, a broken rod tip down in the creek. You think it's William's?"

"We'll find out when we find him. My guess is he probably tripped and fell, breakin' his rod. But God knows why he'd come out right here. Look how thick it is down in there, and steep too! I mean the trail to the creek is only forty feet away."

"You don't think he's hurt, do you?"

Dillon, trying to keep Jay calm and things in perspective, replies, "Naw. I bet he gave it up and walked back down. He's probably sittin' down at the Cherokee waitin' for us right now trying to fend off all the wild animals."

Jay and Dillon quickly walk down the trail heading to the parking lot looking for any additional signs of William.

Arriving at the parking lot, William takes a seat on a bench and puts the finishing touches on his story for the day. He runs his story through his mind.

After catching several trout in the Splash Pool, I worked my way further upstream. I observed something swirling in a dark pool at the far edge of the current. After making several casts with no luck, I changed flies until I tied on a brown one that sinks. On the first cast, there was an immediate swirl. I set the hook and the fish leaped three, no four, feet out of the water. The trout was at least two feet long. A big brown. It swam downstream, where I followed it by running along the bank. Then it headed downstream where I chased it by running into the water along the edge to the next pool. On my way down to the pool, I tripped and fell, tearing my waders and breaking my rod. After picking myself up and grabbing the line, I continued to fight the monster by holding the line in my hand until finally it broke off.

He pauses for a moment and then keeps thinking again. *Yeah, that should have everything covered from my broken rod to my torn waders. Those guys will die of envy when they learn of the day I had.*

As he rehearses his story for the second time, he hears a car coming down the road. It appears to be a park service vehicle. The vehicle stops and out steps Ranger Patterson. Recognizing him from this morning, William smiles as he prepares to test his story on the ranger.

"Good afternoon. I believe your name is Ranger Patterson? I am William Wentworth III. We met this morning in the café. I am up here with Jason and Dillon."

As he prepares to break in to his story, Ranger Patterson cuts him off and asks, "May I see your license?"

"Well sure?" William pulls out his license purchased at The Hatch this morning. "You would not believe the day I have had. A beautiful day of fishing to match this beautiful sunny day!"

As he looks over William's license, Ranger Patterson asks in a stern and serious tone, "So. You caught some trout?"

"Oh you bet, and—"

"May I see them," he asks, cutting William off.

"Sure." Still smiling and proud of the catch he purchased, but his nonetheless, he reaches into his creel and pulls out the bag of speckled trout.

His face turning at first pale, then bloodred, Ranger Patterson grabs them and looks sharply into William's eyes and asks, "Did you catch these?"

"Why, yes, I did, and several more that I let go. Why you should have—"

Ranger Patterson cuts William off again and adds, "Do you know and understand the fishing regulations up here in the Park, Mr. Wentworth."

"Well, uh yeah, I think so. I believe Jay told me that they had to be at least seven inches and that I could keep only five. But to be honest, I do not think he expected me to catch any much less keep them."

"Well, Mr. Wentworth, you are correct in that you can keep five and they must be seven inches, but these are brook trout. It is against the regulations to keep brook trout regardless of their size. They are protected and the only indigenous species of trout in the Park. There is a hefty fine for keeping even one of these. I'm going to have to take you to headquarters."

William, totally confused by what he has heard, replies, "But they are over seven inches. They are not illegal. Besides they are speckled trout, and we are allowed to keep speckled trout up here."

"Did Dr. McMahan or Mister Webb tell you that?"

"Uh no." Not wanting to give away his source just yet, William begins to think of how to explain his viewpoint. Before he can say anything else, Ranger Patterson spins William around and quickly places handcuffs on him and walks him to his car.

"But you do not understand, Ranger Patterson—"

"Well, we'll sort it all out at headquarters."

After Ranger Patterson helps the handcuffed William into the back of the cruiser, he writes a brief note to Jay telling him of William's trip to the Park Headquarters. After leaving the note behind the wiper blade on Jay's windshield, Ranger Patterson places the contraband trout in his trunk and they drive off.

Roughly an hour after William is hauled away, Jay and Dillon make it back to the parking area. They look around the parking area, the benches, and finally walk toward the Cherokee when Dillon notices the note on the windshield.

"Hey, Jay, what's that on yer winder? Looks like a note or somethin'."

Jay walks over, removes the note, and reads it aloud, "Mr. McMahan, I have taken your fishing partner, Mr. Wentworth, to the Park Headquarters. He is under arrest for poaching and possession of brook trout. Sincerely, Ranger Patterson, Great Smoky Mountains National Park."

"Are you serious? Let me see." Snatching the note from Jay's hand, Dillon reads the note. "Well, I'm surprised he even caught anything. Jay, didn't ye tell him 'bout the regs?"

"Yeah, I told him all about them yesterday afternoon. But who'd figure he'd catch anything?"

Jay opens the back of the Cherokee as he and Dillon begin taking off their waders and putting up their equipment. "Well, I guess we'd better go get him. Man, somehow I know I'm gonna catch hell for this."

"You know, Jay, this is one of them times I'm glad I ain't married."

Upon arrival at the Park Headquarters, William is given his one phone call, which he makes to his wife Doris' cell phone. Doris, worried about William, and Debbie, mad at Jay for somehow letting her best friend's husband get into this mess, make the one-hour drive to the headquarters.

As they arrive, Doris looks for William who looks like an unwanted dog in a pound. She rushes to give him a hug. He tries to reciprocate, but the handcuffs prevent it.

Fortunately for Jay, he and Dillon and Ranger Kowalski arrive soon after Doris and Debbie. Another bit of luck is that Debbie is too mad to speak, for now, thus allowing Jay time to assess the situation. Ranger Kowalski drives over after hearing the chatter on the two-way radio. The cooler head and seniority of Ranger Kowalski prevail in getting William out of the handcuffs. Immediately William rushes to the nearest restroom, the women's, to relieve himself from the biological urge created on his bladder by the recent events.

As William steps back out of the ladies restroom, Jay and Dillon grill him over what happened.

Through it all, William has his head down to hide the tears now welling up in his eyes with every hug from Doris, who is now sitting next to him. All of the rehearsing of his big fish story is for naught as William tells of his fishless trial. All he could say was, "No one told me that I could not keep a speck."

Suddenly, Jay realizes something from his sermon last night. "William, why do you keep talking about speckled trout? I never called them speckled trout when I was talking to you last night."

With his head still down and an intermittent sniff, he says, "I know, you never told me I could not keep a speck."

"No. What I mean is, I never said the word *speck*. All I ever called them were brook trout, and I said they were protected. Where did you hear about specks?"

Having finished his paperwork, Ranger Patterson walks up to the discussion and spells out the crime in a stone-cold tone, "Mr. Wentworth, the maximum penalty for this offense is $5,000 and up to six months in jail."

William, only hearing "six months in jail," has sudden visions of being in prison with Ben Dover as a cellmate. "But no, you don't understand, specks are okay, he said…" Then pausing and realizing he has nowhere to go but jail, he finishes, "He said they were the only real trout in the mountains."

Jay looks at William and says, "Who said they were the only real trout in the mountains?"

Totally swallowing his pride to save his hide, William answers, "The man who sold them to me. He said his name was Lester." At the moment the words crossed his lips, William recalls the barrels on the hillside from this morning. He remembers the cockfighting and the poaching. He looks up at Jay who is standing over him, "Lester Blalock."

Ranger Kowalski looks over at Ranger Patterson. The two walk over to the other side of the room to talk privately for a moment. Both believe William's story, his teary eyes and biological breakdown attest to his honesty. Both agree this accusation would be no more than William's word against Lester's, and that will not get them anywhere. They must catch Lester in the act to make the charges stick. Both have tried to snag Lester on several occasions, but without possession of evidence, they have yet to achieve anything. As much as Lester's reputation for poaching in the Park gnaws at Ranger Kowalski, he is patient. Ranger Patterson is not. However, now Lester Blalock has gone beyond poaching a protected species. Now he's selling them!

When they return, they ask William for a description of Lester, which William describes from his greasy hat to his new wading boots. To Ranger Patterson's dismay, Ranger Kowalski drops the charges with a warning to William. No sooner did the pardon arrive than William was out the door, pulling Doris along. After a quick trip to Jay's house to pick up a few things, they were on their way out of the mountains, out of town, and out of the state.

Sadly for Jay, volcano Debbie was still gathering lava as they rode back to Laurel Cove. Dillon sat in the backseat wanting to say something funny but, respecting the life of his best friend and fearing Debbie's wrath may turn on him, contained himself.

A few months later, Debbie's eruption had come and gone, but the memory of William Wentworth III lingered. On a Thursday afternoon, Dillon had taken his Brittany spaniel, Roscoe, for a ride up in the mountains.

Walking around the parking lot watching Roscoe sniff around the woods, Dillon was stringing up his line for an afternoon cast or two. As he stood up from one of the benches that look over Big Bear Fork, he startled Lester Blalock who was walking down the trail returning from a fishing trip. As he was talking to the ever-nervous Lester, Roscoe came running over for a quick pat on the head. Suddenly, Roscoe began digging at Lester's pants' legs, still damp from the day's wet wading. Ranger Patterson, having quietly pulled up in his car, his favorite method of entrance, notices Roscoe's odd behavior as Dillon apologizes and struggles with the typically well-behaved Roscoe. Dillon clips a leash onto Roscoe's collar as Lester quickly walks toward his pickup truck. Using instinct, training, or blind luck,

Ranger Patterson bends down to pet Roscoe with his right hand and unclips his leash with his left. Immediately, Roscoe bolts to Lester and begins sniffing and scratching at his legs. Any more rowdy and Roscoe would've pointed or humped poor Lester's leg.

"Say, Lester, hold on a minute!" Ranger Patterson shouts.

Slowing down but working on the final steps to his truck, Lester looks over his shoulder and replies, "Yeah, what?"

"Why is the dog digging at your leg?"

"Don't know. Ye know how dem huntin' dogs can be."

"Well pull up your pant leg. I want to take a look."

Trying to stutter his way out of a jam, Lester continues to bicker with Ranger Patterson until finally the law and Roscoe's determination prevails. Pulling up his pant legs, Ranger Patterson, Dillon, and Roscoe are treated to the latest Lester brainchild. On each leg is a homemade sock garter. Beneath each sock held up by the garter is a Ziplock bag with three brook trout.

Needless to say, Ranger Patterson has his day of redemption from the "warning" given to William. Not only did he get his redemption, on this day, Ranger Patterson bagged the infamous Lester Blalock, the area's most notorious and craftiest poacher.

Dillon, recapping the story of Roscoe's discovery and Ranger Patterson's arrest of Lester to Jay, finishes with, "Ye know, every dog has his day, uniformed or not."

THE LAST FLY

One of the advantages of a lifelong friendship is the certain knowledge that the other will always be there. Sure, there are good times and bad times, but if one is ever to succeed in avoiding all difficulties in a friendship, the foundation would have to be as sturdy as a bucket of sand in a hurricane. In fact, it's the tough times shared that often form the strongest bond between friends, and it is only the best of friends that possess that certain knowledge that regardless of the bumps and bruises of life, tomorrow they will still be friends. Sometimes, however, others enter their lives, and adjustments must be made, such as when one up and gets married.

Unfortunately, not all marriages survive the ups and downs of life. Dillon is having a difficult time handling the separation. Now that the divorce is final, things are not getting better. Unlike his now ex-wife, Dillon took his marriage seriously and tried to make a go of it, but as he is reminded by Jay, "It takes two to tango." Dillon is low, and Jay knows it. Having known each other their entire lives, Jay knows how to get Dillon out of his emotional slump. Sure, it would take time, but a catalyst was needed. Dillon hates it when Jay gets "all medical" on him, but being a family practice physician doesn't limit Jay to the physical realm of care.

Jay knows that the best medicine is often a dose of laughter or a shot of happiness, but no prescription can guarantee that result. Jay knows Dillon needs something to take his mind off things and get him pointed in the right direction. He has an idea, but this medicine would take time, and time was something Jay wasn't sure Dillon would allow as Dillon never claimed nor demonstrated to be a champion of patience. As with many potential cures, there is also the concern of rejection and possible adverse side effects.

Driving up the gravel road toward Dillon's house, Jay is not certain of the condition in which he would find his friend. Rounding the white-framed house, Jay drives around to the back where Dillon is on the back porch in his favorite rocking chair nursing a long neck. Without saying a word, Jay walks onto the porch, passes by Dillon who is looking straight ahead, yet nowhere in particular. Walking into the kitchen, Jay helps himself to the fridge and pours himself a glass of sweet tea and joins Dillon on the porch. As they look out over the Smoky Mountains through Jenkins Cove and up Balsam Ridge, neither says a word for some time. Finally, as the crickets and cicadas ease off in their pursuit of a mate, Jay takes the cue.

Without looking over, Jay asks, "How's it going?" "Awright," Dillon replies as he tosses back the longneck. "Anything you wanna talk about? Get off your chest?"

Reaching into a small cooler for another bottle, Dillon replies, "Naw. Ain't much left to say."

After a few minutes of looking up the valley, Dillon's gaze never changes. "Ye ever feel totally bankrupt? I don't mean just money. I mean totally empty with nothing left in ye. I guess everybody gets here sometime in life. No more dreamin' those childhood dreams where ye can be anything ye set yer mind to. Does it mean yer all growed up when ye wake up and realize life ain't gonna be a bed of roses and happily ever after? When does a little boy realize he's not gonna be an astronaut or a little girl know she's never gonna be like Cinderella? Hell, I never asked for much, but I sure gave all I had. There's nothing left, Jay. Nothin' 'cept the house, but its empty too. She got all the damn furniture."

Ever the optimist, Jay replies, "Not the chairs were sittin' in.

You got something to start over with, Dillon."

"Well, I'm too tired, too, and I ain't in the mood to start over again. Think I'm just gonna drink myself into the sunset." "Was that a John Wayne movie?"

Dillon cracks a smile that can only be detected by a subtle rise in his mustache over the right corner of his mouth. "No, it was a country song. Probably Merle Haggard or George Jones."

After a few moments and a few more sips, Dillon thinks out loud, "You remember when ye was a kid and ye hurt so bad it was hard to swaller? Ye felt that pain in the pit of ye throat that run plumb down to ye stomach? Ye felt like ye got to do something to make it feel better, but ye never figured out what it was? I think I'm gonna numb it with beer and maybe get a jar of Boots' best shine out to chase it."

"See, Dillon, you've already got your first goal, to numb the pain before you pass out."

Another rise in the mustache on Dillon's face. "Dammit, Jay, you're screwin' up my pity party!"

The next day, knowing the diagnosis and hoping for the right medicine, Jay picks up the package himself before making the house call he'd dreaded all day. As he pulls around to the back of Dillon's house, Jay sees Dillon in the same rocking chair, same stare up Balsam Ridge, and wearing the same clothes as when he left yesterday. The only real difference readily noticed were the numerous beer bottles lying around the porch. Jay opens the door of the Cherokee, thinks about taking the package, but decides to test the waters with Dillon first. Not really sure how to offer his idea of a cure, Jay thinks for a moment. Knowing Dillon will do just about anything for him, Jay decides to ask Dillon for a favor. "Listen, Dillon. I got Debbie something, but it's sort of a surprise. I mean, I need you to keep it for me for about a week."

Taking his eyes off the mountains, Dillon looks over toward Jay. "What's that?"

Jay stands up. "Well, I guess it's easier for me to show you." He walks out to the Cherokee and opens the door retrieving a box. He walks over to Dillon and sets the box down at his feet. The box is moving slightly when suddenly, a small, white, freckled-faced puppy pops his head out of the box.

Jay picks up the tiny Brittany spaniel and looks up at Dillon. "I got Debbie a puppy. I figure if nothin' else, it might curb her motherly instincts a few more years assuring me of at least a couple o' more years of die-hard fishin'."

Dillon, not showing much concern for the little puppy already gnawing at the string on his boot, stares up Jenkins Cove. "Awright. I guess I can put up with 'im fer a week."

Jay, thinking its best to leave before Dillon changes his mind, looks at his watch, makes the first excuse he can think of and replies, "Hey, I gotta go. I'll give you a call in a couple 'o days." As Jay drives away, he can't help thinking about his friend and the "gift." Looking in his rear view mirror back at Dillon's place, Jay thinks aloud, "Lord, don't let him kill the little feller!"

A week has passed, and Jay has avoided making any contact with Dillon. He figures no news is good news, but he knows his time is up, and it is time to try not to pick up the little puppy. Jay has already made arrangements with the owner of the little puppy to bring him back if it doesn't work out. But still, he knows it may not be easy dealing with Dillon. The truth will come out. It somehow always does, and Dillon hates it when someone tries to pull one over on him. As Jay pulls around to the back of Dillon's house, Dillon is sitting on the edge of the first step playing a game of tug-of-war with the puppy. All two pounds of feist is pulling on the little stick. Getting out of the Cherokee, Jay tries to hide his smile as he observes the two locked in battle.

"Hey, Jay, watch this!" Dillon tosses the stick a short distance. Immediately, the puppy bounces over to the stick, picks it up, and retrieves it back, stopping short of Dillon who reaches out resuming the tug-of-war battle. The little Brittany begins jerking backward on the stick with all its strength trying to snatch the stick from Dillon's hand.

Jay forgets for a moment about the deal he's made with Dillon. "Man, Dillon. Looks like y'all been spending some time together. You're already teaching him tricks?"

"A few," Dillon replies as he lets go of the stick. "I thought I'd get his education started fer ye. I guess you're ready to take him home, ain't ye?" Dillon asks with a trace of disappointment.

Jay kicks the dirt a little with his right foot as he pushes his hands further down his pants pockets. It's confession time. "Well, Dillon. Debbie and I are hoping that he is home. We know you're having a tough time with the divorce and all. Hell, who wouldn't. Besides, a dog is man's best friend. Just think about it. Sometimes a dog is a lot better to have around than a woman. A dog don't care if you look at another dog. He doesn't even care how many dogs you've had before. You'll never have to listen to him bitch at ye for all your bad habits. I mean, when he learns that he can, he'll develop his own bad habits, like lickin' himself."

Dillon hands Jay a beer. "Okay, okay, I get the picture. I guess I can put up with him fer a while. He has been a little fun."

Jay reaches out his bottle, tapping it against Dillon's to make a toast. "Well, here's to best friends."

Dillon replies, "Back at ye, buddy."

Dillon knew he had grown attached to the puppy. Now that the divorce was sinking in, he admits to himself that he is feeling lonely at times. Actually, the best part of his day this past week was coming home to see Roscoe waddle out of his box wagging his little stump of a tail. Roscoe. Dillon never consciously named him. It just came out one day, and it felt natural. He looked like a Roscoe. Nothing special, just Roscoe. No longer is Dillon's arrival home to be dreaded. No more cold shoulder, sarcastic remarks, or arguments over anything and nothing. He did miss a woman's touch and a little conversation at night. But he'd been missing those and more for some time now.

Over the next few years, Roscoe grew and learned a few tricks and has even become a good grouse dog making regular trips with Dillon. Dillon also grew. Whereas Roscoe matured into a full-grown Brittany spaniel full of energy, Dillon matured past his torn marriage and moved on to other relationships albeit temporary ones. Some would say that Dillon has difficulty trusting anything without a Y chromosome. Fortunately for Roscoe, that is not a problem that ever comes between the two of them. Few relationships deepened like that of Dillon and Roscoe.

As Roscoe's desire to point game birds grew, Dillon obliged his friend with frequent outings, often just taking walks through the woods. During hunting season, Dillon teamed up with Ernie Ledbetter and his trio of Brittany spaniels. Ernie had his dogs well-trained, taking great pride in the successes of his animals. He also knew the best locales for ruffed grouse, which frequented the rhododendron thickets, sometimes following them illegally into the Great Smoky Mountain National Park.

While Dillon was learning the finer techniques of wing-shooting the elusive and nearly impossible to hit grouse, Roscoe was picking up pointers from his mentors. Beginning Roscoe's third hunting season, the trips with the Ledbetters became essentially nonexistent. The talk down at Smoky's Café was that ole Ledbetter didn't like the fact that "the pup," as he referred to Roscoe, was besting his prized spaniels. As word grew around Laurel Cove and beyond of Roscoe's talents, so did Ernie's jealousy of Dillon and "that pup."

What made matters worse between Ernie and Dillon was the fact that Dillon never cared much for style points or for that matter how many birds Roscoe found, how long he could or would hold point. He just enjoyed the time in the outdoors and watching Roscoe have fun. If asked, he would admit to an occasional smile creeping across his face when Roscoe's performance outshined that of the Ledbetter trio.

It didn't take long for offers to come Dillon's way for Roscoe; although, he had no intention of taking anyone up on them. He would never part with Roscoe, as he'd gotten along better with him than his wife, whom Dillon thought of only rarely now. To him,

Roscoe was not just a bird dog, and a damn good one at that, he was a friend, and he was raised to value friendships, especially good ones, over money even if it was a couple of thousand dollars.

One day, Dillon receives a call from Ernie. Ernie wants to buy Roscoe. He'd even let Dillon keep him. As Ernie put it, "I'd really just like to have him to breed with my bitch. I figure between the two of 'em, I should be able to get a solid white Brittany. A solid white one would be plum purty and easy to see in them thickets."

Dillon sees right through Ernie's pitch, however, and turns the offer down. Besides, Dillon doesn't like the way Ernie treats his dogs, especially when they don't measure up to his expectations. Dillon never wants to force Roscoe to be more than he is. He wants Roscoe to be Roscoe, no more, no less. Having his too-good-too-refuse offer turned down was the last straw for Ernie. He is fed up with all the noise over "the pup." A few months go by before Dillon hears anything out of Ernie. One afternoon, Dillon has just gotten home and is going through his after-work routine, tossing the dirty clothes in the pile, giving Roscoe a good head shake and pat down, which is followed by a quick trip to grab a cold one as Roscoe takes off into the laurel thickets in the backyard. No sooner than he sat in his favorite rocking chair on the back porch looking up Jenkins Cove did the phone ring.

"Dillon! Yer dawg is up here messin' round my quail cages. Now I don't want any trouble, but I ain't gonna let him get at 'em!" Ernie screams on the other end of the phone.

"Well, I'm sorry, Ernie. He is just out burning some energy off. I'll come git 'em," Dillon apologizes.

"Well, don't let it happen agin!"

"Consider it taken care of. Sorry again," Dillon apologizes again as they hang up. Dillon walks back out onto the porch and makes his quick, sharp whistle signaling Roscoe to come to him. To Dillon's surprise, Roscoe comes barreling from around the front of the house, the opposite direction from Ernie's property, promptly coming to a stop by sitting at Dillon's right leg.

"Where ye been, Roscoe?" Dillon asks as he scratches Roscoe's ears. "Ye, gotta stay away from Ernie's birds. He gets a mite ornery 'bout them quail." The same episode happens a few days later, once again with Roscoe still on the edge of Dillon's property. Dillon tries to get across in a nice manner that he doesn't believe it is Roscoe, but all he gets for his pleasantries is abrasive warnings from Ernie.

About two weeks later, Dillon answers the phone, "Dammit, Dillon! I'm gonna burn him up with some rock salt if he don't quit messin' with my quail!"

By now, Dillon knows it isn't Roscoe as he is laying on the rug at his feet in the living room. Dillon is fed up with Ernie's accusations and his refusal to listen to him try to explain that it isn't Roscoe. "Well hell, Ernie, do what ye gotta do!" and he hangs up the phone. A few minutes later, boom! It sounds like a shotgun from up at Ernie's place. Dillon thinks no more of it, and he receives no more calls from Ernie.

The next morning, Dillon is eating breakfast down at Smoky's Grill. Doc Hembree walks over with a cup of coffee in hand and sits on the barstool next to Dillon.

"Did ye hear 'bout Ernie Ledbetter's prized Brittany?"

"No, what happened?" Dillon replies, not really wanting to think about his grumpy neighbor.

"He called me last night wantin' to know if I could work on his bitch. Apparently, he shot her by accident. I put two and two together and figured out that he thought Roscoe was messin' 'round with his pet quail, but he mistook his own for Roscoe and shot her." "Yeah, he'd been calling screamin' at me 'bout Roscoe comin' up there. I got tired of it and told him to do what he had to do." "Well, she's gonna be all right. I had to remove some seven shot from her backside. A bloody mess. He thought he had some rock salt, but he thought wrong. Serves him right." At that, they both have to break out and laugh at Ernie's mistake. However, they feel sorry for the dog, the fact that she got shot but also that she had such a bastard for an owner.

One afternoon, Dillon returns home from a so-so fishing trip, for Dillon, so-so meaning about twenty-five trout. Nothing spectacular, really just meeting his expectations. As with all well-rounded fly fishermen who eventually become fly tiers, he is always looking for the next fly. Perhaps the holy grail of flies that will work under all conditions and will be irresistible to the big ones, the ultimate, the final solution to those sometimes hard to figure out wild Smoky Mountain trout. Deep down, he knows it likely will never exist but feels it his duty to try to make the discovery.

Putting his equipment in its proper place, he feels Roscoe's nose sniffing around on his left hand for the scent of trout. Roscoe wants to know how his buddy's fishing trip went, which he could easily judge by the smell of fish on Dillon's hands. Dillon reaches around to scratch Roscoe's ears, more out of habit than true purpose, when the epiphany hits him like falling into a Smoky Mountain creek on a January morning. Roscoe's coloring is 95 percent white, with a few reddish-brown patches on his forehead and solid reddish-brown ears. Upon closer examination of Roscoe, Dillon notices small pencil-sized twigs of loose hair on the back of his ears. Dillon thinks how they would be just perfect for a number fourteen hook.

After plucking a few loose twigs from one ear, at no disservice to Roscoe, Dillon holds them up to his magnifying lamp at his tying bench. Grabbing the first twig, Dillon ties it to the back of a number 14 2X nymph hook creating a tail of about half the length of the hook using brown thread. Next, he takes the remaining twig cutting it with his scissors into small lengths for dubbing. He then dubs a small abdomen adding some gold tinsel over the back and ribbing it with copper wire. He finishes the fly with a thicker, dubbed thorax, and picks out the fibers giving the fly some added body.

Looking over at Roscoe, who has returned to his nap on his favorite rug, Dillon quips, "Hey, buddy, ye think this fly'll work? Think I'll give 'er a shot Saturday. Maybe you will earn a little extra dog chow fer yur contribution." Hearing Dillon's comments, Roscoe opens his eyes, lifts his head, and turns it from side to side as he so often does when listening to Dillon's words. Just as quickly, Roscoe goes back to his nap, not giving much credence to Dillon's new invention.

Dillon studies the fly again, pleased with his innovation, but deep down realizing few creations truly last the scrutiny of trout over time. If nothing else, perhaps the fly will catch a few trout before being relegated to some corner of his fly box. Still, the fly did look good, even if he wasn't a trout. If he were a trout, he'd take it. He could not resist the combination of reddish-brown hair, whitish tips, and accented with gold tinsel and red copper ribbing. Dillon takes his fly box out of his vest that he has been readying for the upcoming trip and places it where he will be certain to see it.

The following Saturday, Jay and Dillon drive to the South Holston River. As they drive up interstate 81, the sun rises like a fiery meatball over the distant mountains. Just outside of Bristol, driving past the Bristol Motor Speedway, billed as the "World's Fastest Half Mile" and "The Last Great Coliseum," Dillon subconsciously adjusts his camouflage Dale Earnhardt ball cap as his thoughts go to the "Man in Black" intimidating his way to another win on the thirty-six-degree banked curves. Back to the trip at hand, Dillon doesn't care much for tailwater fishing. For one thing, he always feels like he is fishing too close to someone's house. He looks at Jay and says, "Ye never know when some psycho hothead's gonna com barrelin' out of his house with a shotgun screamin' 'bout landowner rights!"

Absent was the beautiful Smoky Mountains with its rhododendron, hemlocks, and waterfalls. They are replaced by rude fishermen, drift boats passing through your hole, and generation schedules. In Dillon's memory is the time he and Jay had gotten trapped on an island when they were twelve years old as a result of a sudden, unexpected rise in the water levels. Making their way to the river, Dillon gets that uncomfortable tailwater feeling. "Hey, Jay, you say the water ain't gonna come up 'til when?"

"Relax, Dillon. They're only gonna pulse one generator. You'll barely notice a rise at all." To Dillon, it just wasn't natural, or as he'd say, "It ain't right!" Still, Dillon knew Jay liked the South Holston and the sulphur hatch, something he picked up while he was in medical school. Besides, the sulphur hatch is really on right now, which might sway Dillon into a little dry fly-fishing, no small feat being the nymphing purist that he is.

While Jay is focusing his attention on a nice, slow run looking for rising 'bows, Dillon eases further upstream and mumbles to himself, "Relax, they're only pulsing one generator. You'll barely notice it as it rises over yer head!" Dillon stops as he settles on a set of shoals where the water is a bit faster and shallower, giving him immediate access to higher ground, just in case.

Looking over his shoulder through the mist hanging just above the river like the fog in the freezer section at Webb's Grocery, Dillon watches Jay, who looks like a ghost in slow motion gracefully casting his number 18 parachute sulphur, laying it ever so softly onto the perfectly smooth surface. Immediately, a nice trout sips the fly and feels the instant connection with Jay's lifted rod. Knowing that Jay has already gotten into his zone, Dillon feels a bit inferior and somewhat overwhelmed by the big water of the South Holston. Not that Dillon hates dry fly-fishing, he just prefers nymphs. Fighting the urge to tie on a sulphur pattern, Dillon opens his box of small nymphs. Small, to Dillon, is anything smaller than a number 10.

Looking over the wide selection of nymphs, mostly tied and weighted with the fast, steep water of the Smoky Mountains in mind, Dillon's gaze stops at his new creation. He studies the color, size, and shape, then glances back into the water flowing by his feet. Not wanting to reveal his secret 'til just the right moment, he chooses a "warm-up" fly. As the water gently rolls by a foot or so deep, he spots a sulphur-colored mayfly bouncing along riding the small waves as it passes by. He keeps his eye on the tiny insect to see if a trout reveals himself by rising for the natural. Suddenly, the mayfly begins skittering across the surface before taking flight. Now, Dillon spots another and another as numerous potential mates join in the midair dance of their reproductive cycle. As he watches the seemingly one-thousandth sulphur mayfly lift off, his upward observation catches two geese flying by in the mist now burning off from the sun's rays, itself now shining through the fog a n d giving the appearance of a full moon. Glancing back downstream through the rolling river mist and over the rumbling rapids, Jay has another bend in his rod.

"Man! I hate dry flies. Too damn small!" Dillon looks back at his fly box. A kingfisher flies overhead seemingly laughing at Dillon with its chatter. This harassment doesn't go unnoticed by Dillon as he shakes his head in frustration at trying to decide which of the little nymphs he should try first. Should it be a number 20 midge pattern or perhaps a number 18 hares ear. Logic tells him to use some form of a sulphur pattern, perhaps of the emerger persuasion. First, he places a small strike indicator onto his leader followed by what he determines to be a good first choice, that being a number 16 bead head pheasant tail. Below the pheasant tail, he drops another two feet of tippet and ties on a sulphur emerger.

After several casts through the run that produced no strikes, he pauses to study the current, his tandem nymphs dragging in the current downstream. Dillon catches a glimpse of a nice rainbow rising just on the far edge of a submerged rock about thirty feet away. As he focuses his attention for a sharper look at the rainbow to determine its size, his rod is jolted, his reflexes automatically setting the hook! Out jumps a small brown, though nothing to brag about, ten-incher. Though being caught accidentally, still Dillon feels a small bit of relief in that he is now on the board.

As he quickly works the trout to his wetted hand, he glances downstream toward Jay, who through the fog can be seen holding his bent rod in his right hand and giving Dillon a thumbs-up with his left. As Dillon releases the small brown, he keeps an eye out for the rising 'bow on the far side of the rock. A steady rhythm of every sixteen seconds reveals a nose barely perceptible as it breaks the surface to sip another mayfly. In the rippled surface along the edge of the currently gliding by the far side of the rock, most anglers would fail to spot the subtle intrusion of the surface film, but not Dillon.

Stripping out just enough line to make the distance, Dillon makes a cast with an immediate upstream mend to compensate for the faster line of current between him and the rising nose. The perfect cast, the perfect drift—nothing! The fishing gods do not reward the perfect presentation, Dillon thinks. Another cast followed by an upstream mend; this time, the nose rises just as the indicator passes. Perhaps he's a little too deep with his nymphs as the water is barely eighteen inches deep. On his next cast, Dillon creates a slight rise in his emerger by quickly but slightly lifting his rod tip, giving the flies the appearance of emerging toward the surface.

The indicator immediately disappears beneath the surface, as the back of the rainbow swirls about the surface of the current. With the current to its advantage, the rainbow saves its strength causing

Dillon to back off on his rod pressure to save his 6X tippet until he can size up his opponent's strength. After several bouts of tug-of-war and two leaps, the 'bow is worked into some slack water along the rocky edge of the river. A nice nineteen-inch rainbow is released and gently glides back into the current disappearing beneath the rippled surface.

Catching several more trout, mostly on the emerger, Dillon continues working his way around the small shoals picking off trout by swimming his nymphs, imitating the action of a mayfly rising from the bottom of the streambed as it makes its way to the surface, where it will dry its wings before flying upward to the mayfly orgy already underway. All this predicated on not being gulped by some ravenous trout attuned to their role in the food chain.

Toward midafternoon, Dillon begins to work his way back toward Jay who has spent the entire day in the same slow run, catching trout seemingly at will. Dillon grins as he thinks of Jay's patience. Dillon prefers to keep his feet moving and not take root in one spot for too long, an old habit too ingrained from mountain fishing. Whether by curiosity, guilt, or some unknown fisherman's reasoning, Dillon stops and takes off the bead head pheasant tail and replaces it with the Roscoe fly, dropping the sulphur emerger off the bend of its hook.

Having caught a good number of trout himself, all on the sulphur emerger, Dillon figures this would be a good test for the Roscoe fly. At least, he knows the trout are actively feeding and has been catching them on a regular basis throughout the day. Walking downstream to the pool just above where Jay has "set up camp" since their arrival, Dillon walks out and away from the river placing some distance between himself and the water to prevent spooking any potential feeding trout.

After looping around for a downstream approach, Dillon walks up below the bottom of the pool and makes a blind thirty-foot cast toward the tail out of the pool. A sudden slight dip in his indicator causes him to lift his rod that is rewarded with another decent brown. Figuring it would be another trout on the sulphur emerger, Dillon is surprised to see the trout dangling from the Roscoe fly. Working his way up the pool, Dillon catches three trout on the Roscoe fly for everyone on the sulphur emerger.

Dillon notices Jay sitting on a rock just downstream and walks down to join him for lunch. Pulling out his RC cola, vanilla moonpie, and can of Vienna sausages, he gives a show-and-tell to Jay of his new creation and its early success. While happy for his friend's newfound success, Jay expresses a bit of skepticism as to the long-term success of the Roscoe fly. Still, as Dillon puts it, "time will tell."

As the summer wears on, Dillon finds his Roscoe fly becoming more of his go-to fly. Typically, his favorite nymph in the Smokies is a big yellowhammer, the very pattern he and Jay cut their fly-tying teeth on and what they used exclusively throughout the first ten years of fishing. He often said, "If they ain't bitin yallerhammers, they ain't bitin!" Jay helps him realize there are flies other than yellowhammers that catch trout, and at the risk of blasphemy, can catch more trout in the Smoky Mountains than a yellowhammer. Jay is more of an experimenter and works more in the field of fly patterns; whereas Dillon practices, and by all accounts has mastered, the art of nymph fishing.

Unlike many fly fishermen, Dillon does not hold his creation close to his vest in absolute secrecy. He figures since he has the sole source of its main ingredient, Roscoe, there is no need to worry. In fact, he often shares his hot fly with fishing friends, or the occasional tourist, who are at a loss for how to catch the wily Smoky Mountain trout, bragging on its source, Roscoe of course, in the process. On more than one occasion, over the course of the next several years, Dillon approaches the century mark on trout caught in one day, albeit a long day, on the Roscoe fly.

It is at these times, that he detects that look from Jay that makes him think of the kid who's just realized he's a nickel short of a pack of bubblegum at the register at Webb's Grocery. And just as Uncle Leroy would chip in what was needed, so would Dillon, slipping a couple to Jay at just the right time. For Jay and Dillon, fly-fishing had become a team sport long before there were fly-fishing contests. To them, it was a tag-team affair, each sharing in the other's success, doubling the joy of each trip. This attitude even found its way into more than one Christmas season as Dillon would tie Jay a couple of dozen Roscoe flies as a gift.

As was Jay's nature, he never takes the gift for granted, especially from his friend Dillon. Sure, to the outside world they are just flies, but as any fly fisherman would appreciate, they are trout flies, and these really catch trout when seemingly nothing else works whether they are fishing the Smokies, the South Holston, Watauga, or any number of trout streams. While they are outperformed on occasion by other patterns, the success rate of the Roscoe flies does not encompass the full measure of the pattern's intrinsic worth. Their true value comes from the source, Roscoe.

Roscoe was a fun-loving dog who never knew a stranger. When someone drove to the house, Roscoe would bark, but only out of the excitement of company and while Dillon wanted Roscoe to just be Roscoe, there were rules which had to be abided by to keep peace in the household. Peace being something Dillon had been without for the majority of his married years. If it were possible for a dog to be psychic, it was Roscoe when it came to reading the mind of Dillon. Roscoe loved the challenge of learning new tricks and could be counted upon to put on a show, something Dillon found to be a good icebreaker for the ladies.

Words were often unnecessary; only a slight movement of the hand, and Roscoe would perform the appropriate action or trick. A short whistle was all that was needed to gain Roscoe's full and undivided attention, and like Dillon, Roscoe became somewhat the mischievous prankster often hiding the ball cap or shoe just as Dillon began looking for it. In return, Dillon too got his fun, often hiding Roscoe's favorite toy. The typical resolution was found in something similar to a hostage exchange where each party surrendered what they possessed of the other in order to regain their prized or needed possession. However, what one gains in the unconditional love of "man's best friend," they lose in the relative short lifespan of a dog.

It has been a month now since Roscoe's death. By everyone's account, Dillon is himself, but Jay knows better. In fact, it is only Jay who truly knows the depth of Dillon's ache. Jay misses Roscoe as well, but he knows his bond was nothing like the one shared by Dillon and

Roscoe. After leaving the clinic, Jay stops by Dillon's house to check on his friend. As expected, Dillon is sitting on his back porch nursing a long neck in his rocking chair. Jay pulls up around back, gets out of the Cherokee, and walks up on the porch passing Dillon who is gazing up Jenkin's Ridge. He walks through the door and pours himself a glass of sweet tea before sitting in the rocking chair next to Dillon. Jay knows the best medicine to start Dillon's recovery, but getting the process started would be akin to giving a child a shot in the arm while convincing them to drink castor oil. As Dillon would say, "It ain't gonna be easy." Still, Jay, knowing Dillon would do anything for him, decides to ask Dillon for a favor.

Looking over at Dillon, Jay asks, "Say, Dillon, how 'bout going fishing Saturday? I've been dying to go over to Deep Creek and fish the upper sections, but Debbie gets all mother hen on me when I mention going there by myself. She's afraid something will happen to me, and nobody will know where I am. Then someday, many years later, my bones will be found with my skeleton hand still clutching my fly rod with a broken leader attached and a smile on my face." Not really in the mood to fish, Dillon thinks for a moment, tosses back the long neck, then agrees to go. Dillon says, "You know. I ain't felt like doin' nothing lately. I ain't tied a fly in over a month. I went to the vice to tie a few 'Roscoe Flies,' but I ain't got no more fur. Not that I'd use 'em anyway, but man, they were always good up on Deep Creek.

The drive over is quiet. On the radio, Garth Brooks is singing "The Dance." Jay reaches to turn it off not wanting to strike a chord in Dillon, but Dillon stops him. For a moment, all the world was right. How could I have known that you'd ever say goodbye…

They arrive and gear up without a word said. The only sounds come from the low rumble of Deep Creek and a lone blue jay searching for breakfast somewhere among the oaks and hemlocks. As they walk up the trail paralleling the creek, Dillon remembers the last time he was here. Roscoe always wanted to go anytime Dillon went, but on that day, he dropped him off with Debbie. Many of Dillon's thoughts come back to Roscoe. How he and Roscoe loved spending time with the outdoors, and enjoying the experience together made it all the better. He is wishing now he had stopped, just stopped to relish the moment. He remembers how he'd fish through Grassy Hollow while Roscoe rounded up a few quail or maybe a grouse. Inevitably he'd hear the bell on Roscoe's collar stop for a brief moment then followed immediately by the thunderous launch of a ruffed grouse or a covey of bobwhites.

To Jay, it is a beautifully painful day. Though growing up in the Smokies, he never grew complacent nor took the mountains for granted. He has always loved the fresh, crisp morning air gently burning his nostrils with every breath, but he also feels the burning sadness within his friend. They are blessed with a sunny day as the fog is pushed out by a cool breeze passing through Deep Creek Valley. On the second switchback, where the trail leaves the creek and climbs up the mountainside before making its way back down to the creek, they stop at a bend in the trail that overlooks a horseshoe on Deep Creek somewhere in the valley below. As always, Jay pauses at this point where he can listen to the roar of the water from the valley below on his left, then taking a few steps over the highest point in the trail, the low roar shifts to the right. "Man, what a beautiful sound." The rumble can be interpreted as wind passing through the trees, but having stood on this very spot many times before, both know it is definitely Deep Creek singing nature's hydrological tune.

To Dillon, no day is beautiful anymore, at least not today. That would take time. Dillon can only think of how Roscoe would love to ramble through the rhododendron to look for birds. He loved to walk the trails with Roscoe. He could complain about or admire anything as he so often did in the mountains, but Roscoe was always there with that joyful panting that gave the impression of a smile, never passing judgment.

Catching a few small rising browns, the fishing is pretty good. About noon, Jay stops for lunch. As they open their Vienna sausage and crackers, Jay looks up the creek for more rising fish. Dillon looks into the water remembering the days he and Roscoe spent bird hunting. The shiny reflection on the water reminds Dillon of the brightness of a snow-covered hillside on a sunny day. He pictures Roscoe running through the snow and disappearing into rhododendron only to reappear again. He remembers how it was nearly impossible to see Roscoe against the white backdrop except for his reddish brown ears. How Roscoe loved the snow and how Dillon misses Roscoe. If only he could relive that day again.

Jay looks up. “Say, Dillon, that’s a pretty good hole up there, ain’t it? Ain’t that where you caught a big brown a few years ago, behind that fallen log?”

“Yeah, it was about this time of year.” Dillon’s mind goes back to thinking about what he was doing, but this time, he isn’t thinking about the large brown, but how when he got home, Roscoe would always greet him at the porch.

“How ’bout we switch to nymphs?” Jay says as he begins looking through his fly box. Knowing the answer, Jay asks, “Say, Dillon. What did you catch that brown on?

“Roscoe Fly.”

“I think I got one left from those you gave me last Christmas. It’s never been used. How ’bout tyin’ it on and giving it a try. Who knows, lightning may strike twice.”

More going through the motions to please his friend than a true desire to fish, Dillon ties the fly on with deliberate care. Holding the fly in his right hand while twisting it to begin his improved clinch knot, he feels the tail of the small nymph with his fingers making an instant connection with his ole buddy sensing a lump in his throat. Dillon tests the knot and strips out a little extra line, judging what he will need for his first cast. He crosses the creek and walks up the side of the stream, careful to stay low and out of sight before positioning himself behind a small boulder in the middle of the stream.

Still sitting on a small grassy patch on the bank of Deep Creek where they had lunch, Jay enjoys the feel of the sun’s warmth meshing with the cool mountain air like hot gravy and biscuits. He is deeply focused on the actions of his friend. At that moment, more than anything, he wants Dillon to catch a big brown. There are times in life when good things are due, if not owed, and now is the time that if possible, Jay would call in a marker from the fishing gods to give his buddy a boost. Dillon needs something, anything, to help him take the next step in the healing process, to take the edge off and have something to rejoice in.

As Jay watches, he thinks of the wound Dillon is nursing. Being a physician has taught him many things, one of which is the error of the often said phrase, "Time heals all wounds." Medically speaking and from experience, he knows that some wounds, both physically and emotionally, never heal. Sometimes, the best one can hope for is a deep scar. His mind wanders back to the day he brought Roscoe into Dillon's world. Back then, Dillon was nursing a wound of a different origin that over time has healed but left a scar nonetheless. In a way, this wound is deeper. For some, wives come and go, but a true unconditional friend is rare for all but the very fortunate, nonexistent for the rest. The depth of the loss is often proportional to that of the wound and, if recovery occurs, the size of the scar.

As Dillon makes his final approach from behind the midstream boulder, his attention and aim is focused on the small eddy behind the log. Though not the prime lie, there's always a chance of a trout behind the log feeding from the softer water next to the bank. A few well-placed casts behind the log has accomplished nothing. For the first time today, his mind is truly off Roscoe and into fishing. With the log lying diagonally from the near righthand side bank to two-thirds across the creek, the main current takes a gradual detour along the upstream edge of the log, funneling its way around the end of the log continuing downstream.

Making a high-stick roll cast in front of the log, Dillon casts just over the fallen log so that his fly is carried along the funneled current as it works its way along the upstream side of the log to the middle of the stream and into the deeper and faster current. He is careful to avoid any limbs that may snag the sinking nymph as it passes by. Using the oft referred to fly-fishing method known as short-lining or high-sticking, Dillon carefully guides the nymph creating a dead drift around the apex end of the log. In doing so, he is able to keep as much slack out of his leader as possible, thus improving his chances of detecting the slightest strike and setting the hook.

Through his polarized sunglasses, which removes much of the glare off the water's surface, he can see deep into the sun-lit, clear water. The only thing he cannot see is the reddish-brown and gold-colored nymph as it drifts just inches in front of and a few feet beneath the submerged log. With his complete concentration on the immediate area around where his leader pierces the surface, his mind imagines his eyes catching a yellowish flash. The movement of his leader tells him it isn't imagination as it suddenly straightens.

Years of fishing this local style results in an immediate and reflexive stiff setting of the hook.

Though some would yell, "Fish on!" Dillon and Jay have danced this dance many times before. No need for excessive celebration, at least not yet, as both know the battle has only begun. After the hook set, Dillon has already begun to fight the trout. He has long ago learned, after years of losing big fish, to take the fight to his opponent. Immediately, he steps around the rock behind which he's been hiding and into the knee-deep eddy of water behind the log, applying enough pressure to get the fish away from the log yet not risk breaking his 5X tippet. In the process, he has already reeled in the excess slack he held in his left hand, getting his line on the reel to use its drag in fighting the fish.

As brown trout rarely break the surface like their cousin the rainbow, Dillon has not been afforded a good look at the size of his quarry. He knows and expects the trout to be a brown based on the flash of yellow he's previously seen. Experience has taught him that when it cannot be seen, to judge the relative size of the trout by the force by which it shakes its head as it attempts to eject the fly embedded in its hooked jaw, while working its way toward somewhere near the bottom of the pool. With the thick overhanging trees shading the deeper part of the pool, the bright sunlight does not penetrate deeply enough to allow Dillon a view of the fish at the end of the line, but the power of the movement tells him it is something big. Very big.

One of Dillon's favorite strategies in fighting larger trout is to move his rod tip from side to side, thus confusing the fish in not allowing it to determine the true direction from which it is being pulled and the location of where he is standing. He believes the insertion of a little bit of doubt into the pea-sized brain of a trout provides him an additional amount of an advantage. This method is much easier on bigger water, but the often tight environment of the Smoky Mountain waters limits his ability to fully implement this strategy. With the ever-moving motions with his fly rod, Dillon keeps his rod tip high allowing the tip to absorb the shock of the trout's many shaking, pulling, and sudden movements, using as much pressure on the 5X tippet as needed to reach and maintain the sweet spot between force, but not too much force that will result in a break.

From his vantage, Jay has seen it all from just downstream, now standing in the creek below to get a better view, "Yes!" he yells. "The Roscoe fly strikes again!"

Suddenly, the game changes. With his total focus on the brown, Dillon had totally forgotten about the Roscoe fly! The only, the last Roscoe fly! Sure, he's danced the big brown tango before, catching many over twenty inches in his years prodding the numerous streams in the Smokies. The excitement and thrill of even the possibility of each battle is as strong as ever. The confidence he has developed in knowing how to fight big trout in the Smokies, a challenge greatly increased by the many boulders, submerged limbs and logs, over-hanging trees, and ever-changing types of water all but evaporates. It was as if he has learned to anticipate the unexpected. But this is different.

The possibility of losing all that is physically remaining of his friend Roscoe has rattled his nerves and shaken his confidence. As if sensing a moment's pause in Dillon's aggressiveness, the brown, as a wise wild trout would, takes advantage of Dillon's lapse and bolts downstream, using the current to its advantage. Standing in the stream, Jay finds himself leaping onto the bank to avoid getting his legs tangled in the line as the brown blasts past him at flank speed splashing water with its massive tail. Though the water is shallow and better penetrated by the sunlight, the water's broken surface and the speed of the trout prevents Jay from getting a good look at the beast. He knows it is big, but just how big, he isn't certain.

With his reel screaming out line, Dillon sprints by Jay, as much as one can sprint on slime and moss-covered rocks of varying sizes, shapes, and dampness in the Smoky Mountains. As it works its way down the rapids, the brown darts between boulders looking for rough edges on which to snag or cut the line to which he is attached. Like Dillon, the old brown has danced this dance before but, unlike Dillon, has never lost a battle in his many years of life. For over three thousand days, the brown has studied and memorized these waters day and night and at all levels and clarity. This gives him a complete knowledge of the exact location of every place to hide, the size of every sharp rock, every submerged root, and every dangling limb on which to break off a fisherman's fly. He has done it more than once. Now with his size and strength, even when fooled, he knows his power and knowledge is a formidable and unbeatable combination.

For Dillon, the goal had changed from catching a big brown to retrieving the last Roscoe fly. Common sense tells him his best chance of getting the fly back is to catch the brute. There is a chance the fly will pop loose on its own, with the help of the trout, but unlikely. It boils down to catching the trout or breaking off and losing the fly forever. The latter is not an option. With this, Dillon clenches his jaw and, with a new determination, refocuses his attention into the battle at hand, albeit a little less aggressively. During his high school football days, where he was an all-state linebacker, Dillon knew the perils of playing tight and being too cautious. Dillon figures as long as he maintains contact with his potential nemesis, he is still in the game and slowly the brown will wear down. He reminds himself that time is on his side as long as he maintains contact.

For the brown, the epic battle between the wise and powerful master of the creek in his domain is life and death. Though he has the home stream advantage, what he lacks he does not understand. The knowledge of his opponent, who like himself, is a master in his own right, possesses the evolutionary advantage of Homo Sapiens, which includes the technological aspects of modern fly-fishing equipment. For Dillon, this is not a physical life-and-death struggle but an emotion struggle of Roscoe's death and his sole remnant of Roscoe's life embodied in the fly now deeply embedded in the corner of the trout's jaw.

Continuing its rapid run downstream, the struggle ebbs ever toward the brown's advantage as he separates himself further from his opponent. After each attempt by the brown to entangle the line,

Dillon's approach forces the trout to bolt to another large rock or limb under which it would wrap itself and work through in preparation for the next escape. It even swims under a partially submerged limb, which is countered by Dillon passing his rod tip under just as quickly. Glancing downstream, Dillon spots a rather large pool with no obvious obstructions. Earlier, as he and Jay made their way upstream, Dillon noted the open area and how it would be a convenient place to lead a trout into the net.

It is here he hopes to settle the battle with the brown and retrieve the fly. As it works its way downstream and over a three-foot waterfall, spilling into the plunge pool, Dillon runs around the pool and along the stream bank. The trout is now in the deepest part of the upper end of the pool, still making every attempt to break loose of Dillon's hold on him. This trout is big enough to have an enormous kype of which he was proud and had used during more than one spawning season to fight off lesser males, thus assuring the continuation of his genetic makeup to the keepers of generations to come.

Positioning himself in the middle of the pea-sized gravel in the tail out of the pool, Dillon feels solid footing for the first time. Applying pressure again, Dillon begins working the trout downstream as he uses his left had to reach around his back to grasp his net hanging handle-down from its magnetic attachment on the back of his vest. As the battle between the experienced gladiators nears its conclusion, the trout catches a glimpse of Dillon through the smooth surface of the water. He is so tired. However, the thought of losing to the predator from above the surface gives him a massive, life-saving surge of adrenalin, allowing him to instinctively bolt from the depths of the pool, leaping up and back over the three-foot waterfall, clearing the surface, thus avoiding the drag of the fast-moving current as it rushes over the precipice.

This leads it back into the rapids upstream of the large pool. Without taking their eyes off the trout, Dillon's and Jay's mouths gape in awe of the power of the leap against the pull of Dillon's line and the fast current of the stream. Never has Dillon ever felt such power in a Smoky Mountain trout! Neither have ever seen a brown of the size they just witnessed as it becomes airborne easily clearing the waterfall and the heavy displacement of water as it splashes back into the current above the waterfall.

Now running back upstream to close the gap, Dillon reels in the slack while intermittently releasing his grip on the reel handle when he feels too much pressure to allow additional line to be released to the escaping trout. More than once the release of pressure just avoided a break in the weakening tippet. Throughout the battle, Dillon has remained visibly calm, if not stoic, but inside, it is a different matter. He is in full panic mode. Again, he considers that never before has he felt this much power during a fight with a big brown. His experience and successes have guided him 'til now, but the power and size of the brown has stunned him, and he is beginning to lose confidence and control of the battle. He knows his tippet cannot hold out forever, and the trout is only getting stronger. The tide is turning.

Sensing the change as only a seasoned angler can, Jay begins to worry as by now it too has dawned on him the coming fate of the last Roscoe fly. Though the fly has successfully fooled such a wise, old trout that has seen and rejected many flies in its time, that success alone is not worth the risk of its loss. All Jay can do now is helplessly watch. There is no advice Jay can give, knowing Dillon is much more skilled and experienced than is he in this scenario.

To Jay, it is like watching a terrible accident in slow motion and unable to do anything to prevent the inevitable. Surely, all the abrasions on the fluorocarbon leader from rubbing against the boulders and logs are adding up ever weakening the tiny connection between Dillon and Roscoe. Stepping up on an exposed boulder, Jay sadly wants to get a better view of the end. Dillon is the best Jay and anyone in Laurel Cove has ever known when it comes to landing large trout. But Jay knows not every battle is a given. Some are won and some are lost.

In this battle, Dillon is losing ground quickly. Jay knows the direction this was heading, and it isn't looking good for his friend. As the huge brown makes its way upstream, with Dillon chasing from a distance well behind, the trout spots something through the broken current. It is another predator, and he is heading directly toward it! Instinctively, he uses another burst of seemingly untapped energy and darts away from the object. In altering his path of escape, the brown surges sharply to his left out of the main current and into a small pocket of water, thus jamming his head into a slot created by two boulders on the far side of the stream away from where Jay is standing.

At last, a drained Dillon has some time to catch up and reel in the slack as he runs back upstream among the loose stones of the creek. In holding his rod tip up to absorb the slack and jolts of the brown, the rod tip has worked its way into one of the many rhododendron branches that hung over the stream. For the first time since his realization of the potential loss of the Roscoe fly, Dillon strangely feels a sense of calm ease over him. Whether it is the acceptance of the realization of the inevitable loss of the fly or some other unknown source of confidence, he doesn't know.

Logically, it doesn't make sense as his line along with the tip of his rod is snagged. A sudden run by the trout will surely end the struggle as it will most certainly break off, and the brown will be gone and with it the Roscoe fly. Ever so calmly, as if to concede, he feeds some slack out so that he can loosen the tangled line from the branches. Once freed, he looks down into the pocket where the brown has fled and is holding. He still has contact! He quickly but gently reels in the slack, without applying pressure. Dillon does not feel ready to continue the battle. He can see the massive tail fin waving gently a foot or so beneath the surface. Dillon notices that as long as he isn't applying pressure on the line leading to the trout, the brown seems to relax with only its tail gently and rhythmically moving. Not wanting to allow the trout too much time to rest, Dillon makes the next move.

As the trout had blasted upstream, whether it was by good luck, karma, or a little assistance from the God of creation, unknown to the parties involved, at that moment, Dillon had been on the brink of losing the massive brown. However, Jay's position standing high on the rock overlooking the stream had turned the ebbing tide of the battle. The effect of Jay's position converging with the path and timing of the escaping trout had resulted in the brown's sole fatal mistake. So often, one seemingly minor decision results in the loss of a battle between two equally matched and equally experienced foes. The aforementioned decision of Jay's standing on the rock altered the path taking the huge trout to a small, shallow pocket of water from which there was little chance of escape.

Whether out of instinct or simple reflex, Dillon neither knew nor considered, he quickly and quietly steps forward, and with his right hand holding his rod, he reaches down with his left hand and firmly but deliberately grasps the brown by its huge tail. Though neither he nor Jay has ever landed any fish, let alone a monster trout, by its tail, Dillon must have seen it done somewhere before, likely in a magazine. Using his powerful arm, Dillon lifts the massive brown up and out of the water. In two steps, he is on the bank where he lays the trout down, quickly retrieving his beloved Roscoe fly. Instantly, Jay appeares from the opposite side of the stream, placing the huge trout into his net, into which only a part of the trout can be secured. Jay feels the net is extremely inadequate. Ever the one to think positive, Jay looks at it as the trout is just that big!

With a loud shout, "Woo-hoo!" Jay is elated with the trophy trout landed by his buddy. Dillon is just happy to have the precious fly safely in hand. Jay quickly carries the net to a safe pool with a little current where he can keep the huge, exhausted brown in the water. After several minutes spent reviving the trout, Jay lifts it up to offer Dillon the release. Dillon, however, is sitting on the log, staring at the treasured fly in his hand.

Glancing over at Dillon, Jay notices a tear trickle down Dillon's cheek, whether a tear of joy, relief, or sadness, only Dillon knows for certain; Jay is thinking perhaps all three. Dillon is busy emptying a box of flies into another, leaving one box empty. It was in this small box he gently lays the fly by itself placing it in his left shirt pocket. Relieved that he has recovered the fly, he knows Roscoe is gone, but his connection is right where it belongs—next to his heart. Jay has quickly changed his glance back to the creek where he takes a brief moment to measure the monster brown. He is in awe as the brown exceeds the thirty-inch mark on his tape measure.

Though once on Little River at Metcalf Bottoms and once above Sawdust Pile at campsite number 85 on Hazel Creek, he believes he he saw a thirty-inch brown; he has never held a trout this size in the Smokies! After a few seconds to measure the trout, Jay snaps a quick photo of it as it lays next to Dillon's rod, giving some perspective to the trout's girth and length. Jay makes another quick glance back at Dillon as he cradles the huge trout in his hands with its massive hook jaw mouthing the current, taking in the freshly oxygenated water, continuing to regain its strength.

For the first time, Dillon looks up as Jay carefully continues to nurse the massive trout. He walks over to look at the old warrior he has just defeated. He is just a surprised as Jay in its size, now getting a good look for the first time at its girth, and notes the colorful red and black dots along its brownish-yellow broad side and massive head. Analyzing its wide tail fin helps Dillon understand its power. The size of the protruding kype in its lower jaw tells him this one is a very old buck that has many years of progeny swimming in the stream.

Still, Dillon wants Jay to have the honor of releasing the giant. To him, Jay's presence is what turned the tide in what had become a losing battle, allowing him to recover his prized possession. If not for Jay, the brown likely would have continued on upstream and broken off, disappearing forever somewhere in the depths of Deep Creek. It isn't the first time Jay has been where Dillon needed him most. After several more minutes of catching his breath and with Jay's careful assistance, the brown regains enough of his strength to ease out of Jay's hands under his own power. With slow, powerful sweeps of its massive tail, it gently but deliberately swims back up into the depths of the pool where he has likely lived most of his life.

Dillon surveys Deep Creek Valley. Looking around at the tall hemlocks and dark green rhododendrons that make up the steep slopes that frame the stream, he takes into his lungs a deep, relaxing breath. The first in what seems like an eternity. "You know. Sometimes fishin' is the best thing for what 'ails ye."

Jay replies, "You got that right, my friend."

Though there are several good hours of daylight remaining in which to fish, an experienced angler knows when to call it a day on a good note, and theirs has sung loud and clear. The purpose in many o' days of trout fishing in the serene Smoky Mountains can be summed up in simply, a refreshing of the soul. Dillon's has been restored, and with it, Jay's concern for his friend has been eased. Today he had entered the water hurting and in need of something good to relieve his pain. The near loss of the last Roscoe Fly had sent him deeper into his abyss, but his perseverance in the battle with the wise, old trout has brought him a long way out.

As they relax on the bank with their feet submerged in the flow of refreshing waters of Deep Creek, both can only sit and ponder the world around them and how blessed they are. With the beauty that can only be found down in the valley where the stream flows, bordered by the beautiful ridges of the Great Smoky Mountains, and topped with a bright blue sky, one can't help but feel the presence of a master creator of all they behold. Surely, there is a loving God that if believed in will eventually make everything right. As both are deeply mesmerized by the sound of the gentle hum of Deep Creek, somewhere off in the distance the sound of a crow can be heard as it darts among the tall trees.

Suddenly, they hear the snap of a twig behind them somewhere in the thick rhododendron. As both turn half expecting a bear, wild hog, or perhaps an otter looking for a meal, they notice something moving just a few steps away. Whatever the source of the sound, it is easing toward them. Hesitant and seemingly in need of contact as conveyed by the shallow whimpering sounds quietly emanating from it over the low rumble of the stream, a small head slowly appears through a tiny gap in the brush just a few feet away. It is small, rather young, lost, dirty, emaciated from hunger, and in bad need of rescue from the abyss. In a last ditch effort for survival and possibly sensing an unspoken kindness in what it sees, the young dog uses its last bit of strength as it emerges from the thicket, wobbling over to the comforting lap of Dillon.

And Jay, sitting a few feet away, senses an immediate connection between two struggling individuals who are seeking to fill an overwhelming void in their lives.

A FORTUITOUS CHANGE

It had been nearly six months in the making, and now Dillon could see the conclusion as a faint light at the end of a long tunnel. From the time he broke ground on the 4,500 square-foot log cabin along the Big Bear Fork, he had spent nearly every day planning, organizing, and subcontracting various portions of the construction of Gordon Smith's new home. He had met Gordon at the auction of the property last year. His first impression, and not a good one, of Gordon was that of an arrogant outsider with more money than sense. The price Gordon paid for the seven acres of farmland, situated along the slow stretch of the river known as Grassy Holler, was well above market value.

It was as if he had money to throw away and wanted to quash any competitive bids right from the start. As Dillon has learned over the years, sometimes the first impression isn't an accurate impression as he soon took a liking to Gordon. Not long after the land was purchased, Dillon received a phone call from Gordon Smith. Gordon said he had heard of Dillon's reputation for building quality houses in the area and would pay top dollar for a house to be built on his property.

Dillon, figuring his first impression was right on the money, agreed to meet his potential client to build what he assumed would be a log-style home. In his mind, Gordon Smith would be the stereotypical city slicker who wanted to buy a piece of paradise in the Smoky Mountains complete with a home in the mountains and a river flowing past the backyard. The trouble is, most clients of this sort are unfriendly, arrogant, and want to share paradise with no one. To date, there had been no riparian rights issues along the Big Bear Fork, and Dillon hoped to keep it that way.

Dillon reflected back to the day when Gordon handed him the blueprints for the house he wanted built. While nothing extravagant per se, the quality of materials and accessories were the best money could buy. To the untrained eye, the house would appear as a large, nicely built log house. A skilled observer would see the spare no expense is too great quality of the materials and accessories including intricate landscaping added to the large log home overlooking the Big Bear Fork.

Fortunately for Dillon, Gordon had already procured many of the more unusual materials such as the exotic plants and water fountains to be placed around the property as well as many of the one-of-a-kind furnishings decorating the interior. Gordon assured Dillon that he would take care of the items not typically found in the area and have them delivered to the site at Dillon's request. With so many items not typically found in a small town such as Laurel Cove, Dillon could not imagine many things that Gordon would not be supplying.

At first, Dillon tried to turn down the assignment, not wanting to deal with another overbearing customer, and an outsider at that. But Gordon's persuasive tone and confidence exhibited in Dillon's abilities somehow made him feel at ease. The final bit of coaxing came in a statement that rang in Dillon's mind frequently throughout the project. Gordon tells Dillon, "If I did not believe in you and your ability to build my house, I would not have asked you." A boost of confidence such as that does not come often enough in the life of a building contractor. Another unusual approach Dillon noticed was the laidback style of Gordon regarding the completion time of his small mansion, a true rarity among customers in the home-building industry.

Finally, after months of work, the house is essentially finished, though a few small items mostly related to the outside and landscaping are still in various stages of completion. The last item on Dillon's long list of things to do today is to check up on the grounds surrounding Gordon's swimming pool. Since a large quantity of clay dirt had to be delivered, packed, and covered with good topsoil for the landscaping, Dillon wants to eyeball the layout before giving his final approval. Pulling into the driveway, he notices Gordon has moved in over the weekend. Opening the door of his truck, Dillon steps out and is closely followed by his friend he found on Deep Creek, Lucky.

"Don't go too far, Lucky. I won't be long," he says more to state a fact than giving instructions as Lucky works his way down toward the river searching for any wayward quail, with whom he's yet to make acquaintance. With Lucky working along the edge of the nearby woods, his stubbed tail wagging like a high speed metronome, Dillon walks around to the back of the house to look at the pool area. Looking over the area, Dillon notices that the concrete walkway down to a gazebo and small picnic area at the edge of the river has turned out very well. Stopping at the wooden wall surrounding the pool area, Dillon pauses for a moment. He could never quite figure out the purpose of the privacy fence. There's not really a house nearby, and it ruins the view of the river from the house. Opening the door of the privacy fence, he walks into the pool area. He is taken back by the sight of a beautiful, young Latino lady sunbathing.

"Uh...excuse me, ma'am." Dillon quickly changes his glance.

"No problem. May I help you?" she replies with a touch of a Hispanic accent.

"Uh…" he replies, still having difficulty speaking with an obvious loss of focus. "My name is Dillon. I'm the builder for this house, and I just needed to stop by to check a few things out."

"Super, you may proceed to do whatever you wish."

As he walks along the edge of the pool, he runs into a concrete statue that is part of the landscaping at the edge of the concrete pad surrounding the pool. In Dillon's and anyone else's mind, she is a goddess, with long, silky, black hair that shows a tint of blue in the sun. But it's not the hair that keeps his attention. She's topless! *Are they real? It's for sure there's no problem with gravity. But who is she? Mr. Smith has got to be pushing sixty. She can't be any more than thirty. Maybe she's his daughter*. His hopes rise, but so does his trouble radar. He's seen enough trouble in his time to be cautious around young, beautiful women, if not downright paranoid. If nothing else, his romantic history has taught him to be pessimistic. If someone appears too good to be true, there's definitely a catch. As he barely avoids another concrete statue of a naked lady pouring water into a small pond, the diva looks up with a smile showing voluptuous, full lips surrounding pearly white teeth. Always a sucker for bright red lipstick, it's then that Dillon becomes self-conscious of his working-man's attire, wearing a pair of soiled blue jeans with worn knees and a Skoal can ring on his back left pocket, his light-blue button-up shirt spotted with stains, the top few buttons have been left undone in an attempt to stay cool on this hot, sunny day.

With a momentary smile, she admires the chiseled features, broad shoulders, slim waist, and muscular arms of the "pool guy." Back home, she had a hunky pool guy but not with the rugged features of this one. Thinking to herself, *Maybe Tennessee is not such a bad place after all.* Knowing how to use her assets to her advantage in gaining and maintaining a man's attention, she sits upright and takes a seductive sip of her drink through the straw showcasing her pouting lips and firm breasts. It's not hard to know where Dillon's eyes are focused. He tries to maintain eye contact, but every man has his limits, and Dillon's have been far exceeded.

Rolling her straw between her fingers and looking seductively with her deep brown eyes, she smiles and replies, "That's okay, do what you need to do."

Dillon, hearing her seductive Latino voice, tries to remember why he's here, wanders around momentarily looking at the pool, and glancing into the water as his mind floats between fantasy and reality. *What if she's single. What did I come here for? How can I find out her name? Where am I? Who am I?* Finally, he's able to get a few words out, "I jest came by to check things out…I mean look things over." Realizing everything he says can and probably should be taken the wrong way, he finally blurts out, "I'll jest be a minute." Still, not remembering why he's here, Dillon makes his way back to the doorway.

Just as he thinks he's escaped without any more embarrassment but not really wanting to leave, she says, "Dillon? Before you leave, would you mind rubbing some tanning lotion on my back? I can't get to it like I need to, and I so hate to have an uneven tan."

Much to his surprise, Dillon gets that "almost got away" feeling; although, why he would ever want to leave this sight doesn't make sense. He turns around, not wanting to make eye contact to avoid the lustful look that he's sure is plastered over his face like an interstate billboard. "Sure. No problem."

As he walks over, she continues her seductive stare and takes another sip of her drink. Dillon, not really sure where to look but definitely trying not to stare at her bosom, instead looks at the top of her head and her beautiful black hair flowing around her shoulders. Dillon pauses on his way to rinse the dirt from his hands in the water flowing from a statue. He takes advantage of the moment for a little self-composure.

Rubbing his hands together under the small stream of water pouring out of the statue, Dillon thinks, *Help me, Lord. Give me strength.* He focuses his gaze on the statue. It's the naked lady. *That don't help none.*

He dries his hands on the only clean part of his clothes he can find, the back of his jeans, as he walks toward her trying to find anywhere to focus his eyes somewhere other than the obvious, at least to him.

She hands him the lotion and rolls over onto her stomach, exposing for the first time that she is wearing a thong. Not too many thongs in Laurel Cove, at least not that Dillon has seen or would care to see. But then again, he's never seen anything like her.

Taking the lotion from her, Dillon asks, "How do you like it?" realizing he did it again and slightly embarrassed as a result.

Her head turns toward him, with her eyes closed, she softly replies, "Heavy, but rubbed in thoroughly."

Dillon pours some lotion onto his hands, rubbing them together as he briefly relishes the moment. The coconut scent of the lotion adds to the difficult situation as Dillon's mind flashes back to earlier days of bikinis and coconut-scented lotion. It would be considered a déjà vu if not for the fact that he has never found himself in this position with such a beautiful object. It has been a long time, too long, since he last laid hands on a pretty woman, perhaps never as beautiful. After a quick check that her eyes are still closed, for the first time, he relaxes slightly and can slowly complete a full body scan. If there is a flaw, he cannot not find it, not even on such a close, thorough inspection. From henceforth, the smell of coconut would forever burn this image in his mind of this very moment. Savoring the moment, admiring her body and trying to remain "professional," he cannot help but compliment the man upstairs as he thought, *Great work, God!*

Feeling the need to break the silence, Dillon quips, "Sure got a nice tan." Speaking more of her physique than her skin color, he follows up with, "My name is Dillon. Dillon Webb."

Opening her eyes for the first time since rolling over onto her stomach, she smiles and replies, "Oh, you built this house for us, didn't you?"

"Why, yes, I just stopped by to tie up a couple uh loose ends," he says, realizing he is looking at hers, which is just the opposite.

She raises up to her elbows, smiles, looks at Dillon, and replies, "I am Gabrielle Smith."

"Well, happy to meet you, Gabrielle. Did I git enough lotion on ye?" Hoping the answer is no.

"Si, gracias, Dillon."

He likes the way she says Dillon, with a touch of an accent.

"There is a towel for you to wipe the lotion from your hands," she says as she motions toward a small table with some towels.

"Sure, thanks," Dillon replies as he walks over to the table and picks up a towel. As he wipes the lotion from his hands, he considers asking her if he could refill her drink, anything to stay another moment or ten. Then realizing his track record with the feminine half of the species, he decides to work his way out while things are seemingly going fine.

"Well, I guess I'd better git goin'. Nice to meet ye, Gabrielle. Perhaps I'll see ye around town."

With a quick wink and a smile showcasing her beautiful white teeth against her dark red lips, Gabrielle replies, "Yes. Yes, I'm sure you will."

As Dillon walks back to his truck, he wonders if Gabrielle is Mrs. Smith or Miss Smith. Fortunately for Lucky, who is waiting for Dillon at the truck; otherwise, he would've had to find another way home as Dillon had already forgotten about his little friend. Looking at Lucky, Dillon states, "What are you looking at? Dang it, Lucky, I didn't see if she was wearing a ring. I'm really slippin'." In response, Lucky responds with an inquisitive rocking of his head from side to side as if he understands his master's dilemma. Dillon smiles as he remembers that his eyes were preoccupied elsewhere. As he drives off in his pickup, he remembers that he was supposed to check on something at the house. As he continues down the road, he is still unable to remember what it was.

Later that afternoon, Dillon stops by Jay's house. As usual, Jay is piddlin' around in his shop out in the backyard. As Dillon walks through the door, Jay looks up from the fly-tying bench as he is in the middle of wrapping the hackle on a number 18 Parachute Adams. Usually in an attempt to belittle Jay, Dillon grins as he shakes his head at Jay for tying something so small, at least to him. Dillon prefers using big nymphs as opposed to small dries.

However this time, something is different. Dillon has no smile. Instead, he has the look that only a lifelong friend will recognize and worthy of stopping midway through the precarious hackle wrapping phase of a Parachute Adams.

Jay pushes himself back from the desk and turns toward Dillon. "Go fishing today?" Jay asks knowing Dillon only gets "the look" from either hooking a big trout or a beautiful woman.

Dillon, looking down, moves some floor scraps that have fallen from the tying bench and onto the floor into a small pile with his right foot and replies, "Nope."

Jay stands up and stretches his back. "Well, who is she? And no BS. Who is she?"

"I'm not sure. I mean, I stopped by the Smith house to tie up a few loose ends. I still cain't remember what I wuz there fer."

Jay breaks in, "She must really be something."

Dillon replies, "Oh man. You won't believe what happened." Dillon goes on to recall his meeting with Gabrielle in vivid detail.

After hearing the finite second by second replay of the topless sunbathing incident, Jay asks again, "But who is she?"

"Her name is Gabrielle Smith."

"Well, is she Mr. Smith's daughter?" Jay asks showing hope for a revitalization of his friend's lackluster love life.

Dillon walks over to grab a couple of beers out of a small refrigerator. "Don't know. I mean she should be his daughter, but with my luck with women, she's probably his wife."

Jay quips, "That'd suck! For you and her. I mean, what a waste for a beautiful babe like that stuck with ole man Smith."

Dillon hands Jay a cold one and takes a sip on his. "Well, I gotta figure it out somehow. Ye reckon I'd be too obvious if I jest drive over and ask?"

"Obvious, but effective. But I wouldn't recommend putting all of your cards on the table at once. Besides, I got the answer." Jay's face changes from his serious thinking expression to a sly grin. "You know, the welcoming committee from the church will take a goody basket over, seeing how they're new and all in town. They'll get the proper invite to church, and Ms. Mitchell will have to fulfill her preacher's wifely duties and get the full scoop on everyone's situation. Fortunately for you, my friend, Debbie is on the church welcoming committee. Between Ms. Mitchell's question and answer session, and a little bug I'll place in Debbie's ear, you'll know everything from her favorite color to her cup size."

"Heck, I already know her cup size. I just want to find out if she's available."

"Well, the ladies are going over Thursday evening. You'll have your answer that night."

Two days later, Jay is in his office playing his daytime role as Dr. Jay, having assumed the family practice of Doc Hembree. According to his schedule, the one o'clock patient is a first-timer and wants to establish himself as a new patient. Looking at the name, Jay knows there can only be one Gordon Smith new to the area. Sure enough, prior to entering the exam room, Jay reviews the patient questionnaire filled out by Mr. Smith: Age, sixty-one; married; wife's name, Gabrielle.

"Damn!" Jay says quietly as he shakes his head in disappointment, standing outside the door—disappointment for his friend Dillon who now has that twinkle in his eye and spring in his step Jay has not seen for some time. Now Jay realizes he will have to give Dillon the bad news. He feels like a Santa Claus on Christmas Day taking his present back from Dillon. *Well, he's a big boy. He'll have to deal with it.* Thinking to himself that a fishing trip will be a good start, he makes a mental note to ask Dillon to go on Saturday as he opens the door with a smile to meet Gordon Smith for the first time.

Though Jay could've given Dillon the news that afternoon, he decided to postpone his friend's disappointment as long as possible. So after the church welcoming committee visited the Smith home and Debbie arrived home that night with the details, Dillon stopped by, and to Jay's surprise, he took the news quite well. Not great but well. It was as if Dillon expected it to be so and resigned himself to the fact that Gabrielle was indeed Mrs. Gordon Smith. Jay went on to tell Dillon the rest of the local happenings as they related to Mr. and Mrs. Gordon Smith and how during the visit by the River View

Baptist Church welcoming committee, Gordon invited them to a cookout down at his river pavilion next month. Jay finished on a positive note in talking Dillon into a Saturday morning trip up the Big Bear Fork.

After breakfast at Smoky's, Jay and Dillon stop by The Hatch to shoot the breeze with Chester and to allow Dillon to top off his morning coffee. On their way out of the shop, they pass Gordon, who is walking in with Melvin Cody. Gordon had met Melvin, the assistant accounts manager, down at the First Fidelity Bank. In setting up an account, Melvin talked about his two favorite subjects—himself and fishing. Dillon and Jay think about the differences between Melvin and Gordon and how they're at extremely opposite ends of the spectrum in nearly every aspect of their lives, yet here they are together.

Fishing has a way of doing that, bringing opposites together for a single goal. They conclude that the only potential exception to their vast differences would be that they both likely share poor fly-fishing skills. Both also agree that it won't take long for Gordon to surpass Melvin in that arena as well. Dillon mentions how it is odd that Melvin is taking Gordon fishing as he mostly fishes alone to avoid verification of his poor skills, although obviously he did make an impression on Gordon with his framed photo from the *Laurel Cove Banner*, which he proudly displays in his office at the bank showing his sixteen-inch brown he caught using, as Dillon puts it, the blind hog theory. The framed photograph had its desired effect on Gordon, tooting Melvin's horn and striking up a conversation about fly-fishing.

By the time Melvin finishes setting up Gordon's account, he has as little of his money and too much of his confidence. Of the two, Gordon's money would last far longer than his confidence in Melvin's fishing skills. A few trips with Melvin would take care of that. Gordon is the kind of inquisitive man who is always interested in seeking new challenges, and for Gordon, the more complex, the better. Having fished mostly for bass with some deep-sea fishing thrown in, Gordon had never trout-fished nor had he ever used a fly rod. Melvin had succeeded in convincing Gordon that he's the local expert.

Leaving The Hatch, Jay and Dillon's conversation naturally turns to Gordon. Jay starts, "You know. As nice as Gordon is and all, he's a bit strange when it comes to being a patient. I know it was his first office visit with me, but based off the medical history he gave me, he has a bit of a heart condition and a touch of high blood pressure. That's no big deal. When I asked about previous medical records, he said they were lost. When I pressed further about giving me permission to try to get them, he would not even tell me his previous physician's name, just that he moved up here from Florida."

Dillon replies with a grunt, still not ready to talk much about the Smiths and not really enjoying the idea of lusting after an "old man's" wife. Something just doesn't feel right about that.

"Well, I guess you'll not be making it to the cookout over at the Smith's next weekend either, eh?"

Dillon lets out another grunt and downs a sip of coffee.

The fishing turns out typical for a summer trip in the Smokies. Early on, Dillon coaxes a few nice browns from some deeper pools and runs known to harbor larger fish. Taking turns, first Dillon swinging streamer patterns, then Jay drifting large nymphs, through likely lies, Dillon has the better success of the morning. As the sun rises over the upper edges of Balsam Ridge, it begins to warm the water. Catching a glimpse of surface activity, Jay ties on a number fourteen Thunderhead; whereas, Dillon remains subsurface where, as he always put it, "where the trout live", with a peacock-bodied yellowhammer. Both catch their share of trout, returning all to grow a little more. While neither keep actual score, it was, as usual, too close to call without an actual count and both feel comfortable in their fishing skills for the day. As the fishing slows, both reel in their lines and walk up out of the creek and onto the trail to make their way back out to the parking lot. On their way back down the trail to the parking area, Jay spies Melvin and Gordon fishing some of the flat shallow runs upstream from Hemlock Falls. Gordon is sitting on the bank working on his fifteenth tangled leader, while Melvin is busy clumsily stumbling with every step in the stream. Instead of gingerly checking the security of each step before beginning the next, Melvin slips with every step flirting with the imminent reality of a Smoky Mountain baptism.

"Ye think he'd learned how to wade these streams by now?" Dillon says as he laughs at the spectacle known as Melvin.

"Oh I don't know, Dillon. I think it's sort of sporting for Melvin to give every trout within a half mile fair notice of his approach!" Jay replies with a grin. "After all, he is the '*Future Fly-Fishing World Champion*'" referring to Melvin's high school claim.

"How's it going, Gordon?" Jay asks.

Gordon turns around and, with part of his leader in his mouth and both hands wrist-deep in a tangled mess, mumbles, "Not very well, Dr. McMahan. I keep getting my fishing line tangled."

"Call me Jay. There are no doctors on the creek, just anglers, skinny dippers, and a few overheated hikers."

Noticing Dillon standing behind Jay, Gordon says, "Well, hello, Dillon. I didn't see you standing there all camouflaged out. Are the two of you coming or going?"

"We're callin' it a day, Gordon. Ye caught anything?" Dillon asks.

"Well, let me think. I caught a couple of tree limbs and several of those bushes over there." He points toward the bank. "And something Melvin calls a 'rock trout,'" he says finishing with a laugh.

"Those bushes along the bank are rhododendrons," answers Dillon. "Thur purty when they bloom, but gobble up trout flies and shred leaders like nobody's business."

"Well, they've certainly kept me busy today," Gordon mumbles as he tries to talk through the pieces of monofilament between his lips.

From across the stream and out of earshot, Melvin continues to stumble. Trying one backcast too many, his fly gets hung up in a low hanging limb of a rhododendron branch as if to prove Dillon's point. As he was turning to work the fly loose, his eyes catch a glimpse of Dillon and Jay watching from the opposite bank. Catching him off guard, his concentration is all but broken, his right foot loses its grip, and he falls face forward into the water, a look of frustration on his face.

As Jay and Dillon try not to set a bad example in front of Gordon, they fight the nearly overwhelming urge to laugh. "Are you all right, Melvin?" Gordon shouts.

"I'm fine! This stupid rock over here rolled on me."

"We got a doctor if ye need one!" Dillon shouts. And with that, the three break out into laughter as Melvin strains to work his dripping torso out of the water.

Turning from the struggling Melvin, who appears to be physically unharmed, the same cannot be said of his ego, Gordon asks, "This sure is a greater challenge than I imagined it to be. If my line's not tangled, it's hung up on something. Otherwise, I'm slipping and tripping over everything."

"Don't get too discouraged, Gordon," Jay advises. "It will take a while to get your wading legs trained."

"I hope it doesn't take me as long as it does Melvin." Gordon laughs.

"What?" Melvin yells from across the stream.

"I said I'm enjoying fishing with you, Melvin!" Gordon yells over the water.

"Well I'm glad to have you along!" shouts back a dripping wet Melvin.

"Have you boys caught anything?" Gordon asks.

"So far, we've been skunked."

"Oh, we've caught a few," lies Dillon, not wanting to injure Gordon's confidence. "Some days are slow, but as we were taught growing up, the good days wouldn't be so good without enduring a few bad ones here and there," Dillon replies thinking of Pop.

"Well, we'd better be heading back," says Jay.

"Oh, before you go, I do hope the two of you will be able to make it to the cookout next weekend. I want everyone to see Dillon's handiwork, and Gabrielle wants everyone to know that the theme to the cookout will be a Hawaiian luau. We're gonna have a roasted pig, tiki torches, and Hawaiian music. If you have a Hawaiian shirt, be sure to wear it, and a grass skirt is optional."

Speaking for both of them, Jay replies, "We're looking forward to it, Gordon. Well, be careful and good luck."

As Jay and Dillon near the parking lot, they meet Wally Jones who is just heading up the trail to fish.

"Hey, Wally. Ye going up for the afternoon?" asks Dillon.

"Yeah, I guess so. I planned on going early this morning, but my car broke down on the way up."

"Is it running okay now, Wally? You don't need any help or a ride home, do you?" asks Jay.

"Naw. I'm awright. Things happen. You just have to roll with the punches," Wally replies with a resigned look.

"Well good luck, and don't catch 'em all," responds Dillon.

"Yeah. Save us a few if you don't mind, Wally."

"Will do," Wally replies with a smile as he heads up stream.

Dillon watches as Wally makes his way upstream. "I don't see how he does it. I mean it seems like there's always something goin' on with poor ole Wally."

Wally Jones comes from a long line of hardship cases. In fact, as Reverend Mitchell once said, "If Wally ever went to Las Vegas, his propensity to attract bad luck would result in such a vacuum removing any trace of bad luck from everyone for miles around so that every other gambler in every casino would simultaneously hit the jackpot." It all started, as best as anyone can trace back, to Wally's ancestor, Henry Jones. Henry was a wealthy river transportation tycoon, making a fortune in shipping goods along the Tennessee River and down the Mississippi to New Orleans. Having a torn allegiance between the North and South during the war of northern aggression, or as Yankees call it, the Civil War, Henry believed a huge financial opportunity lay in assisting the Confederate army in 1862 in transporting war material. Unfortunately, he lost the biggest chunk of his bulging empire at the hands of Union General Tecumseh Sherman as he made his way across the South and into Atlanta.

Enough of his fortune remained, however, to allow Henry's son, John, to build up and invest in the stock market reaching its zenith of value in 1929. The stock market crash, followed by the subsequent depression all but bankrupted John except for several hundred acres of land in the Great Smoky Mountain region. The concept of being land rich but cash poor was passed onto John's son, Woodrow.

Woodrow had the misfortune of having his land purchased for the formation of the Great Smoky Mountains National Park. Though a boon to the citizens of the United States, Woodrow essentially received pennies on the dollar for his property.

If only it had been several miles away in the Gatlinburg and Pigeon Forge area, things might have turned out vastly different, but such is not the fate of the Joneses. Whoever said, "Let's keep up with the Joneses," never lived in Laurel Cove. By the time the small fortune was passed along to Woodrow's son, Wally, he barely had enough money to pay attention. Nevertheless, to the amazement of anyone familiar with the disposition of Wally, he always seems to maintain a positive outlook on life.

Answering Dillon's question, Jay states, "You know. I asked him once how he always stays positive with all the misfortune that finds him. He told me that to be depressed wouldn't change his luck, and he feels better when he stays positive."

Walking toward Dillon's truck in the parking lot, the two walk past Wally's car. Pointing at the flat right rear tire, Dillon asks, "Do you believe that? Poor guy's gonna come back to a flat tire." Reaching under the rear bumper on the driver's side, Dillon finds the keys. It is a common habit among the fishermen from Laurel Cove to leave their car keys in the rear bumper so that if they split up, one can get into the vehicle in the event of an emergency such as getting bitten by a rattlesnake or copperhead. Another reason is they don't have to worry about losing their keys somewhere in the creek.

"Well, Wally may have bad luck, but we can give him the luck of having a few friends that will change his flat tire for him. What do you say, Dillon?" Jay asks.

The two find the spare, and to their surprise, it is fully inflated and not flat as they partially expected with Wally's luck. Changing the tire, they place the jack and tire iron back in their rightful place in the trunk and leave a note on the dash for Wally warning him to get his flat tire repaired.

Driving home, Jay looks over at Dillon and asks, "So, what are your plans for the luau?"

"Don't see that I've got a choice. I've go to be there as he shows my handiwork," Dillon replies quoting Gordon.

As they arrive at Jay's house, Jay steps out of the truck. "Well, don't forget to get ye a purty, flowerdy shirt," Jay says in his best country accent.

Smiling back at Jay, he replies, "Yeah, I got one to match yer purty hula skirt! And don't furget to shave yur laigs! Can't stand to see hairy laigs under a skirt!" Dillon responds in his overdone hillbilly accent.

The following Saturday, Jay and Debbie stop by to pick up Dillon on their way to the Smith's for the luau. Jay and Dillon are in flip-flops, flowered Hawaiian-style shirts, and shorts. Debbie is dressed in a flowered blouse, matching Jay's shirt, flip-flops, and grass skirt.

Looking at Debbie, Dillon sarcastically says, "I can't believe you're wearing that grass skirt."

"Oh, come on, Dillon, this is great! I've got one that will fit you if you'd like. I couldn't get Jay to wear it. Something 'bout having hairy legs," replies Debbie as she smiles at Jay.

Pulling up to the Smith's house at sunset, they see a couple of dozen vehicles are parked along the concrete driveway and around the circle in front of the house. From the front, they can see the glow from tiki torches already lit in the swimming pool area making their way to the pavilion by the river. Opening the door for Debbie, Jay follows just ahead of Dillon. In the foyer are a couple of catering staff directing the arrivals toward the back of the house and to the pool area.

Jay winks at Debbie then glances back at Dillon as he whispers, "I wonder if it'll be as purty back here as you described it." Neither Jay nor Debbie can hold their laughter as they attempt to suppress their giggles. Dillon can barely hide his grin as well but is also feeling a sense of dread.

As they exit the French doors onto the pool area, Jay leans back and whispers to Dillon, "Dang, Dillon. I believed you when you said Gabrielle was hot, but, son…I think you were sandbagging a bit. I mean she's a real knockout!"

Debbie gently elbows Jay in the ribs for his remark.

Looking at the dark-haired beauty in a grass hula skirt and wearing coconut shells for a top, Dillon answers, "Wow! But that ain't Gabrielle. Gabrielle is over yonder." He subtly nods toward the back of the pool area, which leads to the pavilion.

Making their way toward the unknown hula girl, they see her give a lei to a sweating but joyful Reverend Mitchell and a less than thrilled Selma Mitchell.

"I bet Selma's gossiper is about to explode!" Debbie quietly remarks to Jay referring to Selma's chatty nature. "Can you imagine how this is gonna be around by tomorrow?" Giving Jay a serious look, she adds, "Oh, and behave yourself!"

As Debbie, Jay, and Dillon pass by Reverend Mitchell, he smiles. "Praise the Lord!"

Stepping up, Debbie is greeted with an enthusiastic "Aloha!" by the dark-skinned beauty as she places an authentic flower lei over Debbie's head, resting it on her shoulders. Noting a bit of a Latin American accent, Debbie responds, by recalling a bit more of her high school Spanish lessons than either Jay or Dillon, "Aloha and buenas noches."

Jay steps up and briefly tenses knowing the slightest misstep could mean trouble from Debbie and bends over slightly to allow the lei to be placed over his head.

"Aloha!"

Leaning over, his eyes naturally drift to the coconut shells and the firm contents contained within. Raising up, he responds, "Aloha!"

Walking over to Debbie, she whispers, "Busted!"

"Pardon the pun, eh?" Jay grins. "I'm just doing a complimentary breast exam. You know, looking for lumps and all."

"Well, I can see two from over here," answers Debbie. As Dillon steps up, the beauty repeats, "Aloha!"

"Aloha!" responds Dillon just as enthusiastically. Leaning over, Dillon barely hides his visual survey of the Latin cleavage.

Placing the yellow and white lei over his head, she whispers, "Hola, Dillon."

Straightening up, Dillon finds it impossible to hide the stunned look on his face. "Nice to meet ye, ma'am. I see ye know my name, how 'bout sharin' yours."

Also in a grass hula skirt, but more modest, howbeit ever so slightly, black bikini top, Gabrielle walks up to join the two, "Aloha, Dillon. I see you've met my cousin Dominique. Unfortunately, she cannot speak English very well. She is visiting from out of the country and has only been here a few days."

"If ye don't mind, ask her if she'd like me to escort her down to the pavilion."

Without saying a word, Gabrielle looks at Dominique, then back at Dillon, and replies, "Dominique would appreciate that very much."

Dominique smiles, "Si!"

"Ah, my favorite word." Dillon walks up with Dominique at his side.

Jay eases up alongside with Debbie by his side and quietly jokes, "Dude, looks like you done got lei'd!"

Trying to hide her laughter while punching Jay in the side, Debbie scorns, "Leave him alone, Jay."

Jay pauses momentarily, sniffs the air, and whispers so that only Debbie can hear, "Smell that?"

"The plumeria?"

"No. The setup."

Debbie grins as the two continue walking.

As the foursome make their way by the pool, they pass by the naked lady statue. Dillon cannot help but remember his first meeting with "what's her name." His thoughts are now on Dominique. The walkway toward the pavilion is beautifully lined with tiki torches, their glow lighting the concrete path as the post-sunset sky darkens. The evening is filled with Hawaiian music from Israel Kamakawio'ole. The soft guitar and ukulele sounds of "Henehene Kou 'Aka" permeate the evening air. The pavilion table is adorned with Hawaiian-style flowers, pineapples, mangos, and various other fruits, banana bread, raw mahi-mahi, and poi. While the décor and atmosphere is studied by Debbie and Jay, Dillon has yet to notice anything but

Dominique. The aroma of plumeria radiates from the flower behind her right ear accentuated by her long, silky black hair. Though little is said, at least in words, her beautiful smile and deep brown eyes say it all. It may look like Hawaii, but Dillon feels like he's in heaven. Suddenly, that feeling of paranoia creeps over him as typically occurs when he's around a beautiful single female.

Dominique looks at Dillon, smiles, and says, "Uno momento," then walks over to Gordon who is talking to Boots Ferguson.

Dillon, with a worried look on his face, turns to Jay and Debbie. "How'd ye like them coconuts, Dillon?" Jay laughs.

Not really hearing him, Dillon, still with the worried look on his face, asks Debbie, "The flower is behind her right ear. Don't that mean something? Is that good or bad? Which side is it that means she's single? I ain't gettin' all excited over a married woman. Not again!"

"You're in luck, Dillon," replies Debbie. "In Hawaii, single ladies wear flowers behind their right ear."

"You positive? I mean don't mess with me on this one, okay?"

"This is me, Dillon. Not Jay. You can trust me to not mess with your head," Debbie answers in a semi-serious tone. "You know how the wedding ring is on the left hand? The same is true for the flower behind the left ear. Now, that's the tradition and I'm assuming Dominique knows this as well."

As Dillon turns back to look for Dominique, she approaches him with a split pineapple drink in each hand, complete with umbrellas, with Gordon and Boots close behind.

"Aloha, Dillon. Aloha, Jay," says a smiling Gordon.

"Aloha, Gordon. This is my wife, Debbie."

"Aloha, Debbie. Glad you could make it."

"Aloha and mahalo for inviting us," answers Debbie.

"This is wonderful."

"I see you know your Hawaiian, Debbie. Well, if you know your luaus, you know all about the imu. Let me show you. It is just about ready." As Gordon, Jay, and Debbie walk toward the pit containing the buried pig, Dominique hands Dillon one of the drinks.

"Hey, Dillon. This is one of my latest," adds Boots referring to the drink. "It's what I call my Hawaiian punch. It's got one part mango, one part pineapple, and three parts 'shine." Boots Ferguson, in addition to running the barber shop, is well known in these parts for tinkering with moonshine.

"Well thanks, Boots." Dillon takes a drink after tapping pineapples with Dominique. As the two focus on each other, Boots realizes when he should be somewhere else and walks over to join Melvin and his mother.

Moments later, Gordon turns down the music. With Gabrielle standing at his side, Gordon addresses the crowd, "Aloha and good evening, everyone. I want to thank you for joining us tonight. For those of you who have not had a chance to meet her, this is my wife, Gabrielle. Also, we are fortunate to have Gabrielle's cousin, Dominique." He points toward Dominique who steps up alongside Gabrielle.

Standing next to Jay, Dillon whispers, "Man, she's hot!"

Speaking for Jay, Debbie whispers, "They both are."

"Yeah, and it's really an obvious mismatch now that I see Gordon and Gabrielle side by side. I mean he *really* outkicked his coverage!"

Gordon continues, "Please feel at home, and if you need anything, don't hesitate to ask either myself or Gabrielle. Now, if you'll walk this way, we'll uncover the roast pig, or as they say in Hawaii, imu."

Uncovering the roast pig reveals pork so tender it simply falls off the bone.

As the guests begin making their way through the buffet line beneath the pavilion, Jay gets toward the end of the line and notices Mr. Hopkins. "Well, good evening, Hoppy!"

"Buffet!" replies Mr. Hopkins referring to the pork. Mr. Hopkins, a.k.a. "Hoppy," is wearing a bright, aqua-colored cabana shirt covered in 1960s graffiti instead of his usual white long-sleeved shirt, probably a holdover from his college days. However, not one to alter too much from his usual attire, Mr. Hopkins retains the remainder of his ensemble of navy slacks, and vest and navy tie.

At Gordon Smith's request, Jay and Debbie take a seat next to himself.

"So, Gordon. I see you've met Hoppy."

"Why, yes, a delightfully unique individual if ever I've met one. Melvin and I came across him as we returned from our fishing trip. He hitched a ride with us into town." Then in a discreet manner, Gordon asks Jay, "What's the story with Mr. Hopkins?"

Not one to gossip but wanting to answer Gordon's question in an honest manner, Jay begins, "Well, needless to say, Hoppy is an eccentric individual. As they say, he got his money the old-fashioned way. He inherited it. He owns quite a bit of property outside of town."

"But why so, for lack of a better term, strange?"

"It was back before I really remember, but apparently, he was quite intelligent. Some would say a genius. From what I hear, he was pretty normal until he went to college. He eventually made his way to Berkley where he got his PhD in philosophy. He majored in metaphysics, which tries to figure out humankind's place in the universe and questions if the world truly exists outside the mind. He also minored in existentialism, which believes individuals are responsible for creating the meanings of their own lives. The funny thing is, if you believe you're responsible for creating meaning in your life but you're unsure if it truly exists, then on top of that throw in a newly developed compound called LSD, a feller can get a might screwed up. Personally, I believe Hoppy got too much of an education, if you know what I mean. He probably never figured out if he existed only in his mind or all of this is just one big acid trip. Fortunately, he is harmless and gentle as a lamb."

"And also a man of few words I might add," responds Gordon.

Dillon, listening in from across the table, adds but never removes his eyes from Dominique, "Hell, sometimes he goes into a full diatribe and spouts two whole words at a time."

"But why does he spend day after day hitchhiking?" Gordon asks.

"Don't know. Don't reckon anybody knows. I wonder if anybody ever asked Hoppy why?" Jay ponders the thought for a moment, then decides otherwise.

Dillon adds, "As my granddad once told me, there's wisdom and there's knowledge. Knowledge comes from books. Wisdom comes from the proper application of knowledge and life's experiences. If nothing is learned from the experience, either it was a wasted experience, or worse, it was experienced by a fool. And there's no fool like an old fool." He pauses for a drink from his pineapple, winks at Dominique, who smiles back, then adds, "I'm not callin' nobody a fool, but somethin' done went plum wrong somewhere."

Changing the subject, Gordon asks, "So, how did you guys really do on that fishing trip? I know you told me you caught a few, but I'm a man who prides himself on knowing when an individual is hiding something, and I believe you fellows caught more than just a few."

"Well, how did Melvin do?" Jay asks.

"To be honest, I never saw him catch a thing. He said he caught several when I wasn't looking, but like I said, I'm pretty good at reading people and knowing when they're being dishonest."

"Well, you know fishermen are considered the biggest liars," adds Debbie with a laugh.

"So far, I cannot argue that point as I believe all parties involved are being less than honest."

Not taking his eyes off Dominique, who is sitting next to him mouthing a piece of pineapple, Dillon adds, "Let's just say that Melvin has delusions of adequacy when it comes to fishing."

"Or most anything else," adds Jay. "He's always been known to exaggerate profusely when it comes to his ability to catch trout. We've just learned to overlook this flaw."

"Well it seems to me that if two people are talking and one is bored, Melvin is the other one." Gordon laughs.

"Got that right!" adds Dillon, who is still gazing into Dominique's eyes.

"Well look, guys, we need to plan a trip together real soon. I feel the need to get the taste of the bad experience out of my mind."

The remainder of the evening was spent socializing with the other guests, which included Wally Jones who was running late due to having collided with a deer on the way over. Though his truck will make it, the same can't be said about the doe. Gordon and Gabrielle took most of the guests for a tour of their house including a 1,500 square feet toolshed. Contained within were all of the toys of a handy-man's dream including a John Deere tractor complete with a front-end loader. In the garage was a new silver BMW Z4 for Gabrielle to use in her trips into town. When they walked by the naked lady statue, Hoppy stopped, considered its features up and down, and followed the shapely figure with his hands without ever touching it. "Good," he said then continued on his way.

Needless to say, Gordon had it all, a beautiful new house, a beautiful young wife, and on top of it all, an invitation to be the newest member of the old fart's club with a standing invitation to the whittlin' bench in front of Webb's Grocery. For the older set, this is the ultimate symbol that one has arrived and is a welcome part of Laurel Cove.

Though most enjoyed the tour of the grounds, Dillon passed. He figured that he built the place and pretty much knew what it all looked like. Instead, Dillon was more interested in touring Dominique. The evening wound down with Dillon and Dominique slow dancing to soft Hawaiian music as the tiki torches went out one by one. As far as Dillon knew, there were only two at the party, and there was only one word he needed to know—*si*.

The night ended all too soon for Dillon and apparently for Dominique who appeared to reciprocate the feelings of infatuation for Dillon. In fact, few words were exchanged over the next few weeks between Dominique and Dillon. There's something to be said for body language. With time, Dillon did remember increasingly more and more from his high school Spanish class. As he told Jay, "Man, if I knew then what I know now, or if I knew now what I knew then. It's all screwin' with my head, but I like it!"

Dillon didn't get out as much with Jay that summer as he spent most of his time fishing in prettier, more bountiful waters. When Jay stopped by to invite Dillon out for a trip, he developed a "toothache" on more than one occasion. As Jay puts it, "Dillon's got the prettiest damn toothache I've ever seen." This did free up Jay to keep his commitment to Gordon to take him fishing. For the trip, Jay and Gordon hike up the Big Bear Fork to fish Hog Waller Branch, a small tributary of the Big Bear Fork. Though Jay considers himself to be in fairly good condition, he is surprised at how well Gordon keeps up during the hike. When they stop, it is he that is more out of breath than Gordon. Jay finds himself further surprised at how agile Gordon is in hopping from rock to rock and climbing boulders and up waterfalls, even climbing a tree once to retrieve a fly.

"Don't take this the wrong way, Gordon, but you're in pretty darn good shape for your age. I hope I'm as good when I get your age."

Pausing for a moment to take in a breath of cool mountain air, Gordon begins to speak then pauses again as the sound of the rapid-fire thumping of a pileated woodpecker echoes through the valley, penetrating the old-growth forest from some distant branch. The sound could be originating from either ten feet or one hundred yards away, but nearly impossible to tell the difference. "Well, I've always found myself with a desire to stay healthy. Besides, gotta keep the little lady happy, if you know what I mean," Gordon finishes with a grin. Reaching in a pocket he pulls out a cigar. Before lighting it, he looks over at the doctor, "You don't mind do you?"

Grinning, Jay replies, "Well, professionally, I can't say it's okay, but hell, you hiked up here better than I did, and I believe you're a few trout ahead of me right now, so knock yourself out."

Laughing Gordon adds, "You're much too modest, Jay, and a terrible liar to boot. I'll tell you what though, I never realized how beautiful these mountains are and how exquisite these little brook trout are. Only the Almighty himself could paint something so colorful with a dark green back, red belly, and white-tipped fins, without making it look gawdy. I find each one to be an individual work of art."

"Well, Gordon, I'm tickled to death that you caught your first trout today and not just your first trout, but a brookie on a dry fly that you tied by yourself. I can't say I've ever heard of anyone doing all that in one day."

Laughing aloud, Gordon answers, "Well if you asked Melvin, he'd say he did it, and it was a four-pounder."

Jay, also laughing, says, "Yeah, Melvin's something else."

Gordon adds, "Seriously though, I must give a big kudos to Chester at The Hatch. He is one heckuva a fly-tying instructor."

As they make their way leapfrog fishing up the narrow watershed of Hog Waller Branch, the song of a yellow-throated vireo causes Jay to pause and sit on a streamside rock. From the time he was a little boy, it has always been one of his favorites along with the lonely repetitive call of the whip-poor-will. Gordon notices Jay's sudden infatuation with a sound that he otherwise likely would've simply overheard but not taken the time to listen and appreciate. Jay verbally reminisces with Gordon about some of the trips when he just sat and listened but never actually saw one of the little birds. Their focus on the lovely song is broken by the faint sound of a different nature and origin. Somewhere through thick brush and originating from within a thicket of rhododendron, which in this case would truly qualify as a "rhodo-hell," they hear a quiet laughter.

The curiosity of the two fishermen begins to build as Jay says, "It's probably a couple of young ladies skinny-dipping. It's not an uncommon sight to come across on a fishing trip. Over the years, Dillion and I have briefly enjoyed the view of more than a few nude sunbathers then proceeded on up the creek fishing like they're not even there. Sometimes they ignore us, and sometimes they scream and run to cover up." Jay finishes with a laugh.

Realizing the difficulty of an exit strategy in bushwhacking through the rhodo-hell that is densely lining both sides of the stream, and the fact that the source of the laughter far outweighs their desire to bushwhack, both decide to press on to investigate. With the most determined stealth of the day, Jay, followed closely by Gordon, ease their way up the small branch of water. Around the bend of a small rush of water, they see a rather nice-sized pool with a five- to six-foot waterfall at the head of the pool. Jay recalls watching Dillon land a twenty-one-inch brown out of this pool years ago. He always thought this large pool to be out of character regarding its size and depth as compared to the rest of the stream, but such is often the nature of water coursing its way out of the Smoky Mountains. After a few moments of listening and observation, they notice the slender, youthful body of a tanned, young, dark-haired female. Jay looks for towels lying on top of adjacent rocks, the telltale sign of sunbathers. But there are none. What he does see is a single black bikini hanging from the limb of a rhododendron. Additional observation reveals a larger pair of shorts and T-shirt not far away.

With his eyes back onto the young lady as she sits on a ledge beneath the waterfall, the spray of water over her head and around her shoulders obscures any additional visual detail as she falls forward into the depths of the cool, clear water. As she pops back up to the surface, her back is now to them with her long, dark hair draped down her back. Jay looks back over at Gordon, now with a smile on his face savoring the moment. The young lady speaks in a singing tone, which at first isn't understood by Jay, but with a moment for his brain to shift its focus from his eyes to his ears, the words become more clear, "Where are you…my Tarzan?"

Recognizing the voice, Gordon responds, "I know who that is. That's Dominique!"

Suddenly popping up from beneath the surface next to Dominique is a face well known to Jay. "And now there's Dillon." Both use every bit of energy to not explode in laughter.

At times, Jay can't quite make out what the two skinny dippers are saying until he realizes that Dillon is also speaking Spanish and apparently rather fluently! "Well, it looks like those high school Spanish lessons paid off after all, and danged if Dillon didn't remember what he learned," he whispers to Gordon trying not to laugh.

"And then some," replies Gordon.

"What do you mean?"

"Well…" Gordon quietly laughs. "Let's just say that I doubt some of the words they're sharing were in your textbooks. That is unless you guys had the R-rated versions back then."

Joining Gordon in laughing, Jay replies, "And he sure has better motivation to learn it now."

Though every ounce of Jay's body wants to pop up and say something funny, his sense of the "bro code" tells him to ease away quietly and let Dillon enjoy his moment, and what a moment it appeared to be! Besides, doing so allows Jay time to work out the how, where, and when he can use what he has just witnessed, along with the requisite embellishment of details, to get a good laugh at Dillon's expense in the utmost effective time.

While deep in thought, Jay feels Gordon's hand on his shoulder who whispers, "Perhaps a bit of discretion is the appropriate prescription at the moment, Doc?"

Thus, as Tarzan and Jane are intertwined in the cool, clear mountain water, Jay and Gordon make their clandestine exit, crawling their way through the brush.

After making it back to the trail, undetected, they begin their walk back to the parking lot as Jay starts to wonder about Gordon's past. "So, Gordon, tell me your story. Being sort of a history buff, I naturally like to learn the origins of things to better understand it, and being a physician by trade, I always like a good medical history to know where I'm starting from."

Gordon stops for a moment, looks down at the ground, then up at Jay. "Well, Jay, I'd love to tell you about where I came from and about my family, but all I can say is that I'm sort of here for protective purposes."

"You mean like a witness protection program?" Jay asks.

"Something like that. I felt bad that I could not tell you more during my physical, but I'm very limited in what I'm allowed to share. I hope you understand."

"Sure, Gordon. I'd hate to see you get in any trouble. Fortunately, that takes little effort in Laurel Cove. Everybody pretty much keeps things to themselves, except for Ms. Mitchell. Though she doesn't stir up much trouble, she definitely gets things out and around Laurel Cove. Fortunately, as it is to the outside world, we're just some small-town hicks doing our own thing."

Gordon finds the fishing to be easier and much more rewarding than he was led to believe when out with Melvin. Melvin is none too happy when he soon learns that the fly-fishing skills of his protégé has surpassed those of his own. In fact, Gordon took up fly-tying as if it was in his nature to learn all aspects of each endeavor, which he pursued and in doing so easily surpassed Melvin in his tying skills in only a short time. Sadly for Dillon, Dominique had to go home at the end of the summer, staying much longer than expected. By that time however, the two had worked out their communication glitches with a mixture of body language, poor Spanish on Dillon's part, and poor English on Dominique's. It was as if the two had developed a language of their own with equal parts of all three. With his time spent with Dominique, Dillon's little episode with Gabrielle was ancient history. Dominique promised to return as soon as her father permitted, but even Dillon, who hates flying, was planning on traveling to Dominique's home as soon as he got her address. Love, or lust, will cause a person to do many things outside their norm.

The fall colors had settled in over the Smokies. Unlike the Rocky Mountains, the Smokies are blessed with a wide assortment of colors including reds, oranges, purples, and yellows painting the ridges and valleys as only the Almighty can. The sights of the colorful mountains and the smell of the falling leaves create an almost unbearable urge in die-hard trout fishermen in the Smokies. It nearly drives Dillon insane. If he were a whitetail, his neck would be swollen three sizes from his own personal "rut." As the daylight hours shorten, the annual brown trout spawn begins, making the big browns go out of their minds with an undaunted drive to accomplish one thing, the continuation of their species. Having missed most of the summer fishing season, an act for which he is to never second-guess himself, and with his "toothache" suddenly better, Dillon succumbs to his urge to fish and invites Jay for a day of "chasing the biguns." He drives over to Jay's who is still getting dressed. He walks in the back door and pours himself a cup of coffee knowing Jay, as with most physicians, can tend to occasionally run late for an appointment, though fishing isn't the same as an appointment. It's much more important! Pouring the cup, he takes a seat at the breakfast table. Sipping his coffee, his mind wanders to a book on the table. It's a rather old book and makes him think of a book someone would read to their child. Remembering that Debbie teaches young children at Laurel Cove elementary, he assumes it is one she has been using in her class. Having a mind that is seemingly always on the move, his curiosity of the book piques his interest so that he picks it up. Turning it over to see the title, he notices that it says, *Tarzan Lord of the Jungle*, by Edward Rice Burroughs. *Hmm... Tarzan*, he thinks. *It seems forever since I've heard that.* Still deep in thought of some not-so-distant memory, Jay walks down the stairs. Dillon, still with a smile on his face, is brought back to the moment at hand and, without saying much, joins Jay as they walk out the door and into Jay's Cherokee where Dillon tosses in his fishing equipment.

Driving to town, they cross Big Bear Fork, and as by tradition, habit, or a little of both, they slow down to look at the stream, sizing up its potential in its water flow and clarity. Taking an opportunistic open spot just in front of Smoky's Café, Jay pulls in, and both are soon sitting in Smoky's Café for their usual pre-fishing breakfast, where they are soon joined by Wally Jones. Wally has found himself in the midst of his latest crisis.

"Either of you guys ever have a problem with your identity?" asks Wally.

"Every damn day!" Dillon replies jokingly. "Purt near every morning I wonder who that old feller is in the mirror!"

"Naw, what I mean is have either of you ever had your identity stolen?"

"I can't say that I have," adds Jay. "Why do you ask, Wally? Have you had your identity stolen?"

"Apparently so. I got a letter from a couple uh credit card companies that said I owed 'em a bunch of money. Funny thing is, I've never even owned a credit card. Hell, I never had a checking account 'til recently," he says as his eyes wander off somewhere into his coffee. "Apparently, somebody stole some of those stupid credit card offers out of my mailbox, filled 'em out, and run up a bunch uh' bills on my name."

"What 'che gonna do 'bout it?" asks Dillon.

"Well, I've been callin' the credit card people. They don't much want to listen. All they want is thur' money. I called the credit bureau to complain. They said they'd help some, but they won't promise nuthin'. They said I need to git rid of my mailbox. I'm gonna go down to the post office as soon as it opens and get me a post office box down there and probably drop an M-80 in my mailbox at home!" Wally leaves to make his way to the post office in order to be the first one in line. Not that there is a line at the Laurel Cove post office. It's just that Wally is in a hurry to begin getting his newfound credit problems resolved.

Luanne walks up filling Jay's empty cup with coffee and warming Dillion's mostly empty cup that he brought in. "So, what do you boys want today? The usual? Or do you care to look at the menu for our weekend special?"

Dillion asks, "Weekend special? You've never had that before."

Always ready for an opening, Luanne responds, "Well, hon, yur not gettin' any younger, and maybe it's time you think about eating a little healthier. I'll be back to take your order in a minute." With that, Luanne looks at Jay and grins as Dillion reviews the new weekend menu.

Of the new items listed with variations of the same breakfast items offered since the beginning of time which closely coincides with the opening of Smoky's Café, Dillon notices a few "specials" listed such as "the Fisherman," "the low carb," "the gluten-free," "the Tarzan," "the lactose intolerant." *Wait a minute…the Tarzan? What the…?* Dillon's suspicion rises just a touch with the second mention of Tarzan this morning. Not one to believe in coincidences, he doesn't want to become overparanoid and show his hand, at least not yet. He glances up at Jay who is looking at the scores from the high school football games. *Everything seems normal with Jay…but he'd never let on until it's played out…*, Dillon thinks.

Wanting to get his mind off its current course, states Dillon, "Ye know, I can't help but feel sorry for ole Wally. Seems like a single day don't go by that something bad happens. You'd think the way bad luck runs in his family, he'd give up, but it never seems to get him down."

"I know what ye mean. He's the epitome of a positive attitude. Bad things are always happening, always have, but he always looks forward to tomorrow."

After breakfast, Jay and Dillon climb in the Jeep Cherokee and drive by The Hatch before making their way through Gatlinburg, past the Park Headquarters, and over to the Little River. As they are opening the door, the overhead bell rings, notifying Chester of their arrival. As usual, he's at the tying bench. Today's special, streamers! Big flies often grabs the attention of big Smoky Mountain browns as well as Dillon's. "Some new creation, Chester?"

"Yeah. A guy from Knoxville stopped by earlier this week and showed me a fly he picked up in West Yellowstone last year that really worked on big browns that were swimming up the Madison to spawn. He couldn't remember its name, but it was an interesting design. I thought I'd tie something like it. I'm just getting started on this one, but there's a box over there with some of them. You're welcome to take one and give it a try. Sort of a field test."

Figuring he has nothing to lose, Dillon goes over to look at the box next to the "hot flies" box. "Tarzan." Now, really suspicious, he turns to look at Jay who is looking at some new waders for the upcoming cold weather. "Tarzan?" Jay gives no reaction as he continues to browse through the wader section, though Dillon's imagination does perhaps pick up a bit of a smile from Chester.

Ever to go on the offensive if for nothing else but to measure a reaction, Dillon says, "Hey, Jay, you want me to buy you one of these Tarzan flies to use today?"

Without removing his attention from a pair of waders, Jay responds, "No, thanks, Dillon. You know I'm not that kind of fisherman."

Hearing a snort from Chester, Dillon asks, "Chester? You okay?"

"Yeah, I just forgot how *hot* this coffee is."

Ready to get out on the stream and out of The Hatch, the only fly shop that up until now has ever made Dillon feel uncomfortable, both Jay and Dillon soon are on the road.

Wanting to move on from the suspiciously strange and coincidental morning, Dillon starts, "Ye know. The more I think 'bout Wally, the worse I feel," Dillon says still thinking about the frustrated look on Wally's face this morning.

"Yeah, I know what you mean. I just wish somehow we could help him. It seems like anything we do is just a Band-Aid solution to the overall problem. He needs a luck transplant," adds Jay, placing a medical spin on Wally's problems.

"It's like he's got an incurable disease, except it's not anything that would kill him, at least not yet anyway."

"I tell ye. If I could, I'd trade places with him for a day or so if it were possible just to give the poor feller a break."

"Just a day or so, huh?"

"Yeah. Don't know that I could stand bein' him fer much longer. I couldn't keep up his positive attitude. I'd probably curl up my toes and die from frustration, depression, and everything in between."

As they are driving along Highway 321, the road begins to parallel Little River. As is typical this time of year, it is low and crystal clear. Fortunately, the leaves have not begun to fall on the water yet, making the fishing a little easier. However, by the second pullout, Jay and Dillon realize the major handicap of the day will be in leaf watchers. It is difficult enough to catch the large browns, but with tourists walking everywhere, stopping to take a photograph here and there and desiring to include the fly fishermen for that "classic" photo of the Smokies, the degree of difficulty increases five, if not tenfold.

As they cruise by one of their favorite spots, they ease into a small pullout that is big enough for only one vehicle. The two gear up, deciding to wet wade, at least for now. Fishing for large brown trout in the Smokies is much more difficult than many believe, especially for those who have never attempted the hunt. To some, it is referred to as "hunting" instead of fishing as more time is spent looking for browns than actually fishing for them. Spotting large trout in the low, clear water is nearly impossible for some, but to the trained eye, not so.

With every positive, there seems to be a negative to maintain a balanced equation, and nature loves balance. For instance, while it is easier to spot trout in low, clear water, it is also easier for them to spot the anglers. For that reason, Jay and Dillon dress in camouflage, move slowly, using the natural cover as much as possible by maintaining a low profile and hiding behind trees, bushes, rocks, or any other structure provided to them by nature. This process may sound like guerilla warfare, but when taking into account the nature of their quarry, it logistically becomes a requirement if they wish to hook into a trophy brown by any means other than pure luck, or as Jay and Dillon call it "pulling a Melvin."

Since trout have not been stocked in the Great Smoky Mountain National Park since the early 1970s, all trout are wild. And as Dillon's grandfather Harvey "Pop" Powell, who taught Jay and Dillon how to fly-fish would say, "Big fish don't git that way by eatin' flies and gettin' caught." In fact, a brown trout of twenty inches, a minimum requirement to be considered a trophy by Jay and Dillon's standards, would be in the neighborhood of five to six years old. That's roughly two thousand days of on-the-job survival training, of observing and learning from not only their mistakes but the mistakes of fishermen making their way through the creek. Add to that, other predators and old, wise trout become skittish, if not downright paranoid. Through experience, Jay and Dillon have learned many of the don'ts while stalking large trout in the Smokies. It was the do's that they always seemed short on. Thus, they assume anything they can do to level the playing field to their advantage is worth trying.

As they scan the water from the road for targets, though providing a high vantage point for visibility, it opens them to giving away their presence as well—the balance of nature again. Moving slowly, looking at holding lies from previous years, scanning the stream through polarized sunglasses to reduce the surface glare, and staring for long periods at shapes that more often than not are rocks or changes in coloration on the streambed are the required dues. Unlike most times of the year in which numbers of trout are the game plan and if one of those numbers happens to include a large trout, then all the better, now is a time of patience and trade-offs with the trade-off being numbers of trout for size of trout. Whereas in July, thirty plus trout each would make for a good day, today, one twenty-incher or bigger for either of them will more than suffice.

Though numerous trout are spotted, now is a time to get picky and not mess with the juveniles. It is the granddaddies they are after. Unfortunately, the juveniles have to be considered as they will telegraph with their scattering, from Jay's and Dillon's presence if their approach is too sloppy. Scanning the stream adjacent to the pullout does not reveal any targets, so the two move on to the next location a few miles on downstream. At the next spot, the pullout was a little bigger than the previous. Unfortunately, there is already one car parked in it. With room for at least two more, Jay parks the Cherokee so as to take up as much of the parking space as possible to hopefully exclude additional company. Quickly scanning the area, Dillon spots the "intruders." "Looks like a couple of tourons taking photos downstream," Dillon says referring to a local term for "moron tourists." "They'll probably walk up on us. I say let's head on downstream."

"Don't know that we'll find much solitude today," Jay replies as he turns back onto the road to continue downstream, merging into traffic at the first opening.

"Whoa! Stop, stop, stop!" Dillon yells, slapping the dashboard while looking back into the creek.

"What, what is it?" asks Jay trying to see what he's about to run over or otherwise collide with, the sound of screeching tires from cars stopping to prevent running into the side of his vehicle partially out in the lane and partially in the parking spot.

"It's a dang submarine! Back up, back up!" Dillon replies still shouting. Jay quickly shifts into reverse and backs into the parking space. Tourists drive by making various gestures and giving dirty looks for his "slick" move. "I didn't see it 'til we started to pull away! It's huge!"

"Where is it?" asks Jay.

"Right there at the tail out of the pool!" he replies, pointing toward the creek. "See it?"

"Wow! That is huge!" Jay replies now able to see the huge brown trout lying motionless in the clear tail out of the pool. In the bright sunlight, the dark coloration of its long, massive body gives it away. "It looks like a torpedo just beneath the surface."

Dillon slips out of the passenger side trying to limit his motion to avoid spooking the fish from even this distance. Jay meets him at the rear of the Cherokee. Dillon removes his six-weight, nine-foot fly rod, already rigged with his favorite streamer pattern for this time of year.

"There's no way I can approach him from the side or below to get a good cast," Dillon states referring to the overhanging trees and lack of cover.

"I recommend a long cast from upstream and let the streamer drift down to it. Don't let it see your fly line or leader though, or it's over," advises Jay.

"Okay, I'm gonna walk upstream and come down to him. Keep an eye on him fer me." Dillon walks across the two lane road to the far side, bending over as he walks to remain hidden. Jay slowly walks up behind a tree to conceal his silhouette from the target. Watching the huge brown, Jay estimates it to be about twenty-five to twenty-seven inches and close to eight pounds. He then realizes that fish typically looks smaller to him in the water than they really are. As he begins to reevaluate his estimate based on this history, he realizes that with a trout this big, a few inches here or there isn't worth obsessing over.

Much to Dillon's surprise, as he makes his way downstream to the trout, he can still see its dark shape against the light-brown bottom. Even though he is wearing camouflage, Dillon focuses on maintaining a low profile as he walks gently and slowly to prevent any excessive noise or vibrations that may give away his approach. A rolling rock or slip would probably mean game over. A fall, definitely! A wild trout this large has seen many fly fishermen in its time. Even though he might not technically make a mistake, if the trout perceives that something is not quite right, it's as good as gone.

Jay remains behind his tree, observing both the trout and Dillon. Watching the trout, he is amazed how it can remain so motionless in moving water. The mere flip of a tailfin to hold its position behind some invisible hydrological obstruction or a glide of a pectoral fin to help it maintain its position; otherwise, it is perfectly still. He continually finds himself amazed at hydrodynamics and how an object can require little to no effort to maintain its position in the current. Though this one is in a mere two feet of moving water, making it easier to spot, he realizes likewise they too are vulnerable.

With Dillon moving into position, he looks to Jay for an update. Jay merely nods to verify that the trout has not moved. Now, in a crouching position and at about the right distance, Dillon quietly and slowly feeds out what he estimates to be the right amount of fly line. He checks his leader and 4X tippet for strength verifying the absence of any weak spots or bad knots, wishing he could go to a bigger, stronger-sized leader to help him handle the trout but knowing a smaller 5X might prove beneficial in the clear water. "Make your first cast your best," he says to himself remembering what Pop once told him. Realizing that he cannot risk a false cast over the trout, he keeps his rod tip low performing a side cast to feed out line in the current, which he will use to carry his streamer to the waiting trout. He hopes it is either hungry for a small sculpin or too territorial to allow any intruder into its area. Dillon works his fly about ten feet above and about three feet beyond the trout's lie. His plan is to keep it upstream and strip it by the target's nose without it ever spotting his line. As his fly nears the trout's position, he sees the dark object move toward his fly.

His heart begins to pound as the adrenalin rush makes its way throughout his body.

"Hey, are you catching anything?" shouts a man in a white shirt and shorts standing on the highway with camera in hand. Still yelling in order to be overheard by the sound of the stream, he adds, "Don't mind if I take your photograph, do you?" By now, the photographer's two children are walking up the side of the road overlooking the creek with their mother several steps behind.

"Unbelievable!" Dillon says to himself quietly, realizing his chance has been ruined. As tough as it may seem, he knows he must be "neighborly" and exhibit southern hospitality as the man is probably clueless as to what has just happened. Part of him would just love to open a good can of "whoop ass" and use it, but the poor guy is just being friendly. Instead, he just smiles and waves as he reels in his line and begins to make his way to where Jay is standing. Meanwhile, Jay feels saddened by the missed opportunity of such a rare trout of that size and realizes it is one of the many challenges to fishing along Little River Road when the fall colors are in full glory. With nearly ten million tourists, the Great Smoky Mountains National Park remains the most heavily visited park in the United States, a fact that makes Jay both proud of his park but sad that it is potentially being over-loved.

"Tough luck, eh, pal?" Jay asks as Dillon meets him at the rear of the Cherokee. Without saying a word, Dillon walks around and gets in on the passenger side. Joining him at the wheel, Jay says, "Well, let's keep on looking. Besides, we know where the torpedo lives, at least for the next month or so." Jay adds this trying to reassure himself and convince Dillon that another chance will come and hoping that no one else will catch and keep it or otherwise scare it off.

Working their way downstream, they near the Metcalf Bottoms picnic area where traffic comes to a complete stop. A few minutes later, a park ranger works his way by in the opposite lane trying to get to the source of the traffic jam. Finally, after several minutes, traffic begins to ease by. The culprit is a terrified two-year-old black bear clinging to a high branch of a poplar tree with several dozen photographers hovering around the base working for that perfect shot.

"Redneck paparazzi," Jay states as he shakes his head at the foolish actions of tourists. Realizing they've both had about enough, the two head back toward Laurel Cove, to the quieter side of the Smokies, and away from the throngs of tourists making their way between Gatlinburg and Cades Cove.

On their way back, Jay decides to stop by The Hatch to pick up some streamer hooks from Chester.

As Jay and Dillon walk in, the bell over the doorway chimes to announce their entry. The ole farts club is sitting around the unlit fireplace whittlin' on some odd sticks working them down to nothing in particular.

"How ye boys doin'?" Dillon asks as he casually makes his way over to observe their handiwork of smaller versions of what they began with.

"Have ye heard the news?" Chester replies.

"What news?" Jay asks looking over various boxes of number 6 streamer hooks.

"The news about Wally."

"Naw. Dillon and I have been over on Little River all day fishing and haven't listened to the news. In fact, you're our one and only stop since we left the creek."

"Aw, ye gotta hear this," Chester continues. "It seems Wally has been having some trouble with his mail gettin' stolen."

"Yeah, Jay and I talked to him this mornin' 'bout his goin' over to the post office to get a post office box and stop usin' his mailbox," adds Dillon now as he walks over to listen more closely.

'Well, he went over there to the post office and was waitin' to get one assigned. Ye know how Wally is, always curious and all and can't be idle for a minute. He decides to go check out the wanted posters that's always hangin' on the wall to kill a few minutes 'til they get him a box, and somewhere toward the back of the pictures, which had probably been there for a few months, he spies a familiar face." Chester pauses for a moment to maximize the impact. "Who does he spy you might ask? None other than Gordon Smith, 'cept it ain't Gordon. Well it is, but it ain't."

"What are you talkin' 'bout?" Dillon asks, growing impatient.

Chester continues, "Well, apparently, Gordon Smith is actually Gerardo Esteban, and he's on the FBI ten most wanted list for bein' tied up in some South American drug cartel. Apparently, he's a hit man or bodyguard or somethin'. He's wanted for what he may know about the connection to the murder of some DEA agents a few years back."

"No way! Not Gordon. Are you sure?" a stunned Jay asks.

"Oh yeah. You'll see all the commotion when ye get into town, and I 'spect up at his house as well. They'll be up there siftin' through his stuff fer evidence and confiscatin' most everything for bein' tied to drug money."

"Man," Dillon adds, also stunned. "He's such a nice guy. I mean he'd come out and grade the gravel roads for some of his neighbors when they got washboard bumps in 'em. He's too nice to kill somebody. You sure it's him? Ye ain't pullin' our laigs, are ye, Chester? 'Cause this ain't funny."

"Ye know. In a way, I wish I wuz. Gordon is such a nice guy. It's hard to believe all this is true 'bout them."

"What do ye mean them?" Jay asks.

"Oh, I fergot to tell ye 'bout the rest of them. It seems that Gordon, er Gerardo, wuz up here sorta hidin' out fer personally knockin' off some members of a competitive drug ring some time back. But that ain't all. He and his young wife, what's her name?"

"Gabrielle," injects Dillon impatiently.

"Yeah, that's her. Apparently, she and Gerardo were sent up here by their boss to protect his daughter. Sort of uh his-n-her, tag team bodyguard fer their boss' daughter." Not knowing the relationship that had blossomed over the summer between Dillon and Dominique, Chester continues, "Yeah, apparently the real prize was that other girl. Boy she was a looker too. What's her name?"

"Dominique!" Dillon adds almost shouting.

"Yeah, that's her. But her name was really Monique Martinez. Apparently, her daddy is some kingpin drug dealer out of Bolivia. He sent her up here over the summer to protect her from some hit men workin' fer the other drug dealers. Sounds like they're havin' some kinda war down there, don't it?" Chester adds shaking his head.

Dillon leaves the shop, walking back out to the Cherokee and sits in silence as he thinks about the sudden turn of events. Jay pays for the hooks and joins Dillon, sitting in Jay's Cherokee.

Getting in the car, Jay adds, "Man, that sucks, Dillon. At least she's gone now, and you're not too deeply involved in all this."

Still stunned and not really looking nowhere in particular, Dillon adds, "Yeah. I guess things ended 'bout the right time after all."

"Well, you know as our friend Wally is always saying, you gotta learn from the past and look toward the future."

Jay pauses for a moment, then cranks up the Jeep, and heads down the road. Not really wanting to add much more insult to Dillon's current situation, he hesitates then adds, "You know how you were feelin' sorry for Wally this morning, Dillon?"

"Yeah."

"Well, after you walked out, Chester told me the rest about Wally. Apparently, because Wally fingered Gordon to the FBI, according to Chester he's gonna get a one-million-dollar reward! Can you imagine that? One million dollars, tax-free. Ye know, maybe the Jones curse might just have been lifted once and for all."

Looking over for the first time, Dillon adds, "Ye know. It looks like for the first time ole Wally can feel sorry fer me fer a change."

Remembering the conversation earlier this morning, Jay adds, "Maybe your wish came true, Dillon. Maybe today is the day you traded places with Wally. You know, you get the bad luck and lose the girl, and he hits the jackpot, in a manner of speaking."

Trying to find a bright spot in a bad situation as only Wally could do, Dillon thinks a moment, smiles, then adds, "Well, I guess it ain't all a lost cause. I mean I did enjoy the summer with a nice pair of coconuts."

Smiling back, Jay replies, "Well, medically speaking, I'm just glad you got rid of that toothache that kept ye from fishin' all summer. Tarzan must have an awesome dentist!"

THE OLD MAN OF BONE VALLEY

The Hall Cabin, GSMNP

Fall in the Smokies is a wonderfully beautiful time of year. As Boots Ferguson, owner of Boots' Barber Shop, is fond of saying, "Fall is a wondermously, purtiful time when God likes to show off a bit." In the Smokies, showing off is a bit of an understatement. A commonly known fact is that October is one of the most touristy times of the year, typically about the *Third Saturday in October*, which is also known for a "little" football game between the orange of Tennessee and crimson of Alabama. Jay thought it ironic that the same two colors of the opposing football teams are also prevalent in the Smokies just as the game is played. The beauty displayed along the ridge tops and down the valleys is accentuated by the contrast of the dark crimson colors and those of the bright oranges.

Though that contrast is settled on the gridiron to the joy of roughly half the observers, that of the winning side, it continues at the pleasure of all those blessed to be in the Smokies. For anyone having gone through life without a visit to the Smokies in fall, life is simply not complete. Unlike the Rockies that are blessed with cottonwoods and aspens in mostly bright yellows, the Appalachian chain has the full palette of colors thrown its way annually by the master artist. And though most residents look forward to fall when county fairs boast beauty queens, corn dogs, and carnival rides, the mountain folk are busy bringing in their harvest and making apple cider and sorghum molasses. Dillon always finds himself in a bit of a melancholy mood in the fall. He can't help but enjoy the kaleidoscope of colors in the mountain vistas and everything that is autumn in the Smokies, but to Dillon, it also means winter is just around the corner. He never can get beyond the bleak winter days working out on the construction sites in the cold. Each year seems to bring a greater challenge of keeping his fingers and ears warm.

Every year seems colder than the previous, regardless of what the thermometer reads. Jay's medical opinion is that Dillon is simply getting older and with age comes weakening eyesight and decreased circulation exhibiting itself with increasing episodes of cold appendages. There is no way Dillon was going to admit to growing older.

Still, those clip-on magnifying lenses he's seen on the older fly fishermen, those same gadgets Dillon saw as some sort of yuppie fashion statement straight from the catalogue photos, did seem to come in handy for the first time this year while fishing the tailwaters. Lately, those little midge patterns that Dillon so hates to tie seem to decrease at least two hook sizes regardless of what the hook box says. And he still believes the labels on soup cans have smaller writing. He says, "There's a conspiracy going on somewhere!"

In Dillon's mind, it is simply another reason to limit one's fly arsenal to large nymphs. Deep down, Dillon really dreads the coming cold weather this year. Working outside last year in the subfreezing weather really made his knees and shoulders hurt. Old football injuries play hell on the middle aged. A thought that repeatedly crossed his mind last year was, "I'm too damn young to feel this damn old." For Dillon, autumn is not all it is cracked up to be. It is like bad news in brightly colored gift wrapping, and it's difficult to enjoy the wrapping if you know the contents and what consequences it holds.

It had been a difficult summer for both Dillon and Jay. As was typically the case, Dillon had way more work than he needed and definitely more than he wanted, as did Jay who was noticing a minor boom in his medical practice. With the heavy workloads, both had been able to get in a barely adequate amount of fishing and had yet to make their first camping trip of the year. In most years, at least two or three times a year, Jay could coax Dillon into a backpacking trip somewhere in the Smokies. More often than not, they would wind up somewhere on the north shore of Fontana Lake, to fish one of the remote feeder streams flowing out of the national park and into the lake. For Jay, it is a chance to get out of the office and out of range of beepers and telephones to spend some quality time communing with nature and enjoying God's greatest combination, fly-fishing for wild trout and the Great Smoky Mountains. As Reverend Mitchell is known to say, "God may have rested on the seventh day, but to relax, he assuredly fished a little bit and most likely on the blessed waters of Hazel Creek."

Once a small mountain community, Hazel Creek, with its most famous resident Horace Kephart who wrote *Our Southern Highlanders*, felt the world calling in the name of the Ritter Lumber Company in the early 1900s. Reportedly, Horace arrived on the train "well lit," as the ole timers say. He went on to spend a few years living alone in a cabin looking for his "back of beyond" and gaining an understanding of the local mountain people, their customs, and especially their language. While most of the outside world made fun of the hillbillies, Horace developed a large respect for the toughness of the locals in etching out a living among the steep ridges and deep valleys with few modern amenities.

Overnight, the small community was transformed into the bustling logging town of Proctor, with over two thousand residents, complete with commissary, high school, and movie theater all within a stone's throw of the clear waters of Hazel Creek. After the logging was complete, it seemed that Hazel Creek would resume its pre-logging days of a quiet mountain cove. However, when World War II began, electricity was badly needed for the production of aluminum for airplanes at nearby Alcoa, Tennessee. As a result, Fontana Dam was constructed in a few short years to help supply that power.

That, coupled with the recent formation of the Great Smoky Mountains National Park, resulted in the removal of all residents from the beautiful valley. Walking up the old train bed that follows the trout-filled stream, a few remnants of the once thriving community can be seen in the otherwise serene valley. Little has changed in the valley during the last sixty or so years. When the Park was formed, no roads were constructed into the area, thus requiring all visitors to access the tranquil valley either via trail or by boat. This "gift" has kept many of the lesser dedicated hikers and fishermen out of this gem of a trout stream.

From their first visit as teenagers, Hazel Creek has always maintained a spell over Jay. At an age when most boys were running to and fro, the beauty and relaxation of Hazel Creek stopped Jay in his tracks. For Dillon, Hazel Creek is a fly-fishing utopia of beautiful water with plenty of nice pools to hold trophy-sized brown trout. If ever a stream owed him, it is this one. If he were to ever write a book on losing big trout, Dillon's first chapter would be devoted exclusively to Hazel Creek. Dates, like July 6, 1986, and exact runs where lunkers were lost still bore into his memory more vividly than his first kiss, graduation, and wedding day. If asked, Dillon can roll off a list of dates, conditions, and flies used and approximate size of fish lost like an auctioneer at a burley tobacco sale. Nevertheless, he figures he can never get the Hazel Creek gorilla off his back unless he follows Jay on at least one annual pilgrimage to Hazel Creek. For Dillon, however, the lure of backcountry camping is less appealing than for Jay. As a home builder, Dillon spends most every day outside to some degree, and though he loves fishing in the mountains, something about sleeping in a tent, usually a leaky one, on the ground isn't his idea of a high time. However, for the chance at a wild, trophy brown, it is a sacrifice he is willing to make.

Taking the ferry from the Fontana Boat Dock across the lake, Jay and Dillon absorb the breathtaking views with the mountains rising suddenly but subtly for nearly five thousand feet from the glassy smooth surface of Fontana Lake. At over four hundred feet deep, one's imagination is free to roam at what swims beneath the surface among the small towns and farms that remain at the bottom of the lake. Though evacuated, the residents had to leave houses, barns, and other personal items when the flood gates were closed on Fontana Dam in 1944.

Ever the history buff, Dillon voices a thought, "Ye know, I always thought it was the mother of all ironies that in buildin' Fontana Dam to supply power to help make aluminum fer airplanes to defeat Germany and Japan, that a town named Japan was swallered up and covered by the lake. It's like we beat Japan twice, 'cept this one ceased to exist."

The thought is all but lost on Jay whose gaze is somewhere up along some distant ridge as they motor their way across the lake then into and up the cove leading toward the mouth of Hazel Creek.

Words like spectacular, stunning, astonishing, magnificent, and peaceful wind their way through Jay's mind as he attempts to mentally describe the multitude of fall colors splashed throughout the mountains. "Good job, God!" is all he can muster in a low, reflective tone. Overhearing his words and tuning into his thoughts, Dillon agrees, "Amen to that!"

As the cove narrows and the bends tightens, the ferry nears the trail head just below the mouth of Hazel Creek. Arriving at the trail head, Jay and Dillon grab their backpacks and fly rods and begin hiking their way up the five or so miles of trail. By the time they arrive at Bone Valley Campground, late in the evening, the day's sunny skies have become darkened by the setting sun and building clouds. As a breeze signals a likely storm brewing up on top of Clingman's Dome, rain is surely on its way. In a hurry to get their tents up and equipment in the dry, Jay and Dillon hurriedly empty their backpacks, quickly scan the area, and choose their preferred spots to locate their lodging. Preferring to be close to the water and harmonious rumble of Hazel Creek, they look for smooth areas free of roots and rocks that make for a difficult night of sleep. Dillon having spread out his tent is hurriedly connecting the links of his tent poles that will be crisscrossed over the roof of his two-man tent, thus holding it up supporting the domed shape. Once all are connected, he then pushes the pole to his right through the loops of the tent roof, thus providing support for the dome roof.

With his focus on connecting the segments, he feels resistance when trying to push the connected sections away from his tent with his left hand. From his kneeling position, Dillon glances to his left to look at the tree that is in the way of his tent pole when immediately he lunges backward, rolling a complete flip. Jay, wondering what Dillion is up to now, follows Dillon's gaze to where the tent pole points and spies the reason for the acrobatic movements.

It is a coiled timber rattler! Collecting his senses, Dillon realizes how close, less than an arm's length, he'd been from getting bit. Without ever rattling, the large snake uncoils and slithers across a log, disappearing.

"Now that was a close call," Jay exclaims breaking the silence.

Still in shock and breathless, Dillon replies, "I looked around before settling on a spot and I swear I never saw it! It never even rattled… not once!"

"Well, you know we've only ever seen one that did rattle."

"That bigun over at Mouse Creek Falls?" Dillon asks, referring to a long-ago trip when as teenagers they crossed paths with a forty-two-inch specimen crawling across the trail as they were walking down Big Creek trail returning from a fishing trip.

"Yep. To be honest, that big boy was very calm. It's as though he's been around people before. That's good, I guess as he didn't seem interested in taking a bite."

Looking around to make sure it's not sneaking back, Dillon, still catching his breath, asks Jay, "What would you have done if I'd got bitten, Doc?

"Well, depending on where you got bit, I'd try to keep the bite below the level of your heart, use the suction cup out of my snakebite kit to try to extract as much venom as possible, mark the site for future reference, then head quickly downstream to Fontana Lake to see if anyone is there who can call for help," Jay replies with his minimal experience in treating snakebites. He says this both knowing there might likely be nobody with a boat or satellite phone that could reach the "outside world," one of the hazards and attractions to the remoteness of Hazel Creek. Getting his breath and wits back, Dillon replies with a smile,

"Well, if you'd gotten bit, I'd just let you take care of yourself, being a doc and all."

"You wouldn't run for help?"

"Eh…I guess that'd depend on if the fish were biting," he replies, now laughing.

For the rest of the trip, Dillon looks closely at every step he makes around camp fully assured that that rattler is out there somewhere and is going to sink his fangs into his "purty white" calf muscle at first opportunity.

Overnight the storm turns out to be no more than a nice mountain shower, refreshing the cool air. Waking up to sunny skies, Dillon finds the water just the way he likes it, a little dingy and a little high. As he would often tell Jay, "This is when the biguns go on the feed like a fat lady in a buffet line." True to his word, Dillon and Jay have a fairly good day working their way upstream from camp, casting weighted prince nymphs and green inchworm patterns into the pockets and runs of Hazel Creek. At one large pool, Dillon catches two browns nearing sixteen inches, not bad, but not what he is after nor what he is due.

Around two in the afternoon, they make their way back to camp to relax a few hours before the evening fishing. Having kept a couple of trout each to broil in the campfire for supper, Dillon stashes them in the rapids below camp, placing rocks over the creel to keep greedy crawdads out and to weigh them down so they will not be swept downstream by the shallow but swift current.

Relaxing in a hammock strung between two trees within spitting distance of the creek, Jay thinks about Melvin Cody. "Yeah, too bad Melvin couldn't make the trip. We really dodged a bullet, eh, Dillon?"

"More like a pop gun than a bullet," Dillon replies with a laugh as his hammock slowly sways.

"Do ye think Melvin will ever come on one of our camping trips?"

"I shore hope not! I'd be worse than bringin' a two-year-old cuttin' teeth. No, Melvin ain't got no desire to be here. Now getting here, that's what he's interested in. He loves his gadgets and all the preparation and the drama that goes with it, but naw, he'll never make the trip. Its' a bit too fer from momma fer him."

"I heard he bought a new tent and sleeping bag this summer."

"That's what he told me. I asked him how it slept, he said somethin' 'bout his momma's poodle markin' it fer his own and sleepin' on it. You know Melvin, he ain't messin' with momma or Fifi!"

"So what was Melvin's excuse for not coming this time?"

"Something 'bout his momma havin' issues. That boy can't spend the night away from home. He couldn't when we were growin' up. The only time he ever camped out then was if we camped in his backyard."

"Hey, Dillon. You remember the time his momma came outside and tucked him into his sleeping bag."

Breaking out in a hard laugh, Dillon answers, "Yeah. How old was he, fourteen or fifteen?"

Laughing, Jay replies, "Probably." Then he added, "Bet she still does!"

Both are quiet for a moment, then Jay asks, "You know, Dillon, as many times as we've been up here, we've never walked up to Hall Cabin in Bone Valley? What do you say we mosey up there? We should be back in plenty of time to catch the afternoon hatch."

Dillon, trying to doze off in his hammock, stops swinging.

"Dang it, Jay! I thought we wuz gonna relax up here? Now you're tryin' to get me out walkin' again?"

Knowing Dillon's weakness, Jay responds, "I heard there's some beaver ponds up there that hold some good trout. Probably a big brown or two patrolling the deeper end." Suddenly, Dillon springs to life and rolls out of his hammock.

"Well, let's give 'er a shot!"

The Bone Valley Trail makes its way from its junction with the Hazel Creek Trail at the Bone Valley campsite winding its way roughly 1.8 miles up to the Hall Cabin. Hall Cabin was built by Craton Hall, believed to be the first white man in Bone Valley. Bone Valley gets its name from an incident that occurred in the 1870s in which a farmer took his cattle up the valley to graze for the summer.

Unfortunately, a late spring blizzard hit the mountains. In an attempt to stay warm, the poor cattle huddled together but subsequently froze to death. Their white, bleached bones lay around in piles for years, resulting in the valley being named Bone Valley. On their way up Bone Valley Trail, several crossings are made, some nearly knee-deep. As they approach the "reported" beaver ponds,

Jay spots an area of still water on the left side of the trail. Walking back into the woods, the two come up on the first of the beaver dams.

With their combined focus on the beaver ponds, neither notice the dark clouds piling up just over the ridge. Common to the Smoky Mountains, as is typical with most mountainous regions, are sudden changes in the weather. As is often said about the Smokies, "If you don't like the weather, wait a few minutes, and it will change." As Jay and Dillon look for signs of life in the beaver ponds, rain begins to fall lightly on the mirrored surface.

As the two find themselves in the shelter of a tall pine tree, the rain becomes heavier and each drop bigger. Hearing the rumble of thunder approaching in the distance, Jay observes, "You know, this ain't the best place to be, under the tallest tree and all."

"Well, I figger it's either this tall tree or our choice of a thousand other tall trees. I don't see that we can avoid it unless we make a break for the cabin. It's too far back to camp from here."

"How far do you think it is to the cabin?" Jay asks as the rain begins to soak through the overhead branches, making its way to the indecisive pair.

"Don't know, but I say let's hit it!" With that, Dillon takes off running with Jay close behind. As they reach the last crossing of Bone Valley Creek, the water is up over their knees and muddy. Having pushed their way through the fast-moving brown water, they run through a muddy section of the trail until they spot Hall Cabin on the right. Running up the steps and onto the front porch they look at each other, then at themselves and realize they would be no more soaked if they had gone swimming. By now, lightning bolts are flashing across the skies, further enhancing the waves of rain passing through the valley and crashing onto the tall trees of Bone Valley.

"Well, it looks like we might be here for a while," Jay states matter-of-factly as he removes his shirt and rings out the water followed by his socks. He then hangs them both from an overhead beam on the front porch.

Feeling a bit of a chill from the cool damp air, Dillon follows suit by wringing out his shirt and socks as well as removing his hat in a feeble attempt to get them to dry. Realizing they have reached the extent of their clothes drying capabilities, both sit back on the porch and watch the rain fall. If it were possible, the rain was falling even heavier as vertical columns of rain work their way through Bone Valley highlighted with lightning bolts forking their way across the sky and into some not so distant stand of hemlocks. Each boom of thunder vibrates through their damp bones while rattling the very foundation of the old cabin.

Reaching into his day pack, Jay pulls out an apple and rubs it on his pants more out of habit than to clean it before taking a bite. "Well, I'm content to sit here for a while. Sure don't want to get back out into that mess."

Taking a sip from his canteen, Dillon thinks about dinner plans, "I wonder if the trout will be okay? A gully washer like this is liable to wash 'em plum down to Fontana Lake."

"Well, it'll just give us an excuse to fish some more," Jay replies with a smile.

Pointing across the valley, with the far side no longer visible through the heavy downpour, Dillon always the pessimist of the two thinks out loud, "Ye know. I don't expect we'll be able to fish the rest of the day, and probably not tomorrow either." After a few moments of listening to the roar of the rain on the countless trees and the roof of the cabin, Dillon asks, "Ye think the fishin's ruined fer the rest of the trip?"

Of the two, Jay is always the optimist. Trying to spread light where Dillon saw darkness. Perhaps it's in his nature as a physician to believe in change for the good as a student of the healing arts.

"Nah." A few minutes of listening to the driving rain pass. "Maybe."

Watching the unceasing rain a little longer and realizing it is not slacking off, Jay answers more pessimistically, "Probably."

An hour passed by, and the rain continues to fall. Where there was once a trail passing by in front of the cabin, there is now a creek. "I bet there's a fish or two in there." Jay smiles as he points to the trail.

"Yeah, bet they washed down from Clingman's Dome," Dillon replies laughingly referring to the highest peak in the Great Smoky Mountains National Park at 6,643 feet.

Unfinished business is on Dillon's mind. A home builder by trade, he always seemed to fight deadlines, schedules, and missed appointments. But when away from "the job," he hates to not be able to finish what he started. From the time Jay brought up the Bone Valley beaver ponds, ruining a perfectly good midafternoon nap, and in a hammock no less, Dillon has wanted to know if there was any truth to the fisherman's rumor. Truth. The mere thought of the word paints a hint of a sarcastic smile on Dillon's face.

Having been at it long enough to know that fly-fishing is seemingly built around tales and rumors, he knows that any respectable betting man would wager against the presence of "big browns" in the ponds. For all he knows, there may be a few small, dinky rainbows and perhaps a misplaced brookie thrown in for a little variety.

Still it is in his nature, as in that of most anglers, to investigate and discover the truth for himself, thus dispelling the notion of any substance to another rumor. Looking out from the front porch of Hall's Cabin, the rain continues rushing down the trail forming a temporary new fork of Bone Valley Creek. All he could think of is unfinished business and leaving Hazel Creek without knowing the truth, if there is such a thing in trout fishing, of what swims in the depths of the ponds, and that Hazel still owes him!

Though Jay is the more studious of the two, anyone spending more than a few moments around Dillon quickly realizes there is more than meets the eye in the realm of intelligence. Jay's expertise exists more in the scholastic realm than does Dillon's, but Dillon is head and shoulders above Jay in mechanical reasoning and craftsmanship.

If it is broke and part of the human anatomy, you take it to Jay. All else defaults to Dillon. And while Dillon often "plays dumb" about various topics, he has his moments of deep thought and contemplation. Lately, Dillon has been going through a rough time in the construction business, and as his thought pattern progresses, he finds himself somewhere within his current frustration, the Catch 22s of life. His first consideration of any topic, as it evolves through his mental analysis, typically is fishing. Albeit a wonderful example, fishing in the Smokies is difficult. The scenery is sometimes so overwhelming with the thick canopy of trees, multitude of blooms, cascades, and wildlife that it grabs your attention about the same time a trout grabs your fly. Except for the rare suicidal fish, you don't get both. Typically, you lose the fish but are blessed with the experience that is the great outdoors loved by the locals and which the tourists travel from around the world for a glimpse, albeit by and large from the safety and comfort of their cars. And though trout fishing is a great pastime, it would be much less appealing if not for the beautiful stage on which it is played out.

The Catch 22 that's been bothering Dillon lately is that of his other current occupation, building a home for a "half-back." Locals refer to a "half-back" as anyone originally from north of the Mason-Dixon line who has retired to Florida but later discovers and longs for the milder climate and beautiful scenery of East Tennessee, thus moving halfway back home. Wanting their own piece of paradise in the foothills, Dillon is often called upon to build their retirement home or cabin for which they become too impatient and cannot wait 'til the agreed upon time. The catch: does he put up with the half-backs and their Yankee insolence and impatience thus reaping the benefits of their business, or does he tell them to go back to whichever place they came from, on more than one occasion telling them to go somewhere much hotter than Florida!

As is often the case when men find themselves sitting around in the great outdoors with plenty of time and little to do, the conversation turns to either solving the problems of the world or saying aloud what's on your mind.

Looking out over the rain-soaked valley, Dillon asks, "Ye ever get tired of what yer doin fer a livin'?" Sensing the emergence of a melancholy mood, Jay replies, "Well, like anything else I guess, there's good times and bad times in whatever your occupation."

"What about when the bad-uns begin to outnumber the good-uns? It seems anymore all I hear is complaints. Like last week, Martin Jones was complainin' 'bout his wife bitchin' at him 'cause their house ain't done yet. I've got a month left and oddly enough everything's ahead of schedule. I'm sure when I get it done a week early, she'll be gripin' 'bout somethin' else. I guess I just git tired of all the complainin' and nary a thank ye."

"If it helps any, Dillon, I don't see many patients who come in just to say hello. Many come in with some ache or pain and expect an instant cure or pill when all they really need is a little exercise, to eat right, and take better care of themselves. I guess it's all a burden we bear when dealing with people, my brother."

"Sometimes I just feel like there's more to life than buildin' houses and solvin' construction problems. Sometimes I wonder if there's not somethin' else I'm meant to do."

"Well, Reverend Mitchell says the good Lord has all of us where we are for a reason, that nothing happens by accident or without His knowing about it beforehand."

With a smile, Dillon replies, "Ye mean Reverend Mitchell knows everything?"

"No! You know I'm talking 'bout God."

"Well, at least you are doin' people good, Jay. I mean you heal the sick and cure diseases and stuff."

"In a way, Dillon, our jobs aren't that much different." Dillon gives Jay a sarcastic look. "What I'm saying is, people come to me because they want something. Something they believe that I have the ability to give them. People come to you because they want something they believe you can give them as well. I make them feel better physically, and you make them feel better emotionally. I mean building a house is one of the biggest investments most people will ever make. It can be a nerve-racking venture, but when they walk into that new house for the first time or spend that first Christmas there, that's the joy you give them. Think of all the photographs taken of your handiwork and how that will last for years in some family photo album. A hundred years from now, the Joneses great, great-grandchildren will look at photographs of this Christmas and the happiness shared by the Jones family all the subsequent years in their new house that you built."

Bringing Dillon out of his contemplative moment, Jay thinks out loud, "Well, I'll tell you one thing. I'm gonna stay here all night if I have to. No way I'm gonna walk all the way back to camp in this mess!"

"Bet camp is washed away."

Beating Dillon to the obvious conclusion, Jay adds, "Ye think our tents have drifted their way down to Fontana Lake yet?"

Dillon looks across the valley into the white haze of rain. "Nah!" Looking out over the valley, he pauses briefly. "Maybe." Then another moment passed as Dillon resigns himself to the inevitable. "Probably!" Standing up, he adds, "Well, if we're gonna spend the night in the cabin, I suggest we look around, get acquainted with the surroundings."

"Make sure there's no slithering critters around," Jay adds referring to snakes, mostly.

Dillon joins Jay by standing up and begins checking on the status of the clothes drying process, which if any progress has been made it is in the opposite direction of intended result. With the typical humidity in the Smokies and the added downpour, one could seemingly more easily breathe better with gills than a pair of lungs.

Jay stretches a moment and walks over to the cabin door. Opening the door, he tries to look into the cabin, but it takes a moment for his eyes to adjust to the change in light. Keeping his gaze in the area closest to him at the entrance to check for snakes, spiders, or anything else worthy of avoidance, his eyes scans further into the cabin. Over in the corner, Jay looks at what appears to be a dead man sitting in the corner.

"What is it?" Dillon asks peeking over Jay's shoulder from outside.

Taking a couple of steps into the room with Dillon on his heels, Jay points toward the slumped over body. The legs were fully extended out into the room with the left leg crossed over the right leg at the ankles, wearing worn boots with a hole in the ball of one foot and tattered overall pants a few inches too short, a dark-blue flannel shirt covered mostly by a long, white beard culminating to a point at about the level of the belt, which is made of homemade rope and wearing a torn dark-brown fedora hat pulled down low over the face. Old, gnarled hands rested clasped across the lap as the body remains absolutely motionless.

"Ye think he's dead?" Dillon whispers from behind, while looking over Jay's shoulder.

Lying next to the body is a long stick carved in the shape of a snake. Dillon looks at it closely to make sure it's not the real thing then he gently picks it up. Kneeling over the body, but at a safe distance, Dillon uses the stick to gently poke the body on the left shoulder. "Hey, buddy, anybody home?"

With a sudden jerk, the old man's head snaps upright revealing a dark, wrinkled, leathery complexion. Somewhere under thick, white eyebrows, there is a pair of worn eyes.

"I'ma here," answers the old man. "Watch what ye do with ma stick!" Taking the stick with his left hand, the old man stands up using the stick and a little help from Jay.

Releasing his gentle grip from the man's right arm after making sure he's gained his balance, Jay steps back and asks, "How long have you been here, sir?"

"Don't rightly know. A good bit I guess." The old man gazes directly into Jay's eyes allowing Jay to notice and admire his strikingly light-blue eyes. Looking over to Dillon, the old man motions toward a jar on the floor and asks, "Can ye tell me how much water I got in ma jar, sonny? My eyes hain't what they used to be."

Bending over to pick up a mason jar an arm's length away from where the old man was sitting, Dillon takes a sniff to rule out the presence of corn squeezins, a.k.a. moonshine. Holding it up into the light coming in from the outside for a better view, Dillon replies, "It looks about like it's half empty."

"Ye would say that!" the old man says sarcastically as he snatches the jar out of Dillon's hand and takes a long drink. Looking at Dillon, he continues, "I've been sittin in here fer a while now, long before you 'uns walked onto the porch. Ye know feller"—looking into Dillon's eyes—"ye come across as a pessimist, but a purty poor one at that. I've seen plenty uh fishermen in my life and ain't nary of 'em ever wuz a true pessimist. Would a fisherman make the next cast if'n he knew there ain't gonna be no fish, er even a chance of a fish at the other end? Course not! By nature, fishermen are optimists. Jest like gamblers pullin' on a one-armed bandit. They gots to believe that next pull or next cast is gonna be the big un."

The old man takes another swaller from the jar while Dillon looks at Jay and shrugs his shoulders. Jay laughs and adds, "I believe this man's got you pegged pretty good, Dillon."

"No, he don't! I ain't no pessimist, and I don't always see things half empty!"

The old man laughs loudly, "Hee, hee!" Then he asks, "It's gonna git dark directly. Either of you fellers got any vittles fer supper?"

Jay digs around in his day pack and pulls out a few granola bars. "I got a couple of fruit bars and some trail mix."

Dillon looks in the back pocket of his fishing vest and pulls out some beef jerky. "I got a little jerky, but it ain't much."

"Well, looks like you boys are plannin' to go hungry tonight, but you're in fer a treat!" The old man walks over and slowly picks up an old wicker basket creel sitting over in the corner. "I only got two today, but some little voice from way back and beyond done told me I better have enough fer dinner 'cause company's uh comin'." Opening the lid, he pulls out a large brown trout.

"Dang ole timer!" Dillon says with a surprised look on his face. "How big is that un? Looky, Jay, that thangs 'bout seventeen er eighteen inches, easy!" Looking at the old man, Dillon asks, "Where'd ye catch it at? Bet ye caught it in them beaver ponds, didn't ye?"

Somewhere from within the long gray beard, there was a smile as the old man replies, "Naw. I caught it down in Hazel Crick, purely accidental."

Admiring the broad body and dark black spots on the side of the sizeable brown trout, Dillon adds, "I tell you what, I'd like to get one out of here like that."

Laughing, the old man says, "I always heard even a blind hawg gits an acorn once in a while!"

Holding the trout with his left hand slid into the gill plate, the old man hands it to Jay. He reaches back into the creel with his left hand. "Well, I didn't mean to catch that 'un. I was going fer this 'un, and that lit-lun grabbed my fly first." Pulling an even larger trout out of the creel, the old man holds it up at Dillon for the effect he knew was coming.

"Hee, hee! I guess this blind hawg ain't so blind after all, eh, sonny?" The old man laughs as he pats Dillon on the shoulder with the creel in his right hand, his long gray beard swaying from side to side. Holding the big hook-jawed brown with his left hand, he hands it to Dillon whose eyes are round as silver dollars. Dillon takes the fish, moving it up and down and side to side as he admires its large girth and six-inch-wide tail.

"How the heck did you git this 'un?" Dillon asks, recovering from a bad case of jaw-drop syndrome.

Laughing with the old man as much as at Dillon, Jay watches the two large browns come out of the wicker creel, feeling like he was watching a magician pulling rabbits out of a hat, though more impressive.

The old man pauses, picks up his water jar, takes another swig, then answers, "Well, I jest saw his big ole tail fannin' side to side in the current biggern life out the far side of a rock. He had hisself jammed up under the rock purty good, but there was more of him than thur wuz rock." He pauses and winks at Jay with a large toothy grin somewhere within his bearded face. "From thur, hit wuz purty simple. Jest throw the right fly by his nose, and that's purty much hit." After a brief pause, he adds in a nonchalant tone, "Ain't rocket science er nuthin'...jest common sense. Hee, hee!" He finishes as he pats Dillon on the back again and shuffles his feet for a brief mountain dance.

Taking his eyes off the trout he's still holding, Dillon asks, "I thought you said you couldn't see? You expect me to believe ye saw its tail stickin' out from under a rock?"

Looking over at Jay as he elbows him in the side, the old man asks, "He don't listen too good, does he? Ye thank maybe I ought to speak a right bit slower fer 'im?" Looking back at Dillon, the old man answers, "I said my eyes ain't as good as they used to be. Never said I wuz blind." Reaching into his pack, the old man pulls out some cooking gear as he asks Jay to build a fire in the fireplace in the cabin. Jay notices the kindling is already in place as is enough wood to get a small fire going.

"Sure glad I kept both of 'em. I figured somebody would come by fer supper." The old man cuts each trout in half, sprinkling each piece with spices, then wraps each in aluminum foil and gently lays them onto the hot coals. As the water boils, he pours some off for coffee, strong and black, and uses the remaining water to cook rice.

The trout were broiled to a tender perfection as each slab of meat is over an inch thick, plenty enough for the three stranded fishermen to be satisfied. As they sit on the floor in the center of the cabin enjoying the broiled trout and rice, the skies outside darken. The old man pulls out a small lantern from his pack, lighting it to provide just enough light to cast faint shadows within the cabin. Dillon thinks how this is a perfect scene for a slasher movie.

"These trout are heavenly," Jay remarks as he savors each morsel of steaming, tender, trout. "I don't think I've ever eaten trout this large from out of the Park and definitely not as delicious anywhere. My compliments to the chef!"

Trying to chew a piece of fish without burning his mouth, the old man replies, "Well, I don't care much fer keepin' big fish. I respect 'em too much fer havin' lived so long in the crick. But sometimes, ye gotta make exceptions!"

"Well, I'm sure glad ye did," replies Jay.

"I heard dat!" Dillon adds with a mouthful of rice.

"Well, I ain't gonna feel too bad 'bout it. Thur's plenty more out thar biggern these."

As his curiosity continues to work on him, Dillon can no longer resist the question exploding to come out. "Sir, I just gotta ask. How the hell did you catch not one but two trout this big with such ease? I mean I can catch trout, but you make it sound like there's trout this size all up and down the creek!"

Unable to resist goading his dinner guest, he replies, "They is!" The old man asks with a serious look on his face, "Ye mean ye don't catch 'em like this every day?"

"I've been comin up here fer years. I've hooked several nice-sized uns, and lost a few biguns, but ain't had no luck bringin one in. I've even caught several big trout over in Big Bear Fork, on Little River, and one or two up around Tremont, but I can't buy one outta Hazel," complains Dillon.

"Don't need to. I got 'em here fer ye! Hee, Hee!" The old man laughs loudly.

As the evening progresses, Jay's medically honed senses notices the old man's movements. Having experience as a family physician in sizing up the physical attributes of individuals, he is somewhat perplexed by the old man. Thinking to himself that the old feller looks older than dirt, something about him at times reminds Jay of someone much younger. And though the spring in his step is long past, he does not lack for apparent muscle tone and physical agility considering his obvious advanced age and ability to navigate the treacherous rocks lining Hazel Creek. All of his motions are smooth and deliberate. The word that comes to Jay's mind is polished. "Looks like you get around pretty good, sir. Do you always come up here by yourself?"

"Yeah, purty much. Ain't too many fellers my age want to do nothin' but sit 'round and talk about their bowel movements. I git plum tired of hearin' the old folks complain about what hurts and what don't work no more. Ye young fellers don't know how lucky ye are to git round like ye do."

Jay looks over at Dillon and answers in a sarcastic tone, "Yeah, some people think and feel they're older than they are."

"Ain't no reason to git old too fast. I'm gonna stay young 'til I die," the old man says with a joyful gleam of determination in his eye.

Dillon laughs. "Are you sayin' you're young, old man?"

"Shore am! Tell me this, Dillon. Are ye young er old?" he asks pointing a bony finger at Dillon.

"Well, I figger I'm what ye call middle-aged."

"How ye figger? Are ye sayin yer midway to dead?"

Feeling a bit uncomfortable, Dillon sheepishly answers, "Well, I figger eighty is about the life span of a man, and I'm 'bout half way there. So I figger that makes me 'bout middle-aged."

"Who told ye that ye can only live to be eighty? The good book says the days of a man are threescore and ten, but thurs plenty of fellers who outlived that, in fact, Abraham wuz a dad when he's 'bout a hunnert! Methuselah lived fer 969 years. And his daddy, Enoch, still ain't dead!"

Trying to solidify his point, Dillon adds, "Well, there's no guarantee that any of us will live to be a hundred."

"True enough! But thur ain't no guarantee we won't neither, but I'll tell ye what. Ye either git busy livin' er git busy dyin'. I prefer the livin' part!" The old man tosses a small piece of wood onto the fire, then continues, "A feller once told me that he prayed to the Almighty fer all thangs so's he might enjoy life. Ye know what he got?" The old man pauses as he waits for Dillon's reply.

Dillon shrugs his shoulders.

"The good Lord gave him life so's he might enjoy all thangs."

Jay and Dillon look into the small fire. Just as it appears to be lifeless, it is rejuvenated by the added fuel.

The old man sits back, taking a sip of coffee then continues, "When ye first eyeballed me, Dillon, I saw pity in yer eyes. Made me wanna laugh like a cacklin' hen! All ye saw wuz an old gray-bearded, half-blind coot! Fact is, I pity you, sonny. I'm twice yer age and then some, and all ye thank 'bout is some number attached to how many times planet earth has danced 'round the sun since ye wuz born! Don't matter…don't matter uh tall! Ye got plenty o' good years left in ye, and if'n ye don't, is it worth feelin' sorry fer yourself? Course not! Ye too tore up over not bein' young no more when ye don't know what young is! I'll tell ye what, youth is wasted on the young!"

The old man pokes the fire with his snake stick, making sparks rise through the chimney. "It's not 'til ye been 'round fer a while that ye really start havin' fun…hee, heeee!" he adds as he slaps Dillon on the leg with his walking stick. "That's when ye see what's really important if ye open ye eyes. Stop worrin 'bout what ye ain't got, and be thankful fer what ye do got. I ain't no forty year old, but I ain't dead neither! Fact is, I look forward to bein' round fer a long spell yet. I figger I'll be out here doin' what the good Lord lets me git by with…hee, heeee!"

Pickin' up his stick, he pokes at the fire again, further mixing the coals as added life is breathed into the rising flames. "Tell ye what, Dillon. I'll let ye in on my fishin' secret."

Dillon perks up expecting to see the secret fly.

The old man tells Dillon, "Sonny, ye gotta fish smarter when ye git my age. Fer one thing, it takes a while longer to git started, especially in the morning. It also takes a whole lot longer to git over from some foolish move. It's the dumb moves ye gots to stay clear of. Ye ain't gonna see me jumpin to and fro from rock to rock er log to log. I'll take the long way if'n I needs to, but I'll git thur 'ventually… and I'll git that ole granddaddy trout too…hee, heeee!"

Visibly disappointed, Dillon replies, "I thought ye was gonna show me yer secret fly."

"Cain't show ye somethin' I ain't got. Besides, it ain't got nothin' to do with fishin', but everythang to do with how ye see thangs, and I don't mean a trout's tail waivin' out from behind a rock. I sees people like you purt near every day, Dillon. Ye love sunrises and the promise of a new day. A day yet written, and full of promise, like a clear canvas waitin' fer ye to paint the purtiest picture know'd to man, but ye hate to git up to see it! Ye love sunsets, stoppin' at times to appreciate God's handiwork, but when ye thank too much 'bout it, ye git all depressed because ye know the day's almost done over with, and ye feel like ye missed out on somethin'. Dillon, people like you cain't win. In every thang ye experience, ye let the bad parts outweigh the good 'uns, when often times thar ain't no bad parts at all, 'cept what ye conjured up in ye mind. Every minute is a blessin', a gift, if ye let it be." With that, the old man takes the last sip of coffee from his mug, tilts his hat down over his eyes, leans back against the wall, and is soon asleep.

As the sun rises the next morning, they find the old man is gone. Walking down the trail, they come to Bone Valley Creek. It is clear and slightly elevated but in great condition considering the previous afternoons rain. Jay and Dillon find their camp in good condition. Their tents did not make it to Fontana Lake after all. They have been spared the flood, but their stashed fish and the creel holding them are long gone somewhere in the rapids. Packing up camp, they head down Hazel Creek Trail back to the trailhead to catch the ferry back across Fontana Lake. Crossing the second bridge below Sugar Fork Campground, they spot the old man fishing a deep pool downstream. As they admire his slow, steady, but deliberate motions, he hooks into a trout, a big trout! Immediately, he breaks out into a little mountain dance with his rod held high, "Hee, heeee!" They can hear him laughing from fifty yards away.

Standing on the bridge leaning against the side rail admiring the master fisherman, Dillon feels envious. It is an envy that he never saw coming. He realizes he envies what the old man is and what he, Dillon, vows to be from this day forward. Easily half the old man's age, Dillon considers the many years left to enjoy each day the good Lord gives him. If he's lucky, someday he'll be the old man. Looking over at Jay, Dillon pats him on the back. "Better git goin' if we're gonna catch the ferry." With a smile breaking out on his face, he begins walking down the trail.

Following Dillon, Jay shakes his head as he looks back at the old man with his rod bent heavily under the weight of some undoubtedly massive trout, still shuffling his feet in some mountain dance. Over the roar of Hazel Creek passing beneath the bridge, he overhears Dillon, "Hee-heeee!"

THE PROTÉGÉ

Paying It Forward

With Dillon's continuing lack of success in landing a trophy of the female *Homo sapiens* persuasion, specifically one failed marriage and failure to maintain multiple relationships of any appreciable duration, even Jay noticed the sometimes restlessness in his friend's behavior and seemingly impatient and frustrated outlook on life. As friends often do over a beer or two, Dillon has a tendency to share his woes of life with his best buddy. Jay, being a physician of the body by trade, also has a more than reasonable understanding of the human psyche. Though not a professional in the sole treatment and evaluation of human emotions and mental aspects, Jay's time in medical school and time spent working with elderly patients has honed within him a certain ability to recognize particular tendencies, not unlike the tendencies of a trout rising to a mayfly.

Those tendencies more often than not lead to conclusions. The accuracy of those conclusions improving with age and experience.

However, the application of those conclusions is always the dicey part. Jay understanding the connection between physical and mental health of his human patients nearly as well as he does the hatch and rise of the Smoky Mountain trout. Something has been bubbling within Dillon and Jay, being a "fix-it" guy by nature and profession is naturally drawn to the challenge of solving the disconnect. And though Dillon is healthy from a physical standpoint, Dr. Jay knows his patient and friend is prone to periods of melancholy often triggered by the slightest ebb and flow of life.

As Jay is driving to his office, his mind is on Dillon's latest episode of feeling "out of sorts." Deep down as he drives across the bridge and glances upstream at Big Bear, he thought, Water is a bit low, but his mind was at work on solving Dillon's dilemma.

Walking into his office, Jay takes the lab coat off the hook on the back of his office door, and walks to the reception to look at his schedule of patients for the day. "Good morning, Margaret."

Margaret, a well-organized lady in her midfifties, has been the receptionist for Dr. Hembree, since not long after she graduated high school. She is the woman in charge of the office, and Jay lets her do what she does best—maintain order. One moment, she is sweet grandmotherly Margaret, then when necessary can out-bounce any bouncer between Asheville and Knoxville!

As Jay enters, Margaret stands up with a hot cup of coffee just as Jay likes it, fresh brewed with a little cream and honey. "Good morning, Dr. McMahan."

"Good morning, Margaret. Thanks," he replies as he takes the coffee and a sip. "So, what's the schedule like today?"

"It's a busy one! Gotta stay on time today, Doctor. Not too much chitchat and socializing. Not unless you want to work 'til eight o'clock!"

"Well, keep me straight, Margaret," Jay replies with a sneaky smile, knowing Margaret requires no such encouragement.

Jay's first patient is Rachel Cunningham. Rachel is fairly new to Laurel Cove. She moved in a few years ago to teach in the elementary school. She's had a rough spell lately. Being the wife of a naval officer currently stationed in a submarine somewhere in the Pacific, she essentially lives the life of a single mom. For the most part, what she's lacked in her husband being gone, the residents chip in to help out with house and car maintenance as is common in small southern towns. Her son Stevie, a thirteen-year-old eighth grader, is a popular kid at school. Still, life gets lonely at times in the months Lieutenant Cunningham is away. Rachel has been complaining of migraines, and at least to Jay, it is simply the physical manifestation of a many in her position—the scourge of any middle age mother, stress.

With Margaret's prodding, Jay stays on time by working through lunch and was even a few minutes early getting to his final patient of the day.

Jay's last patient is the pastor's wife, Selma Mitchell. She's always scheduled last because of the time required to get her out of the office and finished with the "fellowshipping." As he opens the exam room door, Ms. Mitchell is already seemingly in midsentence taking full advantage of the time allotted to her in the schedule. She reminds Jay of the church homecoming picnic this weekend. Ever the town gossip, she wears out not one but both of Jay's ears, the appointment taking more than the scheduled time, but not all of the expected allowing him out of the office and well before 8:00 p.m.

*****

To enjoy the wonderful afternoon, Debbie has dinner set up outside on the back porch to appreciate the evening view of the Smoky Mountains. Throughout dinner, it was obvious something is on Jay's mind. Debbie feels at times she is talking to herself. She is.

Out of nowhere, Jay takes a sip of iced tea and simply states, "Dillon said something strange yesterday. For Dillon, it was downright enlightening." Debbie sits down her fork and leans back for a moment realizing the topic on Jay's mind is at hand. "Dillon looked me straight in the eye and told me, and I quote, 'I feel like the Good Lord wants me to help somebody.'" Jay pauses for a moment. "Eh… who knows about Dillon though? Lately, he's more down than up. It seems even fishing can't pull him outta his slump."

Debbie, ever the source of common sense wisdom, replies with a shrug, "Well, he'll figure it out. By the way, is he gonna help at the picnic tomorrow?"

"Yeah, but reluctantly so. He's agreed to help the kids with the fishing poles at the trout pond. You'd think he's walking the Green Mile to his execution," Jay states with a laugh and is quickly joined by Debbie.

The next morning, Dillon comes by to pick up Jay and head off to River View Baptist Church to help get things set up for the annually RVBC picnic. A real Southern Baptist affair if there ever was one, complete with music by 3G, a.k.a. the Greenbrier Gospel Gang, a popular gospel bluegrass band and of course *tons* of food! Dillon is busy with anything construction related, including building a wooden "flume" for kids to ride their skateboards down and any other structures needed. Jay is over helping with the tent, all the while wondering when the first smashed thumb will come his way for "emergency treatment." There's a pond where there will be a fishing competition for the kids. After all is set up, Reverend Mitchell gathers everyone around, essentially 90 percent of Laurel Cove for a pre-picnic prayer. Only Reverend Mitchell can pray for everything, from A, avocado dip, to Z zucchini bread, and literally, I mean literally everything in between. Somewhere around the T, tater salad, Jay slightly opens his eyes and glances toward Dillon, who by now is wringing his hat into nearly disappearing into his hand! As a smile creeps upon his face, he feels Debbie, still with her eyes closed using her teaching superpower of detecting mischief, gently squeezing his hand signaling him to "behave."

After prayer, the picnic commences. It's been said that Baptists invented the potluck. Whether that's true or not will likely never been proven, but the evidence is definitely on their side. Beneath the one hundred feet long picnic shed, there's literally every conceivable kind of fried chicken. Both Jay and Dillon, as do most men of Laurel Cove, agree the best of the picnic is in the last twenty-five feet or so. That's where the desserts are. Of course, there are gallons of homemade ice cream in more flavors than at the Baskin-Robbins in Knoxville, plus cheesecakes, chocolate brownies, and too many deserts to mention.

After everyone has eaten, at least the first round, the fun commences. Of course, the "Ole Farts" are there in force. They're whittlin' many creations, mostly sticks. For once, the results of their whittlin' will be put to use as the wood shavings that will later be used to start the bonfire.

There are sack races, horseshoes, three-legged races, races where a raw egg is carried on a spoon as a relay, a greased pole, where $20 was attached to the top of a twenty-feet pole greased from top to bottom. Most of the teenage boys migrate to the pole. Eventually, enough grease is wiped away after multiple unsuccessful climbs to allow one patient climber to reach the prize at the top.

Then there's the fishing tournament for the kids. The pond just down from the campground is spring fed, keeping it cool in the shady areas even in the hottest of summertime. With trout stocked on Thursday, the pond is ready for the picnic. For one hour, each trout caught earns a ticket to be put in a prize bucket. The more trout, the more tickets, the more chances to win! Jay and Dillon naturally migrate to the fishing competition, so does good ole Melvin Cody. More of a handicap that help, Melvin spends most of his time expounding on his skills and the tale of his "monster trout" caught years ago using the blind hog theory. By Dillon's calculation, Melvin's once in a lifetime trout has grown six inches and three pounds at least according to the statistics on the newspaper photo hanging in Melvin's cubicle at First Fidelity Bank. While providing instruction to some of the lesser skilled competitors, they also hand out tickets. As the rules go, the trout must be touched by hand or by land in order to count. During the competition, both notice the skill of the eventual winner, Stevie. Even after the competition has ended and most boys have shifted their full attention to the $20 atop the greased pole, Jay and Dillon stand at a distance admiring Stevie's tenacity as the only one still chasing trout.

"He never stops," says Stevie's mom, Rachel, as she walks up with Debbie joining Dillon and Jay on the hillside overlooking the pond. "I try to get him involved with basketball and baseball. He does ride his bike, but that's to go fishing down at the creek. But I guess it's a good thing though. He could be out getting in trouble."

For a moment, Stevie looks up at the four watching from up on the hill. Rachel motions for Stevie to come up to where they're standing. As he approaches, Jay says, "Congratulations on winning the trout tournament!"

"Thanks, Dr. McMahan," Stevie replies shyly.

"As good as you are, I bet you could teach me a thing or two about trout," Dillon says as he smiles.

"I know who you are, sir. I can't teach you nothing."

The comment takes Dillon a bit off guard as he reaches out to give Stevie a congratulatory handshake.

"Have you ever used a fly rod, Stevie?" Jay asks.

"No, sir. But I'd like to learn how someday."

Jay glances at Debbie. Both are on the same page. Jay looks at Stevie and says, "Say, Stevie. How would you like to learn how? Do you have any plans next weekend?"

Stevie looks at his mom for a second.

Dillon smiles. "You don't have a date, do you, Stevie?"

"Lord no!" Stevie shoots back. "Even if I did, I'd break it to go fishing."

"You're a smart man, son." Dillon laughs.

"To my knowledge, Stevie doesn't have any plans next Saturday," Rachel answers. "Stevie, if you wanna go, it's up to you."

A huge smile pops on Stevie's face. "Yes, sir, I mean, doctor. I'd like to go!"

"Just call me Jay, Stevie."

Later that evening, after the $20 has been rescued from the top of the greased pole, all races won and all desserts gone, the bonfire is lit thanks to the "old farts club" donation of whittlin' shavings, under the direct supervision of the Laurel Cove Volunteer Fire Department. Greenbrier Gospel Gang fires up their mandolin, fiddle, banjo, and base with their rendition of "I'll Fly Away" as the jubilant crowd claps, shouts and sings.

On their drive home, Debbie looks at Jay asking a question to which she already knows the answer, "Why did you ask Stevie to go fishing with you next Saturday? You know you have that medical conference to attend in DC?"

"Oops! It looks like I might've double-booked myself," he replies with a smile. "Hmm…now who could I get to fill in for me?" Debbie and Jay exchange a smile.

The next day, Reverend Mitchell preaches a sermon from Psalms 82. Walking out of church afterward, Jay, Debbie, and Dillon are greeted by the Reverend and Ms. Selma.

"I enjoyed the sermon, Reverend," Debbie states smiling.

"Yeah, after yesterdays' picnic, it was a good follow-up. Really makes a man think, Reverend," adds Jay.

"Glad y'all enjoyed it," Reverend Mitchell replies. "The Lord led me to preach about being a father to the fatherless. I know there's someone out there that the good Lord is speaking to. I just pray they're listening."

As usual, Dillon just smiles and nods as he shakes Selma and the reverend's hands. Not really wanting to get into a last-minute theological or philosophical discussion, he makes his usual beeline to his truck. On the way, he looks at Jay. "Don't you hate it when the preacher is preaching at you?"

Jay with a puzzled look asks, "I'm not sure what you mean, Dillon? Care to enlighten me?"

Dillon simply shakes his head as he hops in his truck and drives away.

"I think we all know what Dillon is talking about," Debbie says, looking at Jay.

Smiling, Jay replies, "Yeah, I'll wait 'til after a while to let it sink in before I lower the boom. Poor Dillon. Knows exactly what's going on yet doesn't have a clue."

That afternoon, the final piece is pushed in place. Dillon answers the phone, "What's up, Jay?"

Wincing, Jay makes the push as Debbie listens next to him. "I need a favor, buddy."

"Sure, Jay. What can I do for you? Need something fixed at your house or office?"

"No. Everything is working fine," he replies, looking at Debbie with the "well, here it goes" look. "I got a call that I'm needed in Washington, DC, to attend a meeting about some medical regulations under review. They want the input of a small-town doc, and I drew short straw."

"So you need me to drive you to the airport?"

"No, Debbie's gonna do that."

"Well, what can I do for you?"

"Well…I sorta need you to fill in for me?"

"Bein' a doctor? I can't give shots, and you know I ain't fond of blood and the smell of rubbing alcohol."

"No, I need you to fill in on Saturday."

"What's happening Saturday?"

"Well, I'd promised to take Stevie on a fishing trip." Without giving Dillon any time, Jay continues, "I feel so bad for the kid with his dad gone, and I can't help but thinking of how we were taken out on our first trip by Pop when we were thirteen. Imagine where we'd be if it hadn't been for that first trip. That's a time I'll never forget." By now, Jay knows he's gotten a good enough swing to at least get a base hit if not a home run, but you never know.

Silence, which seems forever, but in reality, only several seconds in length is interrupted finally.

"You know, Jay. Somehow I knew when I walked out of church, I would end up fishing with Stevie. As you say, 'There's no such thing as coincidences'? Well, I got this voice telling me to take that boy out. You know I'm not the most patient guy in the world."

"Well, you'll work it out. Just go out and give him a good time. Do you remember, when you told me last week that you felt like God is wanting you to help somebody? Well, maybe this is it. Just go out and spend the morning with the kid with no expectations but to let him have some fun. Who knows, you may accidentally have a little fun yourself. I'd really appreciate you filling in for me." By now, Jay is looking at Debbie who is holding up two thumbs and smiling. Jay nods in return like, "Yeah, we got him!"

After a quick phone call to Stevie about the change of plans, Dillon picks Stevie up early Saturday morning. Upon arrival, Stevie is sitting on his front porch with everything Dillon had told him to have ready. As is habit as much as tradition, Dillon takes Stevie down to Smoky's Café. Upon sitting in the usual booth, Luanne comes over with a pot of coffee. "Good morning, Stevie! It's not often I see you here this early in the morning. Did you find a bum on the side of the road and decide to treat him to a decent breakfast?" she asks while nodding in Dillon's direction.

Stevie, not sure what to say and unaware of the history between the ole high school sweethearts Luanne and Dillon, is at a loss for words.

Dillon looks a Luanne, then Stevie, and replies, "Don't worry, Stevie. Years of smelling bacon grease has gone to her head. Besides, the best breakfast she serves is never decent."

"What can I get you, shug?" Luanne asks Stevie.

Answering for him, Dillon replies, "Stevie, I recommend the fisherman's breakfast and a cup of strong, black coffee. That's a piece of tenderloin, two eggs, and biscuits and gravy." Then he looks at Luanne and back to Stevie and adds, "If you'd like chocolate milk, that'd be fine too. Even Luanne can't mess that up."

By now, Stevie is trying not to laugh at either as his breakfast and fishing trip is on the line, so he politely smiles and looks at Luanne, "I'll have what Mr. Webb is having, ma'am."

"Okay, sweetie, I'll get you the fisherman's breakfast. I'll get the bran muffin and skim milk for you, *Mr. Webb*," she replies as she smiles at both and walks away.

To clarify the just completed order process, Dillon goes into the brief history between him and Luanne. "Stevie, do you remember when you said if you had a date, you'd break it and go fishing? Well, that's sorta why Luanne is sore at me. She was my girlfriend in high school, and a few too many broken dates for fishing trips was more than enough for her. I think she's been sore at me ever since," he says with a laugh. "But that's life."

Over breakfast, where Stevie does his best to get the black coffee down, but with Dillon's help in adding some cream and sugar made it a bit more palatable, Dillon asks about school and Stevie's dad and family and anything else of interest to a thirteen-year-old, just getting to know him. Dillon shares some of his family story as well all the while thinking this kid is all right.

As they leave, Luanne gives Stevie a hug and a bit of advice. "Good luck today, Stevie. If you see a bear, just remember, all you have to do is outrun Dillon. As old as he is, you shouldn't have a problem." She smiles and winks as she walks back to the kitchen.

Stevie can take no more and for the first time shows a smile and signs of relaxing a bit.

On their drive to the Smokies, Dillon explains the basics of trout fishing. Mostly, how to approach the skittish wild trout and thus the reason for his instructions to Stevie to wear something dark, drab, or preferably camouflage that will help blend in with the surroundings, decreasing the likelihood of being spotted by the wily fish. Dillon goes on to explain the characteristics of the three species of trout that swim the streams of the National Park. How the beautiful brook trout are the only native, indigenous trout species and are mostly relegated to the higher elevations with the cooler water. Also, they're the smallest of the three species likely due to their life spent in tiny creeks with limited food and short life span. Then come the rainbows, they were delivered to the Smokies by trains during the logging days as a way to supplement the loss of the brook trout. They're more spread out and numerous in the middle and lower stretches of the Park waters. They too have a short life span of typically three to four years and tend to be more aggressive, thus pushing the timid brookies upstream. Then there's the brown trout. Dillon pauses momentarily to reminisce on some battles in the past with big browns. He describes the browns as the "bad boys" of the Smoky Mountain trout. "Yeah, several years ago, the park rangers shocked two big browns out of Abrams Creek. One was purt near thirty inches and was thirteen years old! They're smart and grow faster than rainbows and brook trout. When you hook a big one, whereas 'bows tend to leap out of the water, a big brown typically heads to deep water and shakes his head as he tries to rid himself of the hook."

As they turn up the road along Greenbrier Creek between Gatlinburg and Cosby, Dillon explains the different types of water, the long, slow pools, and the faster shoals and the advantages of each.

After a few miles up the road, it turns to gravel, and not long after driving up over a rise, they stop at a pullout beside a slower stretch of water below some shoals. Dillon talks Stevie through putting on a pair of his extra wading boots, which though a little large, wearing two pair of thick socks will suffice. "Remember, Stevie. Every rock is out to get you and make you fall. It's the sole purpose of why they're in the creek, for you to bang your shins and bust yer butt on!" Dillon pulls up his right pant leg. "See this, I did this when I was a teenager, and this is from two months ago." With a sly smile, he adds, "I have the shins of a ninety-year-old, but they still get me around."

As Dillon rigs up his favorite nine-foot, four-weight rod, he walks Stevie through rigging up the eight-foot five-weight he has for Stevie. Both tie on the fly Dillon likes to use on Greenbrier this time of year, then positions Stevie next to the truck and teaches him a simple roll cast. "This is purty much all you need to do, Stevie. Just roll it over like this, pick up the tip of ye rod to get the extra slack out of your line, and watch your leader for a slight, but quick twitch. More than likely, that's a bite." After of few minutes of practice and a few minor corrections, they finish the short casting lesson.

"You know, Stevie, a lot of guides bring people up here and spend hours trying to teach them how to cast sixty feet!" He smiles for a moment, then adds, "You know, if you cast half that distance in most places up here, you'll wind up in a dozen trees and a messy tangle in one of the rhododendron bushes! I'm not a caster. I am a catcher."

Dillon walks Stevie down toward the stream, pausing several feet back from the edge of the water. "It's always important to scan the water before getting too close to it. You never know when a big ole brown might be hanging out right next to the bank or in the tail out of the pool feedin'. Sometimes, if ye don't spook him, you can get a good shot at him."

Not spotting anything, they gently step into the creek and wade across to the other side through some pea gravel. Dillon carries both rods as Stevie gets used to wading through the cold water, trying to avoid the dreaded crotch chill and getting used to the slick rocks. Sitting down on a rock, Dillon coaches Stevie on how to read a stream, explaining the different types of trout lies, such as out in the current, along the bank, and how to fish around rocks. He also explains how to visualize the entire pool from bottom to top and plan his route so that he can fish the water thoroughly and spook the fewest fish along the way. "In most cases, it's best to fish upstream. The reason is that when trout are feeding, they're looking upstream for the food coming down to them. It's sorta like a conveyor belt. But there are exceptions to nearly every rule as, to be honest," Dillon pauses briefly for effect. "Trout don't know the rules!"

Stevie is quiet for most of the morning trying to soak in the surroundings, getting untangled from trees, and trying not to die by falling on the rocks. All the while, Dillon fishes at a relaxed pace allowing Stevie to watch the simplicity of what most call "high-stick nymphing," and Dillon simply calls "fishin'." Dillon finds himself feeling a bit strange like he is on a vacation day of fishing where there is no self-imposed pressure to catch a lot of trout or a big brown. He is always his biggest critic. Jay has laughed at Dillon many times over the years at how Dillon would talk down to himself if he didn't feel like he'd measured up to his self-imposed standard of getting better and learning something on each trip, even if learning what not to do.

Though Dillon thinks it strange how people talk to themselves, he does not feel the same way about doing it while he is fishing. Dillon spends some time fishing, so Stevie can watch and learn by example and occasionally gives instruction but not in a nagging way. First and foremost, he wants Stevie to learn in his own way and on his own terms. He doesn't want to be overbearing and critiquing or correcting every cast or action that does not match how Dillon would have done it. He just lets Stevie take his own path. What he doesn't realize is how much of a sponge Stevie is in being so interested in something that few kids his age are able to experience. Every sight and sound are being absorbed and catalogued in his young mind.

Dillon is focused on a run flowing up and beneath a large boulder looking for a slight move of a big tail fin or the white of a large mouth open when a sudden flash of activity catches his attention back to his right. It's Stevie! He has caught his first Smoky Mountain trout. Like a proud papa, Dillon is thrilled. What makes him most proud for Stevie's success is Stevie's attitude. Unlike some who yell, "Fish on!" or whoop and holler, that's always gotten on Dillon's nerves, is how Stevie is very calm and methodical, playing the small rainbow and landing it in the net, acting as though he has done it before, which he has, but not in the Smokies. This is likely his first ever wild trout! And the kid did great.

Per the advice of Jay, Dillon has brought a small camera to "capture the moment" to share with Rachel who'd be proud of her little man. Over the next few hours, Stevie catches two more little rainbows, and around eleven o'clock, Dillon sits down on a large, flat rock with a good view of the Greenbrier Valley. Away from the dirt road that paralleled the stream, they are in a good, quiet spot to enjoy the feel of the warm sun and hear the sound of the water as it courses its way over and around the river stones, the occasional Kingfisher chattering its way down the creek and Dillon's favorite the yellow-throated warbler, somewhere back in the woods.

Dillon gets out a couple of peanut butter and honey sandwiches and RC Colas. Also, as a local tradition for first timers, Dillon opens a can of Vienna sausages. Curling up his nose a little at the site of the tiny wieners, Stevie gives Dillon the look like, "What am I supposed to do with those?" to which Dillon answers, "It's an old tradition handed down from the man that took me and Jay on our first fishing trip when we wuz about your age. We liked 'em back then. I can't say so much now, but on a rare occasion such as today when a first timer catches trout, it's definitely something worth remembering."

Slowly taking one with his fingers, Stevie sniffs then takes it into his mouth and chews. After a few chews, he takes a gulp of the RC more to get the taste out of his mouth than a chaser. With a hard swallow, he says, "It's not too bad once you get it down."

Dillon laughs. "Well, the bad news is it don't get no better with the next un!"

Sitting there enjoying the sandwiches and getting his share of the Vienna sausages, that's three, Stevie opines about how pretty the Smokies are and how lucky he is to be able to fish its creeks. "I really appreciate you bring me up here, Dillon. My mom would bring me if she knew where to take me, but she wouldn't let me get to far into the creek if it's just me fishing. I don't think it'd be much fun with her telling me"—in his best impression of a nagging mother—"Not too far now, come on back." Stevie pauses as he imagines his mom saying just those words, "That'd probably scare the fish away."

"Well, you're probably right. But as a mom, it's her job to worry about you a little too much. That's what moms do, ya know."

While sitting on the rock feeling the sun's rays on his face, Dillon's memory goes back to his first trip in the Smokies. His first trip with Jay and his grandfather, Pop Harvey, didn't turn out so well. "You're lucky, Stevie. When Jay and I went on our first trip, it was definitely a lot colder that day. And the trout had a case of lockjaw for me and Jay. But my grandfather, Pop, always caught his limit." Dillon pauses for a moment to remember his mentor. "Pop was the best fisherman I ever saw. It was like he had a solution to any fishing challenge. He was never flashy or anything, but man he could flat catch trout when he took a notion." Somewhere up Greenbrier, Dillon's gaze loses its focus and peers through a window to the past. "I'd like to believe that Pop knows how special that day was for me and Jay. Through all these years, what Pop taught Jay and me has been a bond that will never break. Some would say Jay and I are blood brothers, but in reality, we're trout brothers, if there is such a thing," Dillon finishes with a laugh. Not one to go too deep, Dillon's attention snaps back to the present as his eye is caught by a mink running along the bank on the far side of the creek.

As the day progressed, Dillon finds Stevie's thoughts and impressions not unlike those of his at the age of thirteen as he thinks back on his first trip so many years ago. Pop allowed them to make their own mistakes, and with them, Pop sure laughed a lot. A whole lot. Stevie's first day, though not as humorous as that first day for Dillon and Jay so many years ago, is still by all accounts a success. Stevie did have "the big one," the slip that took him underwater. Fortunately, the shock of the cold Smoky Mountain water was lessened by the sun's warmth. Overall, Stevie wound up with five trout, one a nice ten-inch rainbow.

*****

The following week having come home from his conference, Jay got the lowdown summary from Debbie of last week's fishing trip of Dillon and Stevie. After completing his last medical note, Jay makes a quick stop at Smoky's Drugstore. Stopping by Dillon's house, he notices Dillon has company in his fly shop, a small building behind his house. Jay walks into the fly shed with three bottles in his hand. He opens them, giving one to Dillon, one to Stevie, and one for himself. Stevie takes the brown bottle, then gives Jay a leery look.

Jay smiles. "It's okay, Stevie, Reverend Mitchell won't preach too hard at you for one bottle of root beer. Besides, I won't tell your mom if Dillon promises not to."

Dillon is in the middle of teaching Stevie how to tie a crow fly. Jay walks over to visually inspect Stevie's progress. "Well, if your tying skills are any indication of your fishing skills, the trout are in a whole lot of trouble!" Then walking over to Dillon's vice. "Now with Dillon's fly, there'd be no danger at all except that he can catch a trout with a bare hook!"

"Really?" Stevie asks surprised.

"No, not really," answers Dillon. Then with a serious look off to somewhere unknown, Dillon thinks for a moment then changes his mind. "Well, if I can get close enough with the right cast, I believe I'd have a shot at it." Stevie notices that Dillon's look is still off in the distance as a sneaky smile creeps upon his face. Stevie hopes he too can go there someday.

"And I believe you'd hook it!" Jay adds with a laugh.

"Wow…" Stevie whispers as he takes a sip of the root beer and refocuses his attention on wrapping the split crow feather around the size eight hook.

The following weekend, the three share a trip to the Little River between Gatlinburg and Townsend. Driving along the road, Jay as usual is driving for their communal safety. Not that Dillon is a bad driver; in fact, he's very good. However, his proclivity to scan the creek for large browns more than the curvy road that follows Little River as he's driving has nearly resulted in disaster more than a few times. Finally, Dillon breaks the silence. "I think this is a good spot, Jay. What do you think, Stevie?"

"Uh. Well, today I think I'll defer to your decision," Stevie replies with a thoughtful gaze as he takes in his first sight of Little River.

As the three gear up, tying on their wading boots, assembling the pieces of their fly rods, attaching the reel and running the fly line through the eyelets, Jay says, "Let me show you a little trick, Stevie." Pulling about thirty feet of fly line from his reel, he wraps it around a tree and gently but firmly pulls. "I do this to remove the memory out of my fly line. Do you know what memory is, Stevie?"

With a sincere look, Stevie answers, "It's what my mom says old people lose."

Dillon and Jay both laugh. "Well, Stevie, I guess that's true, but memory in fly line is when it curls up all by itself making it hard to cast far and doesn't float on the water as well, so I am straightening it out so that it will cast better."

Ever the antagonist, Dillon adds, "You remember how I showed you how to make short roll casts last week, Stevie?" Stevie nods. "Well, Stevie, today Jay's gonna blow your mind. But for now, just focus on what I showed you last week, and you'll do fine. Has your mom ever told you to 'Do as I say and not as I do'?"

"Yeah, but I don't like it much when she says that," Stevie replies with a resigned look. "It usually doesn't work in my favor."

"Well, today watch and learn, but stick with what you know fer now," answers Jay.

Stevie notices that though Dillon wears a camouflage Dale Earnhardt ball cap, the same cap he's worn since the late eighties, Jay wears a brown, wide-brimmed hat. He doesn't know, but it is called an "outback" hat. Noticing Stevie's strange stare at his hat, Jay explains, "Several years ago, Dillon tried to make a movie star outta me. You ever heard of the movie, *A River Runs Thru It*?"

"Yeah, I've seen it," Stevie answers still looking at the hat on Jay's head.

"Well, Dillon thought he was giving me a prank gift, but instead, I've come to really like it," he says, taking it off to look it over.

"That makes one of you at your house," Dillon yells from the start of the trail to the creek.

"Yeah, Debbie says I look goofy in it, but I tell ya, it's a pretty darn good hat. It keeps the sun off the back of my neck. It enhances the hearing, which is good when fishing below a dam and the sound of the water subtly increases, giving an early warning of the wave of water on its way because they started generating. But best of all, it is awesome on a rainy day!" Holding the hat to give Stevie a better view, he adds, "Yeah, it's getting old, and it's seen a lot, and I do have to waterproof it occasionally, but the felt really repels the rain. What ole Dillon meant as a joke turned out to be great." Placing it back on his head with a look of satisfaction, he starts down the trail. "Dillon won't admit it now, but when rain is in the forecast, he breaks his out, that I bought him I might add. And he wears it!"

Walking the last fifty feet or so to the creek, Stevie notices Dillon staring at the water, then Jay stopping slightly behind Dillon to stare as well. "You see anything, Stevie?" Jay asks.

Stevie states in a straight deadpan tone, "Water, rhododendron, trees, and a snake on the rock beside Dillon."

Suddenly and without a word, Dillon jumps straight up and runs in no particular direction except away from where he was standing, high stepping and rock hopping as he goes. After about thirty feet, Dillon stops to look for the snake. Jay and Stevie break out into a gut splitting, tear-jerking laugh!

"Oh, that was perfect, Stevie. Absolutely perfect!" Jay yells approvingly as he and Stevie fist bump.

"Oh, I see. A little tag team, pile on action. We'll see how the rest of the day goes," Dillon replies, acting as though he's angry, but all the while trying not to laugh.

As Dillon and Stevie work some shoals, Jay slips quietly upstream to where he pauses to observe the water in a long tail out of a pool. After careful study, Jay strips line off his reel and quickly makes a thirty-five-foot cast into the long pool.

"Whoa...look at Jay!" Stevie exclaims. "I've never seen anybody cast that far before."

"He's using dry flies. When he gets to some of these pools, he likes to cast a dry fly to see if he can get something to rise to the surface. More than likely today, he has a yellow stimulator that imitates a yellow stonefly that's starting to hatch. And I bet he also has a small, number 16 bead head pheasant tail dropped off of it a few feet to tempt something beneath." Dillon continues as he describes what is known as the "dry-dropper" method, "It enables him to cast thirty or more feet while he is way out of view of a trout. If a careful approach is used, he has a dual purpose of the top, dry fly as both a fly and as a strike indicator. If a trout doesn't fully rise to the dry but instead takes the subsurface dropper, the tug on the top fly will suddenly make it disappear beneath the surface where Jay can lift the fly rod, hopefully resulting in a hook set."

After a few casts of his own, Stevie glances upstream to where Jay is hooked into his first trout. Immediately afterward, Dillon, who has crossed the creek from where Stevie is, hooks into one as well. The success of the two refocuses Stevie on his task at hand, "getting on the board" as Dillon calls catching the first trout.

As they work their way upstream through the rapids, Stevie "gets on the board" by catching a nice little brown trout. His first brown trout. Looking across the creek, Dillon gives Stevie a smile and a thumbs up.

Throughout the day, Jay notices the bond already forming between Stevie and Dillon. Dillon slows down to make time to teach Stevie how to approach different types of water, how to adjust his cast to get the fly beneath overhanging trees, helping adjust the strike indicator on Stevie's leader so that he can better detect and react to quick strikes as he high-stick nymphs through the pocket water. Jay admires Dillon's patience in how he isn't too quick to correct and even allows Stevie to make simple mistakes. Though Stevie is likely too young at this point in his life, Dillon and Jay know more is often learned from mistakes than success.

Toward early afternoon, Jay is looking at a nice run along a wall on the far side of Little River. Looking over his shoulder downstream, he pauses as Dillon and Stevie make their way upstream to him. From his angle, Jay is out of sight of trout in the pool. Still he sits down on a flat rock and motions for Stevie to come to where he is sitting. With his best stealth approach and nearly crawling, Stevie quietly reaches Jay's side.

"Wanna see something cool?" Jay asks Stevie. Stevie nods.

"Look over there slightly upstream along that rock wall. Keep watching…there! Did you see that?"

"I saw something, but not sure what it was," Stevie replies.

"Keep looking…tell me when you see it again."

"There! I saw that!" Stevie replies in a quiet excitement.

"That's a pretty good rainbow rising to what we call a mayfly. It's a small insect that swims to the surface. Once on the surface, it must dry its wings so that it can fly off to mate. I can tell how the trout is feeding because only its nose breaks the surface. It's in a good feeding lane and sipping the insects as they drift right to him on the water trying to fly off."

"There it is again!" Stevie notes with excitement.

"What I did is tie on a number 16 mayfly pattern to match that color." With a quick motion of his right hand, Jay grabs a mayfly fluttering by. Holding it on his index finger, he draws it close to Stevie's face to where he can more closely examine the shape of its slender body, long legs, tail fibers, and upright wings. Releasing the mayfly from off his finger, Jay lets it fly off. "Now, let's see what we can do with that trout."

Sneaking a little closer, Jay strips out just enough fly line for the cast he'll make. With a single backcast, Jay gently places the fly several feet from where he and Stevie have noticed the trout's nose breaking the surface. Watching intently from behind, Dillon is looking at the fly as it drifts downstream. Suddenly, the nose appears as the fly vanishes! Jay lifts his rod tip as he strikes home with the hook. Quickly working the rainbow back toward his net, Stevie erupts, "Yes! That was awesome!" Stevie walks over to where Jay is removing the hook from the upper lip of the twelve-inch rainbow.

On their drive back to Laurel Cove, Dillon asks Stevie what his favorite part of the day was.

"When Jay saw that trout rising and put on the right fly to catch it. I want to be able to do that!"

Dillon gives Jay a disproving look. "Well, I think you ruined him."

Jay looks at Stevie. "Yeah, that's always fun, but as Dillon can attest, there's other exciting ways to catch trout. For example, you've not seen it yet, but as much as I love to cast to and catch rising trout, I love using a streamer and feeling the hit and powerful runs and head shakes of a big trout. You feel the wham!" Jay uses his left hand to mimic the head of a trout attacking a fly. "And you know its big, but you're not sure just how big until you get a good look at it, sometimes not until you're bringing it into the net. Sometimes, they get off or break off, and you're left wondering just how big that brown was!"

"You know what I like?" Dillon adds. "I like it when you're in a downpour and the water is getting dingy. You cast a heavy nymph into a shallow run, and the water explodes like somebody threw a five-pound rock into the pool. You set the hook, and it's off to the races as you chase a big brown all over the creek! Now *that's* fishing!" Dillon adds with an excited voice as only one whose experienced such an episode can relate.

A few weeks later, the threesome decide on a trip above Elkmont Campground on Little River. After walking a ways up the Little River Trail, formerly an old train bed from the logging days, they come upon a favorite spot from the days when they were Stevie's age and learning from Pop. Stevie and Jay ease down from the trail to the stream to fish back up to a long, slick pool where Dillon has stepped into the water and into a shallow set of riffles just downstream from the tail out, looking into the water all the while moving slow and deliberately. Mimicking what he has learned over the years from watching the movements of the great blue herons that often feed in the creeks of the Smokies, Dillon suddenly pauses.

He is studying a spot not more than twenty feet from where he's standing. He can't believe what his eyes are seeing through his brown polarized glasses no more than five minutes after gearing up. A large brown trout is lying motionless in a small slot in the tail out just beyond a row of river stones stretching across the creek, below which he is standing. The coloring of the trout is a perfect blend with the brown, stony bottom of Little River. The water surface is perfectly flat and transparent, making it as though he were looking through clear glass. He can easily determine the size and even pick out individual red and black spots on the side of the large brown.

The only movement it makes is a slight wave of its tail fin as it maintains its position on the bottom as no more than two feet of water passes overhead. The fish has no idea Dillon is standing so close as it waits for breakfast to drift from the depths of the pool somewhere out in the distance. Dillon slowly glances around to where Stevie is fishing about thirty yards downstream in the shoals with Jay. Though he wants to yell and wave for Stevie to come up to where he is standing to give him a shot at the big brown, he knows doing so would likely give away his location to the easily spooked ole trout resulting in nobody having a shot at it.

So he does what he must and casts his number eight guinea fly with his nine-foot four-weight fly rod and nine-foot leader tapered down to a 4X about five feet upstream from the nose of the trout. He is standing at four o'clock from the trout's perspective, and though he wishes he was closer to a six o'clock position, directly behind the trout, at least from the side, he knows he's not casting directly over the aged, wily trout. From his position, he can keep his rod tip up in high-sticking fashion, guiding the leader to the side of the fish yet allowing the fly to bounce along the bottom in the clear water right to its nose.

Reflecting back later, he does not remember the actual take of the fly, but something in his senses tells him to set the hook. Immediately, the brown rushes upstream through the tail out toward the head of the pool and to deeper water. Keeping his eye on the moving fly line tracing the direction of the trout shooting through the water as it follows, he lets out a loud whistle, knowing it will pierce through the rumble of the rapids to the two fishermen downstream.

By now, the trout is settled into the deep, dark green depths of the pool as Dillon positions himself in the tail-out of the pool, keeping himself downstream. In a matter of a few minutes, Jay and Stevie are standing on the bank with Jay giving Stevie a play by play of what Dillon is doing to defeat the powerful foe. "Dillon is keeping his line tight to keep pressure applied while keeping himself downstream from the fish. That way, if it tries to use the current to its advantage and make a run downstream and into the rapids, Dillon will be there with his net. As long as the fish is upstream, Dillon has the advantage of the current." Stevie remains silent as he watches the battle between the master of the creek and the master fisherman, both seasoned in their respective skills.

Several feet below the surface, the brown is using a tried and true method in violently shaking its head to dislodge the hook or break the tiny tippet by rubbing it along the side of any of the many rocks along the bottom. Unfortunately for the trout, Dillon has danced this dance many times and remains cool as he is constantly changing his fly rod from right to left. "See how he's moving his rod around? Many fishermen will simply lift the rod tip straight up where much of the tension is against gravity. Dillon moves his from side to side to keep the trout confused, making it second-guess where Dillon is located. Fighting a large trout can be as much a mental as a physical battle. If nothing else, this tends to wear them down faster."

Beginning to feel fatigue, the large trout suddenly bolts downstream, working with the current instead of fighting against it and the pull it senses in the side of its jaw. Dillon uses his left had to strip the slack out of the line as the fish moves toward him. To cut off any chance of escape into the shoals below, Dillon rushes over in the shallow tail out to cut off the trout's planned escape downstream. "Notice how Dillon is making a lot of splash as he runs? That'll scare the trout from coming any closer so that it'll turn back upstream." Realizing its escape has been cut off, the trout turns and works its way over to a bolder on the far side of the stream. Having quickly reeled in the slack, Dillon now has the trout back on his reel where he can let the reel's drag apply resistance. Moving his rod to the left, Dillon skillfully applies more pressure allowing his rod tip to absorb the shock of the continued head shakes as the brown continues to tire. Dillon can now feel the power of the head shakes diminish as the trophy trout becomes ever weaker. As quickly as the fight began, the big brown rolls up on its side, drifting in the current and into Dillon's net.

Finally, Stevie let out a "yes" as he feels relief in knowing the battle is over and runs down into the water to see the trophy brown.

As only a teammate can, Jay has a measuring tape out to quickly measure it. Stevie pulls out a small waterproof camera his dad sent to him to take a photo of the massive trout. "I've never seen any trout like that before!" he exclaims as he gently rubs his finger over its slick side and his finger along the hook at the tip of its bottom jaw while Dillon holds the twenty-one-inch brown down in the water within his net.

"That's called the kype," Dillon instructs as he allows Stevie to inspect his catch. "The big males use that to fight other males during spawning season in the fall."

"I never knew they had teeth," Stevie adds more in a questioned tone.

"Those aren't really teeth as we have, Stevie," Jay replies. "They are sharp little cartilage edges along their jaw, but yeah, they can hurt!"

With a nod from Dillon, Jay reaches over to hold the net. "You wanna release it, Stevie?" Dillon asks. Stevie nods. "Now hold him gently. Never squeeze a trout that you're gonna let go. You can squeeze too hard and kill 'em." Dillon helps Stevie cradle the brown instructing him to hold it facing upstream, so water can flow through its gills.

"That's right. Just hold it upright. When it's ready, it'll take off on its own."

Stevie, watches the large mouth of the brown open and close as he gently cradles its thick body in his hands. Slowly, Stevie feels the large brown regaining its strength. Gradually, with increasing thrusts of its wide tail the trout takes over, swimming free from Stevie's hands. Stevie keeps his eyes on the long, hydrodynamic body as it makes its way upstream to the depths where it had earlier attempted to escape. Eventually, it disappears down into the emerald green depths of the pool upstream. "That was awesome! Thanks for letting me release it, Dillon!"

As the summer fades into fall, with the help of Jay's and Dillon's tutelage, Stevie's skills grow at a seemingly phenomenal rate. As Dillon puts it, "That boy absorbs stuff like mamaw's cathead biscuits absorb gravy."

By now, Stevie is making regular trips to tie flies with Jay and Dillon. One blustery, rain-filled Sunday afternoon, Dillon, Jay, and Stevie have gotten together for some serious fly tying. On the agenda are big streamer and heavy nymph patterns to use on winter trout. As the three are tying flies in Dillon's fly tying shed, they begin to reflect on Stevie's progress over the summer. Stevie, as any enthusiastic teenager would, wonders how he stacks up in his newfound fly-fishing skills. Winding the hackle on a black conehead wooly booger, he pauses and asks, "Do you think I'm as good as y'all were when you were my age?"

A smile appears on Jay's face as he applies head cement to his large rubber-legged Tellico Nymph and laughingly replies, "You're better than Dillon is now!"

Dillon, lifting his head up from his vice where he's tying a number six Jim's Grampus, looks at Stevie, then at Jay, before looking out the window up toward the Smoky Mountains and considering the relative comparisons for a moment. "To be honest, Stevie, yes I think you're better than both of us were at your age. But," Dillon pauses as a wide grin appears, "But me and Jay didn't have *ME* for a teacher!"

WHAT A DAY

Anyone who has fished a reasonable amount of time knows some days just aren't productive. Whether it's the water, the weather, or simply that the fish ain't bitin', it just happens. Ever the optimist, after a slow day Jay would put it like this, "It's the bad days that make the good days great." Having had his share of bad days, Dillon subscribes to that philosophy. However, Dillon's self-imposed standards are much higher than most, if not all. Essentially, unless Dillon is "huntin fer biguns" and instead just going to catch trout regardless of size, a day with less than 20 trout is a bad day. Fortunately, on those occasional, but expected slow days he has the beauty of the Smoky Mountains and the sounds of the birds, the water, and the possibilities that more than make up for the number of trout. Still, he still doesn't like it when Jay says, "Well, it was a good day to be out." To Dillon, that is loser talk.

Sitting in the oak bench pews of River View Baptist Church, Dillon, though not considered a regular church attendee, finds himself awaiting the sermon that has piqued his interest ever since he saw the church marquee earlier in the week that read, "What a day". He has a personal interest in the good reverend's thoughts on how to handle a bad day, of which seems to have become the norm for him lately. Though he would never admit it, not even to himself, it did get his goat just a little that regardless of what happens good or bad, Reverend Mitchell never seems to get upset. That in itself, angers Dillon just a little. He finds himself enjoying the production of the River View Baptist Church choir as they work their way to completion of the **Bill and Gloria Gaither hymn, "What a Day That Will Be**," selected just for the sermon, no coincidence there. As the choir reaches the crescendo by repeating the chorus for a final additional emphasis, Dillon hears the words once more:

> *"What a day that will be,*
> *When my Jesus I shall see,*
> *When I look upon his face,*
> *The One who saved me by His grace,*
> *When he takes me by the hand,*
> *And leads me to the Promised Land,*
> What a day, glorious day that will be"

and finds himself a bit emotional at the sudden relaxed and serene feeling he senses. His serenity fades as Reverend Mitchell walks to the podium and begins his sermon. Being an old-fashioned Baptist preacher of the fire and brimstone persuasion, when the reverend gets going, beads of sweat break out on his forehead requiring constant swipes with his handkerchief as his voice rises. After about twenty minutes, Dillion begins fidgeting like a ten-year-old wearing a constricting necktie on a hot day. Reaching a climax in his message, the reverend's voice becomes stronger and louder.

Having fidgeted perhaps a little too much, Debbie gives Dillon a gentle elbow of acknowledgement that he needs to focus on the message. Debbie has long since made a practice of sitting between Jay and Dillon at church as, though their years upon earth classifies them as adults, more often than not, their behavior belies that classification. It was at that moment that Dillon, Debbie and Jay first notice Luanne and a new beau sitting two rows in from of them. This strategic positioning was no doubt to assure Dillon's observation of said couple. As Dillon is currently going thru an unattached period in his life, there's no doubt the presence of some form of hidden emotion going on within the pokerfaced ex-boyfriend of Luanne. Turning to her left, Debbie nods at Jay, then to the pair up front, to which Jay gives an unspoken "we'll see how this plays out" look. Dillon takes the opportunity to repay the gentle elbow back to Debbie to "straighten up and pay attention," as a slight grin crosses his lips. As the reverend winds up his message, Dillon learns, much to his chagrin, that today's sermon is a two-parter. Thinking to himself, "There's more and I gotta wait till next week to hear the rest of the story?" he drops his head in frustration which brings a gentle conciliatory pat on the hand from Debbie. Being a teacher, she is well adept in reading the body language of disappointment and frustration.

As the sermon and altar invitation run their course, Boots, having made perhaps a bit more moonshine the past week than he ought to have, makes his regular trip up front to the altar to offer his silent confession to the Almighty. Afterwards, Dillon, Jay, and Debbie make their rounds of handshakes to the rest of the congregation. Of course, Melvin Cody and "momma" spend a little extra time "sharing" with anyone that will listen, or can't get away from the trap, the woes of their lives and associated drama, as told by momma and confirmed with head nods of authentication by Melvin. This was a conference in which both Jay and Dillon have no interest in partaking. Jay, as the town physician, has the added joy of trying to avoid "hallway medicine" where members of the congregation ask about treatments for their various ailments, or tell about cousin so-and-so's skin condition. More than a few of the attendees have had multiple cancers that faded away never to be heard about again. Jay recognizes a hypochondriac, but still wonders occasionally about the healing powers at River View Baptist.

Successfully making their way thru the gauntlet, they eventually arrive at the front exit where Reverend Mitchell and his wife, Selma, are greeting the attendees and guests. In a definitive miscalculation of greeting line timing, Luanne finds herself standing in line a few couples ahead of Dillon, Jay, and Debbie. As Luanne and her beau greet the reverend and his wife, the self-appointed and widely recognized town gossip, or "sharer" as Baptists call it, Selma already knows the story. She Introduces Luanne's cousin Rick to those around, including Dillon, Jay, and Debbie. As Selma shares the details of the family reunion this afternoon of the Davis clan, of whom Luanne is a part, the charade concocted by Luanne disintegrates. Refusing to make eye contact with Dillon, from whom she senses a smug grin, Luanne and Ricky make a quick exit.

Now their turn, the reverend makes a point to ask Dillon, "What did you think about the sermon today Dillon?"

Ever the one to evade a direct question, a talent perfected by years of deflecting Luanne regarding the taking of their relationship to the next level, Dillon shakes hands with Reverend Mitchell and replies, "The sanging was right purty pastor. It gave me the chicken skin," referring to the goosebumps from his momentary emotional lift. Dillon smiles as he makes a successful quick exit.

The following Saturday, a planned fishing trip is in the works for Jay and Dillon as they have plans to head to the Great Smoky Mountains National Park. This day, like any other, begins with promise, a day yet to be written, experienced, and lived. A day full of opportunities and unanswered questions. Will today be a good day out on the water or a bad day? Will Dillon get out of Smoky's Drug Store and Cafe without getting bested by Luanne in their verbal sparring? As the years were added and trips between Dillon and Jay increased, so did their simple, mutual appreciation of the time they were blessed to spend together. Both understand the rarity of the friendship they possess in today's modern, social media-based society. On the odd trips they fished without the other, they subconsciously felt something was missing, because it was. Though their styles vary, Jay leaning more toward dry flies and Dillon favoring nymphs, both can easily be persuaded by the success of the other to gladly convert, should the need arise.

Today starts out as usual. Dillon picks up Jay, and they drive down toward town passing River View Baptist, where Reverend

Mitchell has already updated the title of Sunday's sermon, "What a day it will be: Part II" on the sign out in front. Crossing the Big Bear, both look at the water level and find it slightly low and crystal clear. They then turn right at the traffic light and pull over to park in front of Smoky's Cafe. Entering the café, they say their good mornings to the members of the old fart's club who would spend the better part of the morning in front of Boots' Barber Shop whittling creations that were, for the moment, only in their minds. They too were looking at pieces of wood yet to be carved and all the possibilities. Making their way to their usual booth, the one etched with the carving made by Dillon while in high school proclaiming his love for Luanne, both turn over their coffee cups to receive the freshly ground coffee. As Luanne walks up, she says "Good morning Jay. You treating your mentally challenged patients to breakfast this morning?" She smiles at Jay and throws a sarcastic look at Dillon.

Without pause Dillon replies, "If he was, he'd be sued for malpractice due to the service!"

Jay just sits quietly letting his two old friends and ex-lovers get it out of their systems, whatever "it" is, and sips his coffee. He knows better than to get between these two. After the punch, counter-punch of the initial rounds, Luanne takes a momentary step back to ask Jay if he wants the usual while now ignoring Dillon. But today was different. Today was the anniversary of Pop's death. Remembering that breakfast on the April 15th of their thirteenth birthday, now so many years ago, they decide to get the same breakfast as that first day Pop took them fishing. Both order biscuits and gravy, with sausage and strong, black coffee. Without speaking, both know what the other is thinking. Each, is engrossed in his own memories and reflections from that moment so long ago. It is both sad and happy at the same time. Oh how they loved Pop and though Dillon was Pop's grandson, both knew Pop loved Jay just as if he were his own. As both quietly eat their breakfast and wash it down with the coffee, Luanne senses the moment as one of reflection to somewhere she doesn't fully understand. But knowing Jay and Dillon since they were children, she possesses enough intuition of both a woman and waitress to read the two more thoroughly than any fortune teller. As any good waitress realizes, there are times to ease up, even on Dillon, thus allowing them to remain in their memories. Occasionally, Luanne quietly refills the coffee cups of the two silent customers, leaving Jay and Dillon to their own thoughts. After a while, the biscuits and gravy and more than a few cups of coffee have passed the lips of Jay and Dillon and it's time to go.

Leaving Smoky's, Dillon looks over his shoulder, smiling to see Luanne watching he and Jay leave. He gets in a rare last jab in the regular sparring match by adding "Hope the family reunion was successful!", which was followed immediately by the chime of the bell hanging over the door.

Loading into Dillon's truck, they find Hoppy sitting in the middle of the seat staring into a place that only he knows, somewhere off in the distance. "Miss Pop," is all he says before re-joining what is likely a re-memory of a place visited on one of his many, too many, LSD trips taken while at the University of California at Berkley back in the sixties. Through all of his oddities, which include his main occupation, hitchin' a ride with anyone passing by, and his frequent mental trips, Hoppy has an amazing memory and a child-like reminiscence of moments that for many may be the smallest insignificant event. But today, he knows where his moment of lucidity leads. He also seems to possess a sixth sense of the slightest mental aches of those around him where the majority are oblivious to the internal pain of those in their midst. As suddenly as Hoppy's moment occurs, within an instant, his focus returns likely to somewhere in his own personal Xanadu. With Jay's and Dillon's focus now on the Smokies, the threesome are off to one of their favorite stretches of water along Litter River somewhere between Metcalf Bottoms and the turnoff to Elkmont Campground. Well, Jay and Dillon are. Hoppy is off to somewhere not even he knows. Though the traffic and tourons, "tourist morons" as the locals call them, have been more than numerous, Jay and Dillon have a plan. Between the two, it is more often than not Jay who comes up with the strategy for the day with Dillon's confidence noted as he refers to Jay as, "The master strategist." As in their days of playing for the Laurel Cove High Football team, it was often Jay who called the offense and defense alignments, a leadership that more or less defaulted to him. Wisely, he takes the counsel of Dillon prior to making the final decision. Though not one who must be the leader, Jay often found himself the decision maker then and now as he makes his living considering the various physical, mental, and all other known environmental aspects that he can use to determine a diagnosis and course of treatment for his patients. Years in medical school have provided him with the basis for practicing medicine, an art that is never mastered, but that with time and experience, hopefully makes one a perpetual student of the arts. When it comes to the arts of fly-fishing, it is Jay who is the more calculating of the two and Dillon who is the more aggressive go-getter like a linebacker in the creek. Whereas back in the day, whether it was a ball carrier, or a hapless quarterback who had dropped back and stayed in the pocket a second too long holding the ball and paying the price, now many large browns were being sacked by Dillon.

On their drive, both reminisce about that day and how, though up in years from their youthful perspective, they now realize just how relative age is. At that time, they thought of Pop as being so old until they witnessed his agility in chasing that brown. He had hooked it beneath the rock with the current flowing by and with the sudden set of the hook, it hit the afterburners as it plowed its way up the whitewater rapids and into the next long run 50 yards upstream. Though they wanted to go watch the battle and to learn how to handle such a trout, they remembered how Pop yelled, "Youns stay right thar.... We'll be back!" And how, sure enough, they stayed put and in a matter of minutes, but what seemed like an eternity, they saw as they stood high up on a rock, the dark object flash by them as it made its way back downstream in the fast water using the current to its advantage. Looking back upstream, they saw Pop seemingly walking on water hitting every other rock in what seemed like a leap that would be the envy of any Olympic athlete. All the while he kept his rod up and the slack reeled in. As Pop would later say, "As long as ye got yer line in him, ye got a chance."

It was when he finally slid the broad trout over into a slack pool of water and the massive brown had given up, that they got to see the multitude of bright red spots and the massive jaws on what was a twenty-three-inch brown. They remember, and have since practiced, how Pop explained and demonstrated the process of reviving a tired trout so that it would live to pass along its genetic makeup and possibly be caught another day. Pop explained it like this, "This ole feller has been around and seen many a fishermen and flies." They remember how he felt compassion as if the old trout was a long-lost friend who he hadn't seen in many years. Even now they could reflect on how Pop gingerly held the trout in some shallow, moving water gently holding it upright with his left hand and with his right hand on its tail. He'd gently talk, as if on a first-name basis, as the trout's mouth began to open and close breathing in fresh, oxygenated water, and regaining its strength. They remember how they expected the trout to blast away out of fear only to see it gently fin in the current. They recalled how Pop stopped to eat a peanut butter and honey sandwich to watch the trout and make sure it was going to be alright. Only when he was finished with the sandwich and confident his old friend was going to make it would he proceed on. For both, it was probably this day, more than any other that turned on the switch for both as each knew their lives would be incomplete until they too had made friends with such a trout.

Since that time, both had indeed battled and won against such a trout. Though it did take over a decade for both during which several battles were fought and lost with lessons learned on what not to do. One thing they did learn was what Pop would often say regarding large, wild trout, "They don't git big by eatin trout flies and getting themselves caught!" It took them years, but they gradually learned that more important than the fly they used was their approach to the creek. Over their combined years they grew to understand why Pop would always dress to blend into the background. First Dillon, then Jay converted to wearing full camouflage to "improve their chances" against the wary trout of the Smoky Mountains. They also learned the need for a slow, stealthy approach which they remembered by observing Pop so many years ago. Comparing their approach to that of the typical newbie who wears bright clothing and stands upright onto a rock in plain view of every trout for 100 yards, it's not difficult to understand the level of success that Pop, and now Jay and Dillon have in the Smokies.

Another addition to their attire over the years is the use of polarized glasses, which they refer to as their "fish finders". Somehow, they could never quite figure out how Pop could spot seemingly every trout of a keeper size in the creek through his old prescription glasses. Never used by Pop, they find the use of good, brown toned polarized sunglasses help them immensely, though they still feel inadequate against the old, honed eyes of Pop. Aside from the lackluster comparison to Pop's ability to spot trout, they feel good about the skills they have jointly developed over the years and both are driven to be ever improving. Jay has even developed a computer spreadsheet documenting numerous aspects of the creek and atmospheric conditions along with the number, sizes, and species of trout, and most importantly what they caught the most on. Being the problem-solver by nature, as in the diagnosis and treatment of his patients, he enjoys the bits of information he is able to glean from the gathered data and appropriately and effectively applies it to his future trips. He feels he is getting close, not to finding the Holy Grail of trout flies that would work every trip, but knowing in advance what would be the best fly to use based off the time of year, creek fished, and conditions. Years of fishing have convinced Jay and Dillon of the lack of existence of such a Holy Grail fly. Put that up there with Sasquatches and the Lock Ness Monster. Many have claimed to have found the perfect fly for all occasions, but all have yet to pan out. The program definitely helps Jay and Dillon in spending their time most effectively in tying the said flies that most often prove to be the fly du jour. This is not information needed so much by Chester Barnes down at The Hatch. Chester's business relies heavily on customers buying flies and of course, the more different choices in patterns added to the many sizes of hooks the flies are tied on, the more flies the customers must purchase to make sure they have their bases covered when chasing Smoky Mountain Trout.

Having lost Hoppy at a traffic light while passing thru Gatlinburg, Jay and Dillon approach the somewhat hidden stretch, meaning away from Little River Road and away from view of the aforementioned tourons who have a tendency of unknowingly spooking the quarry for which they seek, so Dillon slows down the truck. Pop had his favorite spot on the Little River. Today, in his honor, Jay and Dillon would visit those waters they spent fishing with Pop so many years ago. It was that day that both saw their first trophy sized trout landed and though one of many for Pop, it was far from his first rodeo with one of the wild browns that reside in the pools along Little River. They each remember the day they first saw pop catch a trophy brown. That day, Pop hooked, and after a long fight, landed a powerful twenty-three-inch brown on his favorite go-to fly the green yellowhammer.

The day was set to be clear and sunny with the bluebird skies of perfection. However, Dillon and Jay rarely have great days on the stream on such days unless it was after a hard rain the night before. For Dillon it has always been a dysfunctional relationship between a beautiful day, the perfect cast, and a great day of fishing. As Dillion has stated before, "It is rare that the fishing gods reward a perfect cast." For him, the same goes for perfect days, weather-wise. Additionally, today, they know the water will be as clear as a jar of Boots' best moonshine, making their approach to the pools all the more difficult if they wish to maintain a stealthy approach. Reminiscing about that day so many years ago as they drive toward their destination, they recall that on that day, it was indeed a bluebird day of nearly identical conditions. Both can recall the exact spot where that monster brown was hiding when Pop's fly bounced along the bottom and along the edge of the rock under which the trout lay looking for breakfast. Their reflection of that day moves to their mutual progression over the years and how Pop's lessons, though not realized at the time, was one of many building blocks for what they would learn over the years. During that time, Jay has become a bit of a dry fly aficionado whereas Dillon remains true to the high stick nymphing style as perfected and taught to them by Pop. Ironically, both are a bit envious of the path taken by the other, with Dillon wishing he were a better dry fly fisherman, especially when casting a number eighteen sulphur mayfly pattern on the South Holston River, and Jay wishing he had the innate ability to work a deep pool or pocket in the Smoky Mountain streams with a heavy nymph or streamer like Dillon. Still, both have their advantages and unlike most in the world of sports and hobbies, they rarely partake in trash-talking between themselves. From Jay's perspective, he remembers well their senior year during a pre-season football scrimmage a certain running back from Oak Ridge mouthed off at Dillon's football talent only to find himself riding in the back of an ambulance before the night was over. Dillon, ever the quiet one, had taken enough verbal abuse when he decided to dish out a little physical abuse of his own exhibiting the mantra, "Actions speak louder than words," when the over-confident tailback broke through what he believed to be a wide, gaping hole in the defense only to find everything suddenly dark due to a high speed freight train of a middle linebacker. With that memory forever engrained in his mind, Jay remembers observing the impact from his position of safety about fifteen yards downfield and the loud pop and launch of the tailback's helmet. He remembers thinking to himself, "Lord, don't let his head be in his helmet!" Thus, not willing to risk the wrath of the once all-state middle linebacker, Jay and Dillon took to praising the other's skills way beyond that of their own as well as any future skills or talents the other may develop. Thus, unlike the exuberant back and forth jib-jabbing and taunting, Jay and Dillon developed a mutual repertoire of praising, lauding, and magnifying the other's fly-fishing skills over those of their own. For example, Jay might say, "You know, if I were a 25 inch brown and I saw you sneaking up the creek, I'd just go ahead and curl up my fins and give up, cause you know, it's like game over man!" To this, Dillon would respond, "But where they'd see me coming, because of my clumsy wading skills, you'd make a perfect two hundred yard cast from the parking lot, thru the trees, off a boulder, nothin' but creek, using a size thirty-two parachute Adams and the poor trout would never know what happened!" Even when at The Hatch, when asked, one of them might say he caught three, when in fact he'd caught many more, only to exclaim that the other quit counting at 50. All of this was in jest and mutual admiration for the other.

But back on that day, so long ago, both reflected how they too have caught many trout some days and very few on others. They mutually agree that all of their skills, though self-developed through years of practice, boil down to the foundational knowledge passed to them by Pop and how he shortened their learning cure, but sadly passed away far too soon to see their development. For that, they'll forever be regretful. Both can, though they do not, boast of having released numerous large trout in the Smokies of which Pop would be proud. But neither has come close to three large browns in one day at Metcalf Bottoms as Pop had relayed to them during one of many stories he told them of the old days. To them, that was their ultimate remaining goal, not so much to match Pop, but to reach that pinnacle as a tribute to him. They did have a day a few years back where both broke the twenty-inch range the same day, but they concluded that if and when one caught such a trophy, they would gladly sacrifice their opportunity to assist the other in catching a similar trophy that same day. To them, it was not a major issue who caught what as long as the other was there to share in the experience. In fact, the day of the double, Dillon had caught a nice twenty-one-inch brown that was holding on the bottom about half-way up the pool between the tail out at the lower end of the pool and the head of the pool where the water flows in. He was fortunate to be able to work it to the back end of the pool where he stood, and away from the area the trout had been resting. Doing so improved the chances of catching another by not spooking any other large trout in the area of the pool where the larger trout seemed to be holding. After landing that trout, they spotted another that was lying in the similar spot, not far from where the first had been. Fortunately, the other trout had remained essentially in the same location. As few fishing friends would do in today's overly, self-centered, competitive world that has invaded the gentleman's sport of fly fishing, Dillon stepped back and directed Jay to where the other large trout lay. The location of the trout and the clear, calm characteristics of the long pool required a long and precise cast. As too often seems to happen, the dreaded last back cast got hung up in a tree, breaking off Jay's fly. Without taking his eye off the trout and not wanting to risk something happening while Jay took a few moments to tie on a new fly, Dillon simply handed his fly rod to Jay. Not wanting to make the same mistake twice, Jay made the perfect cast of the Grampus Fly, which sank at the perfect rate and right in front of the remaining trout's nose. Too much temptation resulted in the telltale white flash of the trout's mouth opening to take the weighted offering. After a lengthy battle in the deep pool, Jay landed a near identical brown of twenty-one inches. Though they rarely boast to others, other than providing a little insight to assist Chester with his business at The Hatch, they do enjoy the occasional "sharing" of their dual successes with Melvin, if for no other reason than to counteract his boasting, which has a low to no probability of reality.

Still, the holy grail of three in one day was doubtful to ever present itself to them in the Smoky Mountains. Here, though in some areas can be somewhat plentiful, twenty-inch trout are not everywhere and due to their wild nature, can be difficult to approach, cast to, fool with the correct fly and hook into. In fact, it is likely that ninety-nine percent of fishermen to ever cast a fly into the cool waters of the Smoky Mountains never encounter such a trout.

Jay's mind must always be active even when fishing. Since he was a teenager, he always had a song running through his mind when he fished, mowed the yard, or during any of several other activities of a physical nature. He could even hone into a specific tune that, if the fishing suddenly turned hot, he would stick to that song for the duration of the trip. He even went so far mentally as to repeat a song from a previous trip during the next trip, thinking that since it worked once, it may work again. That theory has yet to be proven totally successful, but he's still in the testing phase. Since last week's sermon, of which the conclusion was scheduled for tomorrow, the choral special of last Sunday was going through his musical mind today. And by some incredible coincidence, he and Dillon had determined that the song, "What a day it will be," was Pop's favorite song that he loved to sing while fishing. Though he never shares his mental jukebox with Dillon, he remembers how Pop would sometimes sing out loud, and Jay too hits an occasional, discernable note when the sound of the stream softens. That song is still running thru his mind when his train of thought is broken with a sudden rant from

Dillon who is eyeballing his rear-view mirror. Turning around, Jay sees the blue lights flashing on the National Park SUV.

Dillon pulls over at the next pullout on Little River Road. "I bet that's that jerk Patterson! He probably pulled me over for being a local," Dillon said in a not too pleasant tone.

Walking up to the driver's side of Dillon's truck, the ranger has his head down covering his face with the brim of his hat and is wearing dark sunglasses. Looking up with a grin, the ranger states, "I need to see your fishing license and your can of worms."

With a serious face Dillon replies, "Sorry sir. My license was revoked for failure to catch and release last year, and the worms are asleep in their Prince Albert can. You see, we only use NIGHT crawlers," emphasizing the word night!

"Well if Prince Albert is in the can, you better let him out or I'll have to arrest you for kidnapping," the ranger replies, referring to the old local joke about Prince Albert tobacco in a tin can that was often used to sneak live bait into the Park. As all three laugh, it turns out to be Ranger Kowalski who they haven't seen since last fall.

"What are you fellas looking for over here?" he asks as if he doesn't already know.

Jay speaks from the passenger side, "Well, we thought we'd fish the favorite stretch of water of Dillon's grandfather, Pop Powell, who taught us how to fish when we were kids."

"Well, I won't ask you where that place is, but I know you guys will do well today. The fish really seem to be biting this week."

After a bit of catching up on local news, Ranger Kowalski relays an incident that happened to him last week. "I was patrolling over at the Metcalf Bottoms picnic area last Saturday. There was one heckuva a tuber hatch!"

By a tuber hatch, Ranger Kowalski was comparing the number of tubers floating on the water to aquatic insects hatching. This sudden hatch of insects sometimes occurs along the streams of the Smokies and in other areas especially on the South Holston River just outside of Bristol, Tennessee. During such a hatch, millions of insects suddenly appear on the surface of the water. As in the case of the South Holston, the sulphur mayflies, as they're known locally, drift helplessly on the surface of the water, drying their wings so they may take flight to continue their mating process. It's during the drift that trout tune in to this abundant food source and go into an absolute feeding frenzy. Since before the days that Izaak Walton wrote his book, *"The Complete Angler"* in 1653, fly-fishermen have been taking advantage of this phenomenon in their pursuit of trout.

"There were tubers everywhere on Little River. It looked like an invasion of overweight tourists and sunburned locals," he added laughing. "Anyway, I park my vehicle in the lower parking lot and walk upstream along the bank."

It was at this point Dillon broke in with a smile, "To harass innocent fishermen no doubt," adding a dig to his friend behind the badge.

Continuing, Ranger Kowalski added, "Anyway, before I was RUDELY interrupted, this healthy-looking middle-aged lady of about three hundred pounds sees me standing on the bank. She had been floating down from the bridge and she begins flailing her arms and kicking water. I figured she'd seen a snake."

Breaking in, Jay asks, "If a copperhead had bit her, would she have bled bacon grease?", he laughs referring to her weight.

"No, more likely sausage gravy," Dillon adds.

"Guys, you're sad, and you're killing me. You ever thought of doing comedy over in Pigeon Forge?" Ranger Kowalski asks then continues his story, "This lady she makes her way over to me in her innertube that was WAY too small to keep her afloat. She yells up at me and says, "Hey! Do you work for the Park Service?"

Obviously, standing there in my ranger uniform I want to say something like, "No ma'am, I only dress up like this for photos with visitors", but I don't. Anyway, I respond very politely, "Yes ma'am. Can I help you?"

The lady then asks, "How long does it take to get back to here? I ain't got all day. I've been floating for fifteen minutes and ain't got back to where I started yet!"

"I'm not sure what you're asking ma'am."

Then she repeats her question real slowly as if I'm too dumb to understand,

"How…long…will…it…take…me…to…get…back…to… here?"

I pause a moment thinking she can't be serious, so I answer as best I can, "Well, if you keep floating down the creek, you'll wind up in Townsend which can take all day and I wouldn't recommend that." I then ask, "Do you have someone who will give you a ride back up stream?"

At this point, she's wondering if I'm giving her a smartass response, so she says, "What do you mean?"

Finally, I try to be as clear as I can and say, "Ma'am this isn't a lazy river ride like at the hotels. This is nature and the creek flows downhill due to gravity and only takes you downstream.

She gives me the most puzzling look and says, "I don't understand."

At this point my only reply is to say, "Well ma'am I can't fully explain gravity, but that's how it works." At this point, I just have to walk off.

During the telling of the story Jay and Dillon are in the truck laughing till both have tears rolling down their faces.

"Well, I guess I'd better get going. I have to check out a bear issue over in Cades Cove. My guess is another photographer forget how to use their camera zoom, so they walk right up next to the poor bear for a close up shot," he says sarcastically.

"Hey, Kowalski! You're not going to check us for our licenses?" Dillon asks.

Laughing as he walks away, Kowalski says "Not today, I'll just give you a warning this time. But be sure to let Prince Albert out of that can!"

Dillon waits to pull back out until Ranger Kowalski is on his way toward Cades Cove. "It'll take him 45 minutes to get there and the rest of the day to get around the loop road," Jay says referring to the common bumper to bumper standstill traffic that is common to Cades Cove this time of year.

Driving downstream, the river goes from their left to their right. Dillon pulls the truck into a pullout as the two get out to gather their fishing gear. Being a warm day, they both gladly "wet wade" wearing no waders, and pull on their LL Bean Aqua Stealth wading boots. Both are dressed in brown Columbia pants that zip off at the legs and dry quickly with long-sleeved, breathable camouflage shirts, making sure their arms are covered so they're not seen by the trout. Remembering back when they were young, they recall wearing old work boots and blue jeans, and how those boots were slippery on the wet rocks of the streams and their blue jeans would still be wet when they got home. Those old fly rods, bought for them by Pop have long since worn out. Today, they use nine-foot, four weight graphite rods. Now geared up, they pull on their fly-fishing vests, each with a net hanging off the back, and with various line snippers and hemostats, compliments of Jay from his medical practice, and more than enough flies. Both throw a cold drink and a small metal can each into the large pocket on the back of their vests. Making their way down the side of Little River Road, cars and RVs pass by on their way most likely to Cades Cove, and groups of motorcycles head over to US Highway 129, aka "The Dragon" noted world-wide for its 318 curves in a mere eleven miles and raced over by thousands of motorcyclists and sports cars every year. It's not uncommon for several to lose their lives due to high speeds on the precarious curves and adjacent drop offs down into the valley some distance below where the Tennessee River flows.

Stepping off the road, they pick a good spot, one hopefully without snakes of the fanged nature, and make their way down to where they wish to begin fishing the Little River, Jay and Dillon pause to look at the water conditions, listen to the sound of the rapids, and take in a deep breath, feeling the cool of the morning mountain air deep down in their lungs. Both pause to think back to the time Pop brought them here. Never did Pop take them anywhere without sharing a story or two of trout caught and lost, often accompanied by a humorous incident that occurred along the stretch at some point. Due to his sudden passing, they were only blessed to fish with Pop for a few years, but what they learned during those few, precious years was incredible. Often have they wished for more time, but likewise have never take for granted the opportunity they had, thanks to Pop. To them, Pop will always be the standard by which they judge themselves. Though Dillon exceeded the length of the largest trout ever caught out of the Smokies by Pop, neither has ever caught more than one trophy trout in a single day like Pop did. They too consider a trophy to be twenty inches or larger. But today is not about large trout, or a large quantity, it is about remembering Pop. While looking up the waters of Little River, each mentally plan their approach to fish the various runs and pools. A toss of the coin reveals who gets the pleasure of crossing the creek to fish the other side since they enjoy fishing together from opposite sides.

Standing at the side of the stream, Dillon says in a solemn tone, "This one's for you Pop".

Jay concurs, "This one's for you."

Jay crosses over to the other side, which he prefers as he finds it easier to cast right-handed from the left side of the stream. Both maintain the same pace with the other as they slowly make their way upstream. When approaching a long run, both will pause and not proceed until the other is satisfied that either they have spotted a nice trout in the shallow tail-out of the pool, or fairly certain there's nothing to visually target on their first cast.

The first hour passes remarkably slow with each having brought only a few rainbows to hand. Having made a few changes in fly pattern in the hopes to improving the number of strikes and fish caught, Dillon finds himself with a number eight weighted Guinea Fly and a small, number fourteen bead head prince tied off the end of the Guinea. Jay has kept his favorite heavy nymph for summer on, a number eight weighted Grampus and attaching a dropper fly off the end of the Grampus, he remembers Pop's favorite fly, a number ten green bodied yellowhammer. As Jay works his way up the left side of the stream, they each approach a set of rapids. In the rapids, there is a nice, but small pool of about three feet deep directly upstream from where Jay is standing. Just to the right of the small pool is the fastest part of the current. He realizes this is going to be a difficult cast to make with two flies as there is a mid-sized tree that has fallen from somewhere up the left bank and down into the rapids. Not only will he have to cast under the tree, but if he waits too long in pulling his flies out of the water, it is likely they will be swept around and into the fast water getting caught on the submerged log. If that happens, there's little chance of retrieving his flies.

Squatting down, he grabs his bottom fly, the green yellowhammer, pulls back on it to create a slight bend in the tip of his rod building resistance, and uses the "bow and arrow" technique, to make a good cast under the log and to the head of the small pocket of water. Interestingly he can see well into the pool nearly to the bottom, but there is a rock perfectly perpendicular to the current at the lower end of the pool creating nearly a vertical wall that a thin sheen of water passes over. It is in front of this rock that he has no visibility. Suddenly, his line twitches and he sets the hook, missing the trout that appears to be about ten inches. Still with his eyes on the pool, he suddenly spots a large brown rising up into view just in front of the vertical rock. Thinking to himself, he wonders "Which one struck my fly," knowing it is rare for a wild trout to bite a fly twice. Experience has taught him to cast quickly as doing so can, though rarely, elicit a second strike. If it was the smaller trout that struck the fly, that means the large one is likely still there. An identical quick cast a bit to the left in the pool where the larger trout briefly appeared, receives an immediate hard strike followed instantly by a lift of his rod tip. He's hooked it! The large trout drops to the bottom of the pool as Jay considers his next move. If Pop, and experience, has taught him anything, it is when fighting a large trout in the Smokies, if at all possible, take the fight to it, by going on the offensive. Realizing he's in a bind as it would be extremely difficult to reach up over the rock at the back of the pool and down into the water to net a large trout, he still applies pressure up and back hoping to get keep the trout away from the current. What sometimes happens with a smart trout is if you pull one way, it runs another. It swims into the current. For a brief second, Jay has no say in what is going to happen next. Miraculously, the trout avoids going under the log and stays on the same side as where Jay stands, taking him down to a larger pool below. After a brief fight, he lands the nice brown and with Dillon's help measures it at twenty- and one-half inches on the ever-dependable Grampus! Gently handling the trout to quickly return it back into the water, they notice it has a humped back similar to that of the sockeye salmon of Alaska, though not as extreme. This is a physical characteristic neither have ever seen in a trout in the Smokies. Just upstream, the river makes a slight turn to the right where it widens a bit, revealing numerous sections of shallow pocket water. It is as if the large brown signaled the turning on of the appetite of every trout within a mile! Seemingly any trout to which they cast explodes on the fly, any fly, that they tie on.

Though Jay is already on a roll, Dillon is struggling a bit with the ever-formidable rhododendrons seemingly getting one snag after another. Having found himself about 20 yards upstream from Dillon, Jay stops to survey the next pool which is long with a wall along the right side at the upper end. The tail out of the pool is fairly wide and shallow, with a large, flat boulder about 20 feet up from the lower end of the pool. Looking over the area, Jay looks back at Dillon, who is battling some form of extreme bird's nest in his leader, trying to untangle the latest mess. Jay can easily see into the shallow water from his low profile, except for the area on the far side of the flat boulder. The top of the boulder is out of the water, but there appears to be a darkened area where the current moves at a slightly higher rate on the far side. Slowly kneeling down, he strips out some additional line to make his first cast just beyond and above the boulder so that his flies will drift through the current. As Pop would say, "Make your first cast, your best cast." Making the cast, a near perfect one, Jay remembers what Dillon typically says in such a situation, "The fly-fishing gods do not reward a perfect cast." As the Grampus and green yellowhammer make their dead drift around the rock and towards him, Jay lifts his rod up to pull the flies out for another cast. Suddenly, his eyes tell his brain something the brain pauses before believing. A huge mouth opens up wide and is swimming toward the files, which he is pulling toward him to make another cast. He is too far along in the process before his brain yells, "STOP", but it is too late. The flies have come out and are making their way behind him. Keeping his eyes on the large brown, he quickly looks over his shoulder and considers yelling at Dillon to give him a crack at this one, since he's already got his trophy today. In what must have been the mother of all tangles, Dillon is still sitting on a rock with his head down trying to free his line. Knowing that any arm motion, such as throwing a rock to get Dillon's attention or yelling to him so that he could be heard over the sound of the water has a more than average chance of spooking the large trout, he chooses to make another cast.

Turning his eyes back to where the large brown has settled after chasing his flies, he no longer sees it! Did it see him as it was chasing the flies? It had happened before. He knows he needs to make a cast quickly while the trout is still interested, if it is interested. So, he makes a cast about three feet upstream from where he thinks it has settled, which is less than fifteen feet from where he is kneeling from his position below the pool. Suddenly, his line makes a sudden and hard twitch signifying a forceful strike. Setting the hook, he misses!! Quickly, before considering the old adage of a wild trout never strikes twice, Jay immediately makes another cast. It hits again and this time he has it! Having just finished freeing his tangled line, Dillon sees the hook set and quickly makes his way up stream to where Jay's rod is bent and water is splashing from something he has hooked, something that looks big.

After setting the hook, the large brown makes its way toward the far bank. Unlike the earlier trophy, this one has no major obstacles to consider. No fallen logs to avoid, no fast current, it would either run upstream into the large pool where the fight would be a little easier, or it would make a run down the shallow shoals, which could become a problem if it went far enough to get back down to the rapids. Chasing it over to the far bank, Jay makes a quick, unsuccessful attempt to land the trout with his net. By now, Dillon is just across the creek on the side where the trout has swum. After a brief pause in the upper shoals behind a pocket of water, the trout makes a run downstream with Jay chasing behind, keeping slack reeled in and his rod up to reduce the likelihood of the line being snagged on a rock. After the trout has trapped itself in a side pocket, one final swoop of the net reveals his second trophy trout of the day! Bringing it back upstream to get Dillon's assistance in a quick measurement and release, Jay is yelling, "What a day! What a day!" Having his tape measure in hand for a second time in less than an hour, Dillon measures this one and finds it to be another solid twenty-one inches!

Having seen his friend meet a goal they'd both had, and one they felt selfish about, Dillon realized between the two of them, he is happy it is Jay! He thoroughly enjoys how Jay is so happy and surprised at what has just happened, that he is shaking as if he'd caught his first trout over twenty inches, which had happened long ago.

As the day continues, the trout are in a constant feeding frenzy. Before noon, both have agreed to stop counting at over fifty trout each. To Dillon, hearing Jay singing "What a day" makes him join in though he doesn't fully know the words. All he knows is "What a day, glorious day that will be" which he keeps singing over and over.

Nearing the end of "Pop's stretch" as they refer to Pop's favorite stretch of water they are enjoying today, they come upon another long, clear pool. With both on high alert and using their fish-finders, what they call their polarized glasses, they fail to spot any trout of size in the lower end. Casting their way carefully up the slick surfaced, clear water, both pick up several small rainbows each. About half way up toward the head of the pool where the rapids poured in the cool, gin-clear water, Dillon spots a large trout on the far side against the bank in about four feet of water. Because the sun is now directly overhead, the trout is easily seen as it has a dark body while gently finning on top of a light tan colored stone in the slow current. Pointing it out to Jay, they both observe it feeding as they watch the flash of its white mouth open to take some likely subsurface nymph. Though they are within thirty feet of where it lies feeding, both know that the wrong step, banging two rocks together or the subtle push of wake, will signal their presence and they will likely lose any opportunity to land the feeding brown.

"Go get it Dillon," Jay urges. "I've gotten mine, today. Now it's your turn."

Looking down at the bottom of the stream at his feet, Dillon shakes his head and sings, "What a day glorious day it will be." He turns to look at Jay smiling. "No, my friend, this one is yours. We've both caught trophy trout on the same day up here before. You take this one."

Jay looks at Dillon and says, "True, but today I've caught two, Dillon, two in the same day. That's a goal we both have."

Countering the argument of his friend, Dillon says "True, but you can match Pop's three in one day. We may never have this chance again in the Smokies and I want you to do it." Then, after a brief pause, he adds "For Pop."

Stepping forward, Jay begins to make his approach and determines the best location to cast his Grampus and green yellowhammer. While appreciating the gesture and opportunity given to him by Dillon, Jay feels a sudden pressure that he hasn't felt since catching his first trophy trout many years ago. Sure, trout like this do not come along every day, for most people they never do, but even less likely is what he is about to attempt, catching three in one day. He pauses to take an extra check of his leader and make sure his knots are strong and secure. He does not feel any weaknesses along any section of the leader. He pulls out his hook sharpener to make one last swipe or two then verifies the sharpness of both hooks by running them along the top of his thumbnail. Both dig in, meaning they're sharp. He looks over his shoulder and around to make sure there are no tree limbs or anything else that he needs to consider in making his cast. He re-checks the position and that the brown is still feeding and seemingly unaware of their presence.

Dillon, not risking a false step, sits down on the rock next to him to watch his friend do something, that to his knowledge, only Pop has accomplished. Not saying anything out loud, the words "What a day glorious day, this will be", runs through his mind. He doesn't know that the same tune is going thru Jay's mind on his mental jukebox as it has all day.

Like Dillon, Jay has also changed the line to "What a day glorious day, this will be" as both realize how glorious this day has already been and each hope it will get even better.

Jay makes a near perfect cast, though perhaps a foot to the left. Hoping the brown will drift over to inhale either of the two nymphs, he watches as they drift within two feet of the large trout. Making a second cast, both nymphs go seemingly within inches of the brown which still appears to be feeding.

"Why not try the Guinea and maybe a small bead head prince?" Dillon quietly asks.

Jay nods and cuts his line, removing the two flies.

"Try these," Dillon whispers. Having cut the two flies that he has used so successfully today to give to Jay to use, knowing it will save time. This will only require Jay to tie one improved clinch knot, instead of the three knots required to tie the top fly, then the tippet line onto the bend of that fly, then to the second fly.

Taking the Guinea Fly and bead head prince, Jay gives Dillon a nod of thanks and ties the flies on. Both Jay and the large brown are still in their respective positions, so Jay makes another cast about four feet upstream and slightly to the left, nearer him, to the brown. He keeps the cast more to his side to prevent his leader from rubbing the trout as doing so would likely spook it, losing any opportunity to get a strike. As the flies drift in the clear water, the hackle of the guinea flairs out, undulating in the appearance of something neither Jay nor Dillon would recognize. Both have always assumed it is just something that looks tasty to a trout.

With a gentle roll of its body, followed by the white flash of the open mouth, the large trout inhales the Guinea Fly. Immediately, Jay sets the hook into the left corner of the trout's jaw, embedding the sharp hook into its hard cartilage lips. The brown bolts upstream into the deeper section of the pool. For once, the clear water works to the advantage of the anglers as they can see the absence of any trees or major boulders which the trout could rub and wrap the line around to break off, a common tactic among the wiser trout. Fortunately for Jay, all the trout has is its strength and the deep water to which it attempts to escape. For Jay, he has confidence in the 4x tippet tied, and as long as he keeps the slack out of his line and takes the fight to the trout with constant pressure, he will eventually wear it down. Moving his rod tip from side to side, he continually alters the direction from which the trout feels the pull and thus keeps the trout guessing the direction from which the resistance originates. This guessing game wears the trout down mentally as much as physically, thus speeding the conclusion of the battle to Jay's advantage. Jay's reel screams as the large trout makes multiple runs up toward the head of the pool. Fortunately, Jay keeps the slack line reeled in forcing the trout to fight against the drag of the fly reel. Each attempt to get away saps more and more energy out of the trout. As the fight slows and moves back to the middle of the pool, Jay eventually works it into his net. "What a day…what…a…day!" Jay yells as he carries the trout filled net to where Dillon has been watching his friend complete the trifecta.

Measuring the trout, Dillon says, "And that's ANOTHER twenty-one incher! Wooo!! What a day!" as he walks over to give his friend a fist bump! "Unbelievable!"

Jay, at a loss for words from what has just happened, can only muster a smile as he has yet to comprehend what he's just accomplished, even though he witnessed the process unfold throughout the day.

Having been too consumed in the incredible fishing of the day to pause for lunch, both sit down to take in the moment of what has unfolded on this incredible day, on Pop's favorite stretch of water, in what they agree is the most beautiful place this side of heaven; a creek in the Great Smoky Mountains National Park. Though the cars have been passing by all morning up on Little River Road, between their focus on catching trout, and the sound of the various rapids through which they have fished, neither has permitted a mental consideration of said traffic. Today, all of that congestion could have been a thousand miles away for all they were concerned. How lucky they were to experience such a day within a hundred yards of the thousands of visitors passing by, making their way to some part of the Smoky Mountains, never realizing what a day had transpired down in the little creek just off the highway.

Taking to heart another lesson taught by Pop, "Know when to call it a day", both reel in their lines and sit down on a nice flat rock. For fun, both take off their wading shoes and socks and as they had seen Pop do on occasion, dangle their feet in the cool Smoky Mountain water. There is a peaceful sensation on such a warm day as today, with the gentle, refreshing breeze of mountain air coming off the water, the beautiful bluebird skies, and the sounds of the occasional kingfisher chattering as it passes by making its way to somewhere downstream. Adding to this symphony of sounds, is the yellow-throated warbler that is sharing its beautiful song somewhere back among the trees, and the distant pileated woodpecker playing a tune on some distant hemlock. This all serves as a sweet layer of icing for what has been a wonderful day, perhaps the most wonderful of all days. For lunch, in honor of Pop, they each get out Pop's favorite, a RC Cola, which Pop always pronounced "R-O-C Coler" and Vienna sausages, which Pop called "Viener". Though neither really appreciate the flavor of Vienna sausages, both have a certain level of pleasant familiarity in paying homage to their mentor.

Sitting there sharing in what Jay has accomplished today, neither Jay nor Dillon see it as either of them, nor for that matter the two of them combined, have achieved the fly-fishing skills of Pop. Not at all. With Dillon having exceeded the length of the largest trout caught by Pop not too long ago, and Jay matching the three in one day feat of Pop today, both simply see it as a continuation of what Pop passed along to them in what he had learned from his mentors so long ago; the passion and love for fly fishing in the Great Smoky Mountains.

Both readily agree that things have changed from those early days. Starting in 1992 with *"A River Runs Through It"*, referred to in the fly-fishing world simply as "the movie", it seemed everyone wanted to be Brad Pitt, except for the ending. The movie led to the influx of new fishermen and their money, which due to good ole American capitalism led to newer, better, and more expensive equipment. True, there has been much progress in fly rods, fly reels with smooth drags, leader line that is smaller and stronger, and the availability of better hooks and synthetic fly-tying materials. Thanks to Chester at The Hatch and the many other fly shops, as well as the internet, knowledge is more quickly shared, though mastering the knowledge of those techniques still takes time. All of this has allowed the learning curve to be dramatically shortened in time. Still, there's no replacement for time spent on the creek, chasing the wild brown, rainbow, and brook trout. For those who spend any amount of time in the pursuit of trout, each feels a certain draw to its waters and the wild trout swimming here that survive by their wits and their wariness of predators. To man, the ultimate predator, this natural wariness requires an extra level of stealth rarely seen in waters outside the Great Smoky Mountains National Park. To a few, they leave the Smokies and upon returning to their homes will reflect on a particular day and think, "what a day, glorious day," they had.

ABOUT THE AUTHOR

Jim Parks, a native of Newport, Tennessee, has spent forty-three years fly-fishing in the Great Smoky Mountains National Park, which he considers his home waters. During that time, he has taken self-guided trips to Alaska, Arkansas, Hawaii, Montana, Virginia, Vermont, Wyoming, and Mexico. He also enjoys occasional fly-fishing trips to tailwaters in Tennessee and North Carolina.

Jim graduated with an MBA from the University of Tennessee in 1992. He has written articles for *Fly Fish America* and various fly-fishing newsletters and has worked as a volunteer for the National Park Service. Jim has given fly-tying demonstrations, taught fly-fishing courses, and given talks to civic organizations where he shared his experiences. Those who know Jim know his skill in catching numbers of and releasing trophy trout in the Smokies. He enjoys remembering those who taught him by being a mentor in sharing his knowledge with the next generation of fly-fishing enthusiasts.

Jim currently resides in Kodak, Tennessee, with Trena, his wife and best friend of thirty-three years.

CPSIA information can be obtained
at www.ICGtesting.com
Printed in the USA
BVHW012316070722
641302BV00027B/397

9 781644 686867